Graveside Reunion

Also by Maureen Klovers:

Hagar's Last Dance (Jeanne Pelletier Mystery Series, #1)

In the Shadow of the Volcano: One Ex-Intelligence Official's Journey through Slums, Prisons, and Leper Colonies to the Heart of Latin America (memoir)

Graveside Reunion

Maureen Klovers

Chesapeake Books

For my daughter Kathleen—may you be as brave as Jeanne, but less reckless...

ACKNOWLEDGMENTS

This book would not have been possible without the assistance of numerous friends and family members.

First and foremost, I would like to thank my husband, Kevin Gormley, who is not only an indefatigable reader and editor, but also an incredibly supportive husband and hands-on, can-do dad.

The members of my mystery writing critique group, Eileen Haavik McIntire (author of *The 90s Club* mystery series) and Mary Stojak, as well as my friend Shelby Hagenauer, provided invaluable feedback and proofreading. My sister, Christelle Klovers, generously shared her expertise on federal investigations into pill mills.

Christine and Michael Glenn accompanied me to Oak Hill Cemetery on a beautiful fall day. (Yes, it really does exist, and Union Major Willard and Antonia, his Confederate spy wife, really are buried there!) Christine's arm is dangling over the tombstone on the cover photograph, and Michael snapped the shot and turned it into my spookily beautiful cover.

Finally, Chris and Christine Ware saved me from making some very embarrassing mistakes regarding Civil War history and reenactors' garb.

That said, all mistakes in this book are my own.

Chapter One

In fifth grade, in the throes of an obsession with ancient Greece, Jeanne Pelletier had delighted her classmates by transforming an old mine shaft into the Oracle of Delphi. Draped in an old white sheet, her mousy brown hair arranged in a Princess Leia braid, she had been the high priestess. Jeanne had drunk from a bowl of bubbling, burbling apple cider, her face dramatically lit by some artfully placed birthday candles and wreathed in clouds of incense, while raking her fingers across the moose antlers cradled in her lap. She had not made her cryptic announcements in ancient Greek, but rather in the antiquated Acadian French of her grandparents' generation. Her classmates had more or less understood, or at least enough to get a vague presentiment of their fate.

Nineteen years later, the roles were reversed. Jeanne was the supplicant; the high priest was her next-door neighbor, Jerry. At first glance, he did not play the part well. The white robe had been replaced by a ratty undershirt, from which a decidedly hirsute beer belly protruded, in addition to the tattoos of swirling Arabic

1

script and blocky Chinese characters that surged down his beefy forearms. His potion of choice was thick, black Turkish coffee that tasted like sludge, which he imbibed in between long drags on hand-rolled cigarettes. The smoke wreathed around his head like a slightly off-kilter halo.

He swilled the Turkish coffee in his "Kiss Me, I'm Italian" mug and peered into its murky depths. "What we have here, Twinkletoes, is a classic case of a disconnect between expectations and reality."

Jeanne's shoulders slumped.

"The reality," he continued, "is that you live in one of the most expensive cities in the world, and have the misfortune of being grossly underpaid for the use of your brilliant mind. The reality is that all you can afford is a studio condo, far from public transportation, with a psychedelic bubble gum pink 1970's bathroom, an avocado kitchen, a view of a brick wall, and a few resident rats."

He really was a mind reader. "My real estate agent showed me that exact unit today," Jeanne said. "Minus any obvious rats—although I did spot a few mouse droppings on the microwave—but plus a mold infestation." She cocked her head. "Did I mention that the young couple upstairs was throwing out all of their possessions to get rid of the bedbugs?"

Jerry shrugged. "I hear that even the top hotels in New York City have bedbugs now." He leaned a massive forearm on the table, and Jeanne's hot chocolate sloshed in her cup. "There is of course a way you could afford a one-bedroom, maybe even a townhouse. Maybe even with a tiny fenced-in yard for Scarlett." He sat back and regarded her intently.

"Rob a bank?"

"No," he said slowly. "I was thinking of something much less illegal, although possibly just as dangerous." He swilled his coffee again. "You could just postpone your house hunting until you marry Braveheart. Two incomes are definitely better than one."

Jeanne was midway through a gulp of hot chocolate, which she hastily spat out into her mug. "Jerry! You can't be serious."

"Of course, I can. You've been dating for seven months. You obviously like—dare I say love?—him. He's trying to get a green card. He keeps dropping all of these little hints about your future together. Trust me, once his visa situation is resolved, he will propose."

"If Fergus's visa situation is ever resolved," Jeanne shot back.

"It will be," Jerry said firmly, but at that moment, she was suddenly less convinced of his predictive powers. INS was a nameless, faceless bureaucracy, full of people trained to say "no" as impersonally as possible. They might as well just staff it with robots.

"He could get a visa," Jerry added slyly, "if he were to get engaged. But there's the catch-22. He won't ask you until he has a visa, because he wouldn't want you to think that's the reason he wants to marry you."

Jerry was making her head spin. "So you think I should propose?"

"Why not? Unless you have doubts."

The trouble was that Jeanne did have her doubts. She loved Fergus, but was not sure that was enough.

3

Maybe she was not cut out for marriage at all. Being married sounded so conventional, so staid and boring—so proper. All things that she was not.

And she never, ever wanted to depend on anyone. Not for money, not for a house. Not for anything.

But Jeanne did not say any of this to Jerry. Instead, she just gave him an enigmatic little smile. "Oh, look at the time!" she exclaimed, making a big show of checking her cell phone. "I need to get ready for Vivienne's Charity League ball. I'm her date tonight."

"Way to change the subject, Twinkletoes." He grunted. "Say hello to your hottie of a sister for me."

She took a final swig of hot chocolate, got up, and placed her mug in the sink, which was overflowing with dirty dishes. "Will do," she promised as she rushed out the door.

In truth, she had ten minutes to spare, and she used the time to take Scarlett, her three-legged, one-eyed Golden retriever, out to pee.

On the way back in, she dug a small gold key out of her pocket, inserted it in the mailbox marked "305," and pulled out a wad of envelopes. Mostly, it was the usual—charity appeals featuring starving African children and sad-eyed puppies, credit card offers, and the odd Chinese takeout menu. But two envelopes in particular caught her eye.

The first was an odd square shape, addressed by hand in beautiful calligraphy, with a return address that she did not recognize. But it was from her home state of Maine, from a town perhaps twenty miles from the bend in the river where she had grown up, and that fact alone made her pulse quicken. Tearing into it, she extracted a

4

glossy, rather childish card, emblazoned with green and red balloons. "You're invited!" it announced.

She could only assume that someone had made a mistake. She hadn't been back in eleven, almost twelve years, and she'd cut ties to everyone and everything she knew there—everyone, that is, except Vivienne and her grandmother. She couldn't fathom how anyone had found her and, more importantly, why they'd want to.

She nearly threw it straight into the trash, unheeded, unread. But her curiosity got the best of her, and so she opened it slowly, almost furtively. She hoped old Mrs. Berenstein would not stomp through the lobby just then, muttering about Russian spies poisoning her Siamese cats. Jeanne wanted only Scarlett for company when she read the mysterious summons.

To her surprise, it was an invitation to her tenth high school reunion. Jeanne found herself envying people who went to their high school reunions anxious that they were single, had gotten fat or bald or both, or had a job at Walmart. Jeanne had a boyfriend, a dead-end job by D.C. standards but a pretty decent one by Maine standards, and, while she was as Fergus charitably described it, "Rubenesque," she was not technically fat. No, she did not have those sorts of pedestrian concerns. She wasn't worried about being pitied, just hated. Hated because of who she was, and whom she was related to. She didn't believe that the Russians were actually poisoning Mrs. Berenstein's cats, but she did believe that her classmates might slip a bit of arsenic into her rum punch.

Or a lot.

The second letter was more troubling. It looked very official, with a pre-printed address label and the seal of the State of Maine. With trembling fingers, she ripped open the side, and the contents—a single sheet of paper, with a neatly typed letter—came tumbling out.

Clutching the letter to her chest, Jeanne leaned against the mailbox and gasped. Oh, the irony—another invitation.

But this one was to appear before Maine's parole board.

Jeanne was acutely aware of each raised eyebrow. The gesture was subtle and refined, a mix of bemusement, titillation, and self-congratulation. With a quick appraising glance from Vivienne to Jeanne and back to Vivienne, followed by a sagacious nod to one's companion, the distinguished ladies of the Charity League confirmed that Vivienne's protracted divorce had turned her into Sappho on the Potomac.

Jeanne was not surprised that they failed to see the family resemblance. Vivienne looked like a Walt Disney version of a Celtic warrior princess. Tall and statuesque, her reddish-gold locks perfectly set off her emerald green eyes and flawless ivory complexion. Jeanne was more like her homely forest animal friend—short and a little lumpy, with piercing dark eyes and a shock of brown hair that shot out of her head like a bushy squirrel's tail.

"They think we're lesbians," Jeanne muttered as she slid a tiramisu, two petit fours, and a chocolate mousse on her plate. "And they think I'm the butch one."

"Nonsense." Vivienne slid a single petit four onto her plate. To Jeanne, it looked lonely. She couldn't understand the point of paying an exorbitant sum to attend a charity soirée if you didn't at least enjoy the desserts. "They know I was married to a man."

"Operative word: was."

"Whom I divorced," Vivienne said pointedly, "because he was an asshole. Not because I decided to switch teams."

Mitch was, indeed, an asshole. But he was rich. Unlike Jeanne, Vivienne never had to worry about money. Courtesy of Mitch, she lived in a two hundred-year-old mansion that oozed stodgy, old-money Georgetown charm.

"Did you get the letter?" Vivienne asked in a low voice.

Jeanne gritted her teeth. She thought about playing dumb ("what letter?"), but there was no point. She'd only be postponing the inevitable. "Yes."

"And are you going?"

Jeanne wanted to reply with an emphatic "no," but it stuck in her throat. If she said "no," Vivienne would try to argue with her to do the right thing, to get closure, blah, blah, blah. Better to be noncommittal.

She was unexpectedly saved from having to answer by a barrel-chested, silver-haired gentleman in a tuxedo. He took Vivienne's right hand in his and pumped it vigorously, while squeezing her shoulder with his left. "Vivienne," he crooned, "it's so wonderful to see you."

7

To Jeanne, he looked very familiar. Where had she seen him? On TV, perhaps? Squinting, she tried to imagine him in a boring navy blue suit. When she added a red tie and the obligatory American flag pin, turned the smile into a bit of a sneer, and imagined one of his thick, pale fingers jabbing in the air, his image matched that of the angry congressman she'd seen on TV this morning. And last night. And the night before that. This was the man who seemed to immediately blow up like a puffer fish at the mere mention of the name Edward Snowden. "Traitor!" he had roared over and over, startling Scarlett out of her slumber and prompting Jeanne to change the channel.

But now he was all rainbows and butterflies, the charming, calm sort of fellow that Fergus's Aunt Margaret would love to invite for tea.

Vivienne kissed him on both cheeks. "It's good to see you too. Jeanne, I'd like you to meet Congressman Mason Richardson from South Carolina. Congressman, I'd like you to meet my sister, Jeanne."

He took her hand and gave her the power squeeze. "And are you a member of the Charity League as well?"

"Oh, no. I wouldn't have the time," Jeanne said. Nor, she might have added, the money, the social standing, and the influential husband. There were plenty of career women in D.C., but they had no interest in the strange, insular world of the League.

"So, what do you do?"

Ah, the dreaded question. It was a staple of D.C. party conversation and it did not, regrettably, refer to the individual's hobbies. The right answer was generally not the truthful answer. No one said, "I sit around googling exotic destinations in Africa while pretending to write policy briefs—otherwise known as lies—about why ketchup should be considered a vegetable in school lunch programs." Instead, they waxed poetic about their important work to protect American family farms and, by extension, all of rural America.

"Law," Jeanne said vaguely, and then silently rebuked herself for playing the game. "I'm a legal temp, actually, at Higgins, Higgins, and Applebaum. You know the drill—lots of drudgery, little pay." The congressman nodded sympathetically, so Jeanne went on, ignoring Vivienne's pained expression. "And—it seems—a professional house hunter because there is absolutely nothing in my price range. Maybe if I never eat out again, and never go on vacation again, I'll be able to afford a condo when I'm sixty."

"She's also quite an accomplished belly dancer," Vivienne interjected briskly. "In fact, she's going to perform at our Halloween party benefitting the children's hospital."

Jeanne smiled weakly. Her sister was making it sound much more impressive than what it really was—the result of her sister's maneuvering to get Jeanne a paying gig. Her down payment had to come from somewhere.

The congressman beamed. "Excellent," he boomed, and Jeanne had the distinct impression that this was the stock phrase he employed at every campaign event, whether presented with a prize-winning tomato or a spelling bee winner.

"And," Vivienne suddenly added, as if desperate to further plump up Jeanne's résumé, "she's also a sleuth."

Now she had his attention. "Well in that case," he said, his eyes narrowing into little slits, "take a last bite of mousse and come dance with me. I've got a business proposition I'd like to discuss with you."

He led her far away from the dessert table, so close to the band that she could see a bead of sweat rolling down the singer's face. The congressman was surprisingly light on his feet, effortlessly leading her through the cha-cha. The slightest lift of his calloused hand, the softest little push, somehow told her to turn, which never happened with Fergus.

But the congressman did not turn her too many times. He held her close, almost too close, although it did not feel sexual at all. It felt, rather, like the embrace of a drowning man reaching for a life raft. He spoke directly in her ear; the combination of his warm, tequila-scented breath and his deep baritone drawl would have been soothing were it not for his message.

"I need your help," he said, "and I'm willing to pay. For your time and your discretion. No matter what you decide, you won't breathe a word to anyone about this, right?"

She nodded slowly and felt his stubble brush against her cheek.

"Even if you do," he continued, "I'll deny it." He gave her a little push, slightly harder this time, and she turned.

One-two. Cha-cha-cha.

"I'll give you twenty-eight thousand as a gift. Fourteen from my wife, fourteen from me. As you know, that's the legal limit."

Jeanne felt suddenly woozy. A congressman—a stranger—was offering her the equivalent of half her down payment. All on Vivienne's word that she was a sleuth. But perhaps what struck her most of all was his tone. He seemed so commanding on TV; he told people what to do, and now he was asking. Pleading.

Three-four. Cha-cha-cha.

"Look over to your right, but don't make it obvious. See the woman in the red dress?"

Out of the corner of her eye, Jeanne spotted an elegant, raven-haired beauty at least twenty years the congressman's junior. "Yes. She's very attractive."

"That's my wife, Meaghan. She's a friend of Vivienne's. She seems perfectly normal, right?"

One-two. Cha-cha-cha.

Jeanne was not quite sure how to answer. She couldn't tell much without talking to her. "I guess."

"She's gone loony tunes."

Jeanne pulled away from him and gave him a searching look.

"How so?"

"She claims we have a ghost."

They came to a standstill. "A what?"

"A ghost. A poltergeist. A spirit. Whatever you want to call it." He took her by the hand again. "She says that the ghost of Lucinda Cartwright has been visiting her—tormenting her really."

"Who's Lucinda Cartwright?"

"The daughter of a congressman and a good friend of Dolley Madison's. She was engaged to be married to a rich merchant in Alexandria. Before the wedding, he sailed to Barbados to settle some business affairs, and he ended up bringing a new wife home with him. And that was the end of their engagement."

Jeanne frowned. "I'm an amateur detective, not a ghostbuster. I only have experience bringing live bad guys to justice."

"I know that, and you know that. But"—his warm air shot into her ear—"my wife does not. I want you to get to the bottom of this."

"You want me to find out if your wife is delusional."

"Yes. Or if someone—some live person—is tormenting her and making her think there's a ghost. Maybe someone who has a grudge against me."

"Do you have enemies?" Jeanne asked.

"All congressmen have enemies."

As Jeanne considered this, her gaze wandered back to her dance partner's striking wife. Smoothing a strand of silky dark hair behind her ear and chatting amicably with a woman in a lavender sheath, Meaghan certainly didn't look crazy.

"You said Lucinda is tormenting her. What do you mean by that?"

Jeanne felt the congressman tremble slightly in her arms. "Lucinda," he said between gritted teeth, "is making Meaghan paint her body like a cow."

Chapter Two

"Painted like a cow?" Jeanne's best friend Lily shrieked as they cruised down Wisconsin Avenue in Lily's battered Crown Vic.

"That's what he said."

"What kind of a cow? A Holstein? A Hereford?"

Jeanne looked over at her friend and sighed. "He didn't say. Really, Lily, you're going to have to calm down. We need to take her claims seriously, or she's not going to tell us anything.

"Oh, I am serious," Lily said as she tucked a bright pink hair extension behind her ear. "I just watched a whole *Ghost Hunters* marathon. The details are very important. One time, they figured out that a ghost just wanted her wedding ring to be buried with her. After they did that, she stopped haunting them."

Lily swung a left at the Georgetown Library, headed past the imposing metal gates of Oak Hill Cemetery, and stopped in front of a large red brick Georgian mansion that occupied nearly a whole block.

"According to Zillow," Lily murmured, "that pile of bricks is worth seven million."

Jeanne stepped out of the car, opened the door to the backseat, and hauled out Vivienne's video camera, a tripod, and Jerry's high-tech audio recording equipment. She figured that if she was going to play the part of a ghost hunter, she might as well have the right gear. Jeanne tossed a couple of sawed-off old belly dance canes to Lily. "Your divining rods, Zelda."

"Thank you, Imogene. Ready?"

Congressman Richardson's house made even Vivienne's look like a hovel. They sat in the library, which was at least twice the size of the condos Jeanne's realtor had been showing her and featured gleaming hardwood floors and floor-to-ceiling bookshelves. Friezes of nymphs cavorting in gardens of pineapples and roses stared down at them from the crown molding. The walls were a rich cranberry red, dotted with silvery beams from the enormous crystal chandelier, and all of the furniture was leather.

"Darling," the congressman said as he patted his wife's knee reassuringly, "I want you to meet the"—he swallowed hard and looked at Jeanne—"paranormal investigator that I've hired." He gripped her knee tighter. "To investigate Lucinda Cartwright's ghost."

Meaghan looked at them dubiously.

Jeanne took Meaghan's limp-wristed, slightly clammy hand in hers and tried to shake it authoritatively. She noticed how delicate Meaghan's hands were; she had the long, thin fingers of a pianist, and the raw, red fingertips of a nail-biter. "Imogene Coakley," Jeanne said. "I've got a Ph.D. in paranormal psychology from the University of Singapore. And this is Zelda Lee, a renowned medium. We work together often. We've led investigations at Eastern State Penitentiary in Philadelphia—"

"Old prison. Capone stay there," Lily suddenly interjected, and Jeanne nudged her lightly with her foot. Adopting a bizarre Chinese accent was not part of the plan. But then Jeanne should have known better; with Lily, nothing ever seemed to go to plan. "Many people go crazy," Lily added. "Many, many ghost."

"And I've investigated the Lee mansion in Arlington cemetery," Jeanne added quickly. "Plus, a lot of old mansions in Savannah and New Orleans."

"Alcatraz." Lily held up a hand and started ticking off imaginary highlights from their ghostbusting careers, while Jeanne began to sweat. She felt safe talking about Eastern State, a two-hundred-year-old star-shaped prison founded by the Quakers that loomed over the streets of Philadelphia like a medieval fortress. Endowed with America's very first flush toilets and reputedly haunted by the ghosts of prisoners driven mad by the Quakers' enthusiasm for solitary confinement, the place seemed to exert a magnetic force on every ghost hunter in the country. But now Lily was veering into unfamiliar territory.

"London Bridge—many virgin buried alive in bridge, just like song say. Many unhappy ghost. Coliseum. Many people hear lion at night. Bastille."

Meaghan frowned. "The Bastille burned down," she said. "There's just a traffic circle there now."

15

"Ghost still there," Lily parried. "Many, many accident in circle. Before many accident driver hear sound of guillotine." She clapped her hands and the congressman started. "Bang. All die, more ghost."

"Zelda did a wonderful job on that investigation," Jeanne said brightly. "She convinced the ghosts to leave the circle if the prime minister went there and apologized for the excesses of the French Revolution."

"And that worked?"

"Like a charm." Jeanne selected a lemon macaron from the silver platter on the coffee table and offered it to Lily. Maybe if she had her mouth full, she wouldn't talk. "Which is why," she said, "it's so important for us to understand the context. We need to get into the mind of the spirit. And in order to do that, we need to know when she appears and what she says or does. Anything you can tell us, Mrs. Richardson, would help our investigation." Jeanne nibbled on a mocha macaron. "Now your husband tells us that she wants you to paint your body like a cow."

Meaghan nodded.

"And how does she communicate this? Verbally?"

"Yes. In a whisper. Sort of a hoarse whisper. Almost as though she's about to burst into tears."

"What does she say exactly?"

"She instructs me to go into my study—I'm a historian, and I write all of my books in that room—take off all of my clothes, take black paint—"

"What kind of paint?"

"Well, she didn't specify, but I use my son's finger paint."

The congressman reached into his pocket and took out an expensive leather wallet. "This is our son Grayson," he said, pulling out a snapshot of a towheaded toddler with a gap-toothed grin. "He's two."

"Do you have any other children?" Jeanne asked.

"Cassandra, my daughter from a previous marriage. She's sixteen and lives with her mom, but she spends summer and Christmas with us."

"And how well do you get along with Cassandra?" Jeanne peered at Meaghan.

"Well enough," she answered, but Jeanne thought she detected a hint of hostility. "She's a typical moody teenager. One day she likes you, one day she doesn't."

"But you hear this even when she's not here, right?"

"Oh, yes. I hear it often. Especially when it's raining."

Jeanne jotted that down. "Okay, so she wants you to get naked, cover your body in black paint—"

"Black spots," Meaghan corrected her. She unbuttoned the cuff of her jade silk tunic and rolled up the sleeve. "I've taken two showers since my last encounter with Lucinda, but you can still see them faintly."

"And then what happens?"

"That's it," Meaghan said in a small voice.

"Now, be honest, darling." The congressman leaned forward and dropped his voice. "Lucinda makes her say, 'I'm a fat, disgusting cow, and nobody will ever love me.'"

"Very mean ghost," Lily observed.

"And when did this start?" Jeanne asked.

"Around the middle of May."

"And how do you know it's Lucinda?"

"Good question." Meaghan crossed the room and rummaged through the top drawer of an antique mahogany desk. "As a historian, I'm pretty well connected in history buff circles. A couple of years ago, I was working on a biography of Henry Clay." She must have noticed Lily's blank expression, because she hastily added, "Whig congressman from Kentucky, Speaker of the House, mastermind of the Missouri Compromise."

"I remember he was always running for president," Jeanne said.

"Exactly. But he was a perennial loser." Meaghan extracted a small, leather-bound volume from the drawer and returned to the sofa. "One day, while I was knee-deep in Clay's biography, I got a call from a book antiquarian who claimed to have in his possession a diary written by Lucinda Cartwright. Needless to say, I was floored. Not only was Lucinda Cartwright the daughter of Congressman Cartwright, an important Whig ally of Henry Clay's, but she was also an occupant of this house from 1811 to 1814."

"So, you purchased the diary."

Meaghan nodded. "Which turned out to be a very wise investment. It's full of perceptive and witty observations about the political climate of the time."

Jeanne took the diary from Meaghan and slowly turned its rippled pages. "But I still don't understand how you know that the spirit is Lucinda."

"I know it sounds crazy, but I see her apparition. Not distinctly you understand, but enough to get an impression of what the spirit looks like. A long gown, lace collar, strong jaw line, button nose, and a mass of light-colored curls piled on top of her head."

"And how do you know what Lucinda looked like? There are no sketches in the diary."

"But there is a portrait of her at Tudor Place. And I swear it's the spitting image of the ghost."

Jeanne savored a bite of a chocolate macaron. "But why is she so angry? Why is she still haunting the place?"

Meaghan looked behind her, and Jeanne had the distinct impression that she was afraid that Lucinda might overhear. She dropped her voice to a whisper, and Jeanne had to strain to hear her.

"Her family had a huge plantation in Tennessee, and her father was one of the biggest slaveholders in the state. Even though she was not terribly good-looking, she was considered a very eligible bachelorette because of her father's wealth and prominence. She had three suitors— Thomas Hardwick, a Georgetown dry-goods merchant; John Marbury, a dashing young rake from Alexandria; and Andrew Parkhurst, a well-known physician who was the scion of a wealthy, slave-owning family in Kentucky that was related to Henry Clay."

"I can imagine which one her father wanted her to choose."

"And you would be correct. But Lucinda detested Andrew. She found him conceited, proud, and no match for her wit. She was wildly infatuated with John and apparently trysted with him on the banks of Rock Creek when she was supposed to be riding with her friend Dolley Madison. Just as she was beginning to suspect that she was pregnant, John went to Barbados on business. Before his departure, they were secretly

19

engaged to be married. But when he returned two months later, he was on the arm of the daughter of the richest rum merchant in Barbados."

"I can imagine how desperate she felt then," Jeanne commiserated.

"Exactly. Three months pregnant, about to start showing, and no husband. So, she turns to her second choice, Thomas, who is all too happy to propose. But it's 1814 and the British are ravaging the Potomac, so Thomas is called out to defend D.C. along with the rest of the ill-trained militia."

Jeanne picked up the story now. Unlike Lily, she had actually paid attention in history class. "The British and the Americans meet at Bladensburg, six miles from Washington, but the battle goes very badly for the Americans, who beat a hasty retreat."

"Thomas is shot in the leg," Meaghan continued, "and evacuated with the retreating troops. His blood loss is extensive and later that night, he is proclaimed dead by none other than her detested suitor, Andrew Parkhurst. He's hastily buried, and Andrew begins to press his suit with her. She's starting to waver when, one day, she visits Thomas's family mausoleum, which has been damaged by a recent storm. She sees a strange white rabbit and, out of curiosity, follows the rabbit down into the crypt, where—to her horror—she sees the badly decomposed body of Thomas, as well as some tell-tale scratch marks on the now collapsed inner wall of the mausoleum."

Lily's jaw dropped. "He buried alive?"

Meaghan lowered her gaze. "Unfortunately, not that uncommon of an occurrence in those days."

"So, what does she do?" Jeanne asked.

"She tells her dad that she and Andrew will announce their engagement at a party that her family is hosting later that week. Then, the night of the party, she greets everyone calmly, then accuses Andrew of burying Thomas alive, says that she would rather die than marry such a man, douses herself in alcohol, and—to the horror of everyone present—lights herself on fire."

For a moment, no one spoke. In her mind's eye, Jeanne could see it all now—the horrified servants; the bewildered, anguished Andrew, who expected a betrothal, not a self-immolation; the guilt-ridden father, who had pushed his daughter into the arms of a man she hated. She could almost smell the burning flesh and hear the frantic footsteps of the guests as they raced about trying to find something, anything to smother the flames. And all the while, the nymphs—the very same nymphs who watched them now—kept vigil.

Rain began to pelt the windows, and a peal of thunder nearly sent them flying off the couch. It was almost as if Lucinda wanted to underscore the drama of the moment. And, Jeanne remembered with a shudder, Lucinda liked appearing when it rained.

"Where did she die?" Jeanne finally asked.

"Right here. This used to be the ballroom."

"But she doesn't appear here."

"No, only in the study, which used to be her bedroom."

"And where exactly does she appear in that room?"

Meaghan swallowed, hard. "The fireplace."

21

Chapter Three

Jeanne and Lily dutifully set up their equipment in the study, while the congressman and his wife attended a fundraiser for a fellow Republican congressman. The Richardsons assured them that Grayson would be blissfully asleep in the next room and that, in the off chance that he did awake, Jorge, their Colombian au pair, would come running to comfort him.

"I wonder if Jorge's a hot manny," Lily whispered as she helped Jeanne set up the video camera to face the fireplace.

Jeanne hoped they wouldn't find out. The last thing she needed was a crying baby and a highly distracted partner.

Lily pulled her long black hair into a ponytail, the hot pink extensions shooting out like fireworks. Her eyebrow ring glinted as a mischievous smile played on her lips. "I'm just going to take a look around," she said.

"You're going to snoop, you mean."

Lily shrugged. "Your words, not mine."

Cradling a steaming cup of tea, Jeanne plopped into the deep, pillowy well of a brown leather armchair and patted the well-worn cover of Lucinda's diary. "I'm going to catch up on my reading."

As Lily padded off down the hall, Jeanne turned the stiff, rippled pages, and inhaled their slightly musty scent. It was a tactile, almost sensual experience, and she felt a certain pang as she realized that this joy would be denied future generations. Scanning two hundred-year-old emails just wouldn't be the same.

June 28, 1814

Cousin Martha arrived this evening, fleeing the advance of the British. She was midway through a breathless account of the burning of St. Leonard's, which she observed by climbing up on the roof of her home—not three miles from the now destroyed town—when vile Andrew put a stop to the conversation, claiming that ladies are too delicate to endure talk of war, to which I offered the rejoinder that if Joan of Arc could lead an army into battle, he could rest assured that Martha and I could at least contemplate the thought of war.

"Yes, but Joan of Arc was burned at the stake," he said in a most patronizing manner, "and you are far too precious to suffer that fate."

Before he could lecture me any further, or hold forth on cotton prices or Kentucky thoroughbreds, I gave him my most brittle smile, crossed the room, and began to pound out a tune on the piano forte—although I must say that the song was more forte than piano.

"Liberty, Mr. Parkhurst," I shouted above the din, "liberty is what is most precious!"

Oh, how I loathe the man! If only father did as well.

Jeanne took an instant liking to the unfortunate girl. Lucinda's personality leapt off every page, which sparkled with her wit, intelligence, and righteous indignation. She was a bit angsty—as Jeanne supposed all teenagers were—but this tendency was tempered by her biting sense of humor; Lucinda was a most entertaining guide to Washington's high society.

Jeanne skimmed several entries describing an endless succession of teas, balls, dinners at the "President's House," and outings on horseback with Dolley Madison. Lucinda deftly made her way through what seemed to be a very violent era, replete with cockfighting, brawls that ended with gouged-out eyes and mangled ears, and the occasional duel in the woods beyond Boundary Street. Jeanne found Lucinda's description of the graveyard on Twenty-Fourth Street to be particularly grisly—"a denuded hill, perched above the street, its sides sheared away to reveal open graves and rotting coffins, pieces of skulls falling to the sidewalk." For a moment, Jeanne imagined it to be the very same cemetery where Lucinda had stumbled upon Thomas's corpse, but then she realized that they were two distinct places; the former was a burial ground for Robert Peter's slaves—"denied dignity in death as in life," as Lucinda observed—while Thomas had been buried in the whites-only Holmead's burial ground, then at the very edge of the city. Based on the crude map in Lucinda's diary, Holmead's was about a mile from Lucinda's house—about where the Dupont Circle Hilton now stood.

Jeanne was struck by Lucinda's compassion. While not exactly an ardent abolitionist—which could hardly be expected from the daughter of a slave owner—Lucinda was relatively enlightened for her time. She expressed revulsion upon witnessing a slave auction just a few blocks from the White House, slipped her father's slaves extra rations from the pantry, and taught the cook how to read on the sly.

She found it most unlikely, then, that Lucinda would have turned into such a mean-spirited ghost. And "fat cow" seemed like an odd taunt from a woman who lived in an era in which "Rubenesque" was the ideal of beauty. Lucinda described her rival for John's affections as "a pale, twitchy woman with a permanently upturned nose," but she failed to remark on her weight. The only person she described as overweight was her friend Dolley Madison, whom she characterized as "growing more delightfully plump by the day, with a full face and an ample bosom"—which sounded quite complimentary.

Nor could Jeanne find any reference to "cows," unless she counted Lucinda's rapturous passage about the dessert served at a dinner in honor of an emissary from the Ottoman Empire. Lucinda had enjoyed Mrs. Madison's strawberry ice cream—her first—immensely, almost as much as the emissary's astonishing request that President Madison furnish him with four wives for the duration of his stay.

Jeanne was just turning her attention to Lucinda's entry for August 24, 1814, the day the British army under General Ross torched the city, when Lily returned.

Jeanne forced herself to tear her eyes away from the journal. "Anything interesting?"

Perching on the arm of a red velvet loveseat, her knees tucked up to her chin, Lily looked like a cat ready to pounce. "Nothing that directly explains who—or what—is tormenting Meaghan." She flashed a wicked smile. "But I did find something that you might not expect to find in the home of a man who won his last primary by trashing his opponent as a twice-divorced, home-wrecking, pill-popper."

Lily held up an industrial-sized Ziploc bag, across which was scrawled "oregano" in black marker.

"Let me guess," Jeanne said. "They don't do nearly as much Italian cooking as that bag suggests."

"Well if they did," Lily said, "they'd be high as a kite after dinner."

Lily took the next shift in front of the fireplace, while Jeanne stole silently into Grayson's room. She peered into the crib and watched his tiny chest rise and fall. Wispy little blond curls framed his round face, and his little fists were balled up by his chin. She saw no signs that he was the offspring of drug-addled parents. In fact, the nursery—just like the house—gave off every air of tasteful, old-money respectability. An appropriately masculine mobile, swirling with fire engines and rocket ships, hovered above him. The walls were some sort of soft pastel shade—Jeanne could not discern the exact color in the dark—and decorated with stencils of Thomas the Tank Engine and his friends. A video baby monitor rested on a small table across from the crib.

Tiptoeing to the closet, Jeanne pried open the door. Luckily, it had been oiled and made no sound. Bending down, her head brushed a phalanx of tiny wool sweaters and brushed cotton onesies. She reached up and felt the back of the closet, which was directly opposite the fireplace.

But she felt nothing—no trap door, no opening. There was no way for someone to enter Meaghan's study through Grayson's closet.

She tiptoed out of the room and padded down the hall to the master bedroom. The ancient floorboards groaned beneath her, and she silently cursed the Richardsons' zeal for historic preservation.

Gritting her teeth, she slowed to a crawl as she crossed over the threshold and sighed with relief as her toes sunk into thick, plush carpet. At the center of the room was an enormous four-poster bed draped with a silvery gossamer material. A round mirror rested above an armoire inlaid with mother-of-pearl, and what looked to be a Tiffany lamp was tucked in the corner by an end table stacked with appropriately weighty policy tomes. The Richardsons were no lightweights in that department.

Jeanne turned the crystal knob of a door just to the left of the armoire and found herself in a walk-in closet nearly the size of her studio. She was surprised, since she had always heard that old houses had tiny closets, until she realized that this had once been a separate bedroom. Now, it was brimming with fur coats of every length, shimmery floor-skimming evening dresses, and an entire wall of shoes. Backing out slowly, she shut the door and wiped the doorknob with her sleeve.

She crossed the room and approached a door opposite the closet. A faint light emanated from the bottom; apparently the Richardsons had left the light on in their haste to make the fundraiser.

She turned the knob slowly, stepped onto the black marble floor, and gasped.

"Who are you?" she demanded as she locked eyes with a handsome, dark-eyed man. Clad in a tight black T-shirt and black jeans—neither of which left much to the imagination—his sideburns disappeared into a forest of stubble, which spread over his strong jaw line and around his full fleshy lips. "And what are you doing here?"

His nostrils flared. "I might ask you the same thing."

Chapter Four

"Imogene." Jeanne cleared her throat and tried to appear more authoritative. "Imogene Coakley. I'm a paranormal investigator hired by the Richardsons. I thought I heard something in here."

A hint of a smile played on his lips. "Do ghosts often use the restroom?"

He gently pushed a drawer shut, leaned his long muscular frame against the sink, and cocked his head towards her. Jeanne forced herself to avert her gaze from his bewitchingly deep liquid brown eyes, only to find her eyes wandering to his suggestively tilted pelvis. Jerking her head upwards, she stared resolutely at the medicine cabinet, silently reminding herself that she had a boyfriend.

"Um, no," she stammered, "ghosts, as a rule, do not use the restroom. They don't have our, uh, biological needs. But sometimes they might haunt a bathroom if something significant happened there."

"Like the shower scene in *Psycho?*"

"Yeah, something like that."

"Huh." He didn't sound convinced. "Well, I'm Jorge."

Jeanne frowned. Could he really be the Colombian nanny? She detected just the slightest trace of an accent, but he spoke perfect colloquial American English.

"Your English is excellent."

"Thank you. I would hope so since I went to the American school in Bogota. And now, if you'll excuse me, I need to finish cleaning the restroom before they return."

Jeanne skulked away, and the rest of the evening passed quite uneventfully. Jeanne and Lily neither heard nor saw any sign of Lucinda.

"What a pity," the congressman said when he returned, as if he had actually expected them to come to some kind of understanding with their resident ghost.

Old Town Alexandria, just down the river from Georgetown, was teeming with ghosts. If you could believe the tour guides, no one slept peacefully in its moldering graveyards; from the richest, meanest slave trader to the humblest scullery maid, they were all wandering around its cobblestoned streets. Jeanne did not, of course, believe in ghosts—or so she repeatedly reminded herself—but she found herself enraptured by the stories nonetheless. In front of Gadsby's Tavern, she and Fergus learned that in colonial times, an important beauty tip was not to sit too close to the fire, lest the wax covering your face melt off and reveal your smallpox scars. A few blocks away, they learned that Alexandria housewives used to buy ice from the morgue—which after all did possess the largest blocks of ice in town, albeit ones that were a bit blood-stained—thus setting off a craze for pink lemonade. "I knew it," Fergus muttered just loud enough for Jeanne to hear. "You Americans really are all vampires."

And in front of a narrow brick townhouse across from City Hall, they heard the tragic tale of a young woman whose wedding dress caught on fire.

"She died right here, on this very spot," the tour guide intoned solemnly, adjusting his wig, "with all of the wedding guests watching."

A hush fell over the tour group. "It's a candy store now," the guide continued in a low voice, indicating the gumball display in the window, "but it used to be a bridal shop. And do you think the ghost liked seeing women in wedding dresses?" He lifted his lantern and gestured at a teenaged girl in a pink T-shirt.

"Noooo," she said and her friends giggled.

"That's right. If a woman looked particularly lovely, sometimes the woman would feel a strong push." He paused for dramatic effect. "One day, a woman was pushed down the basement stairs. And that was the end of the bridal shop."

"Did the ghost ever say anything?" Jeanne asked.

"Not that I know of."

"Did the ghost ever force the bride to do anything?"

He pushed his spectacles up his nose and adjusted his wig again. "No, not that I know of. But perhaps you could ask in the gift shop...."

The rest of the tour was entertaining, but hardly informative. Afterwards, Jeanne and Fergus got ice cream cones from Ben and Jerry's and sat on a bench by the water. Lights twinkled on the far shore of the Potomac, and sea gulls circled overhead. The fog was rolling in, and for a moment, Jeanne felt as if they were the only two people in the world.

"You've got New York Super Fudge Chunk on your nose." Fergus's gravelly Scottish brogue filled her right ear.

"Do I?"

He licked it off, then gave her a long lingering kiss on the lips. He tasted like Cherry Garcia, but there was also something more—a slightly spicy, slightly salty taste that was all his own. Jeanne had always been one for wild fantastical stories, but never sentiment, which she considered a luxury reserved for those with happy childhoods. But now, to her irritation, she found herself growing increasingly sentimental. The Fergus Effect, she called it. And, at that moment, the Fergus Effect was telling her that right here, right now—with this skinny guy with the blue-gray eyes, copper-colored five o'clock shadow, and funny accent—she was home.

As if he could read her thoughts, he suddenly asked, "How's the house hunting going?"

"Not so great."

He pulled her closer and kissed her on the forehead. "Well I'm sure any day now you are going to find a reasonably priced castle, with a turret lined with books, and a dumbwaiter that connects directly to a Ben and Jerry's, plus a full-sized belly dance studio and an entire wing for Scarlett."

"Yes," Jeanne cackled, "once I convince the sheikh that New York is a much better location, his Great Falls estate will be mine!"

"Well, in that case, I'd like to apply for a position as your pool boy, masseuse, and dog walker."

"Only if we can have a completely inappropriate employer-employee relationship."

"Agreed."

An image of her and Fergus lying by the pool of her Great Falls estate flitted through Jeanne's mind. In this fantasy, he didn't look much like a bronzed, waxed Adonis of a pool boy. Swim trunks emblazoned with the Scottish flag hung loosely on his pasty white frame. As he belly-flopped into the pool, sunlight glinted off his wedding band, which jolted Jeanne back to reality.

"But seriously, Jeanne," Fergus was saying in the gravelly soft voice he used to signal that, for once, he was not kidding around. "You will let me see the places you're seriously considering, right? To at least give you my opinion?"

She could not bring herself to look directly at him, but out of the corner of her eye she glimpsed a deep pink flush beginning to spread across his cheeks.

"I mean," he continued, "in case I—in case we—in case I ever move there. Someday." He cleared his throat. "With you."

He looked at her hopefully, but Jeanne resisted the urge to hug him. Because that might give him false hope. The truth was that she just didn't know if she could marry him—or anyone else for that matter.

"Of course," she said carefully, her eyes fixed on a sailboat bobbing up and down in the harbor. "I'll be sure to get lots of opinions. From you, from Lily, from Viv. Everybody."

"I was hoping my opinion might count for a bit more."

The hopeful inflection had gone out of his voice and been replaced by a hint of anger.

Squeezing his hand in hers, Jeanne murmured, "I just—"

"Need more time. I know." He squeezed her hand and added in a lighter tone, "But I'm sure Lily and Vivienne have better decorating tips."

Jeanne felt her shoulders relax; the tension that had built up in her began to ebb. She laughed, much louder than she intended to. "I don't know. If I let Lily choose the color scheme, I'd end up with a tiger skin rug and a zebra-print couch."

"Like an African safari lodge designed by Liberace. Absolutely horrid."

"Speaking of pool boys," Jeanne said, anxious to change the subject, "the Richardsons have some rather attractive household help."

"Does this household help have a name?"

"Jorge."

Fergus groaned. "What is it with you and hot Latin men?"

Jeanne knew that he was referring to Carlos, her friend who happened to be a very attractive Salvadoran ex-con, but she decided to play dumb. "He's not as attractive as you, of course—"

"Of course."

"—but he is rather more attractive than the job of nanny would require."

"Ah, but Jeanne, as a barrister, you should know that you can't discriminate against someone because of their looks. For all you know, he could be a worldwide authority on CPR, speak flawless French, and have a track record of getting all his former charges into Harvard."

Jeanne bit into a white chocolate chunk with gusto. "All true," she said, "but that doesn't explain why he was poking around the master bathroom."

"Leaving love notes for Mrs. Richardson, perhaps?"

"That's my theory."

"Well, in exchange for the payment of a little tax"—he leaned over and took a lick of Jeanne's ice cream—"I'll give you mine: he was stealing pills. Vicodin, Percocet, that kind of thing. No one would be daft enough to leave notes in your lover's husband's bathroom."

"Unless he knows about it."

"Doubtful." Fergus frowned. "Jorge may be eye candy, but I have a feeling he has nothing to do with Lucinda's supposed appearance."

"But he's the only adult living in the home. And I checked the walls pretty carefully. There's no way for someone to sneak in."

"What about the window of the study? Or what about through the chimney that leads to the fireplace?"

Jeanne shook her head. "They've got motion-activated spotlights all over the yard. There's one tall tree in the backyard that might be out of range of the sensors, but it's too far from the house. There's no way someone could climb the tree and then jump onto the roof."

"But maybe they could swing from the tree on a rope."

Jeanne supposed that anything was possible. "Maybe."

"How is Mrs. Richardson's mental stability?"

"She doesn't seem crazy to me. A little anxious, maybe, but not crazy."

Fergus looked at the boats bobbing in the harbor for several moments, and Jeanne could almost see the wheels turning.

"One thing stands out to me," he finally said. "Mrs. Richardson did not hire you, nor did she attempt to hire anyone else to drive away Lucinda."

"Maybe she doesn't believe in paranormal investigators."

"She doesn't believe in paranormal investigators, but she does believe in ghosts? Come on, Jeanne."

"So, you're saying she doesn't want these visits to stop?"

"Maybe. Or maybe the only person she needed to be convinced of Lucinda's visits was Congressman Richardson."

"To what end?"

"That, love, is what we need to find out."

Chapter Five

"Some female spirits," Jeanne said apologetically as she, Lily, Fergus, and the Richardsons crowded into the study, "feel more comfortable talking to a male ghost hunter. So that's why we've brought along Lord MacAlester."

Fergus bowed slightly and re-adjusted his kilt. "The pleasure is all mine," he said in his deep, raspy baritone, his brogue thicker than ever.

Meaghan twisted her wedding ring and clenched her jaw. "I appreciate your efforts—really, I do—but I think she may only like to appear to me."

"We've thought of that," Jeanne reassured her. "So, this time, you're going to be an integral part of the search. And, in case it doesn't work, we'll leave the audio and video recording equipment behind so you can make recordings when you and Lucinda are completely alone." She took a deep breath. "Now, let's start with your saying what Lucinda likes you to say."

Meaghan swallowed hard. "I'm a fat disgusting cow and no one," she said in a hoarse whisper,"—here, her

lips trembled and the congressman squeezed her arm—
"will ever love me."

"Thank you, Meaghan," Jeanne said brightly. "I can
appreciate how difficult that was for you. Now let's see
what Lucinda has to say about that." She raised her
voice, as though she were an irritatingly peppy mother
talking to a hard-of-hearing toddler. "Lucinda?" she
shouted in the general direction of the fireplace. "Did
you hear that? Meaghan says she's a fat cow and no one
will love her. But someone does love her, obviously.
Congressman Richardson. He loves her and wants you
to leave her alone."

As Jeanne turned around to face the couple, she
caught them exchanging a furtive glance that she could
not quite decipher. They seemed to have a close,
companionable marriage and yet there was something
about their relationship that bothered her. But she could
not quite put her finger on it.

"Do you hear or see anything?" she asked Meaghan.

Meaghan shook her head, shaking loose a few more
tendrils from her perfectly tousled dark ponytail. Jeanne
noticed that the tendril fell into a single bead of sweat
that ran down her temple.

Suddenly, Lily flinched. "I feel tap on shoulder!" she
exclaimed. "Spirit very angry. Bang! Spirit want my
attention."

Meaghan's eyes darted from Lily to Jeanne and back
again. "But I don't see or hear anything."

Jeanne waved her hands dismissively. "That's not
necessarily unusual."

Lily stretched out her hands so that her two
divining rods were parallel. "Spirit, this is Zelda Lee. I

want to ask you some question. First, are you Lucinda Cartwright?"

For a moment, nothing happened. Then, slowly, Lily's hands trembled and the divining rods slowly began moving towards one another. They crossed and then suddenly stopped. Lily's eyes were glazed over, glassy, and completely immobile, as if she were in a trance.

"Yes," said Lily in a strange, high-pitched voice. Then, in her own voice, she continued, "Are you jealous of Mrs. Richardson?"

As if of their own accord, the divining rods moved apart, in one single fluid motion. Lily's delicate little hands, adorned with gaudy costume jewelry and accented with her trademark black fingernails, seemed to glide effortlessly through the air. The effect was mesmerizing. If she and Lily hadn't planned it all beforehand, Jeanne might have been fooled too.

"No."

This answer seemed to catch Mr. Richardson by surprise. "Well why, then," he sputtered, "is she torturing her?"

"Only yes or no questions," Jeanne reminded him.

Fergus interjected, "Are you angry with Mrs. Richardson?"

The hands jerked for just a moment and then stayed put—uncrossed.

"No," Lily intoned, expressionless.

"Is someone else bothering Mrs. Richardson?"

Lily's hands moved together.

"Yes."

Mrs. Richardson's lower lip trembled. "Who?"

"Is it an enemy of Congressman Richardson?" Jeanne asked.

The rods uncrossed.

"No."

"An enemy of Mrs. Richardson?"

They all watched as the rods moved slowly together. This time they crossed at a nearly ninety-degree angle. "Well that looks like an emphatic yes," Jeanne remarked. She shuddered in spite of herself. Lily's performance was almost too convincing.

"This is preposterous," Mr. Richardson thundered, jabbing a finger at Jeanne. "My wife has no enemies."

Nor, he might have added, had he hired her for the purpose of terrifying his wife further. His bulging blue eyes and flared nostrils told Jeanne that perhaps she should have given more specific instructions to Lily.

All eyes were on Jeanne. "Well, just like people," she stammered, "ghosts sometimes get their facts mixed up. It may be that Mrs. Richardson is mistaken. Maybe the spirit causing these problems looks like Lucinda, but is in fact someone else. Or maybe it's a real live person with a grudge and a talent for holograms."

As they continued to stare at her, Fergus reached under his kilt and slid his fingers along the hem until he extracted something soft and pliable. With a deft flick of the wrist, he scooped up a tiny amount, took a step towards the window, and pressed it gently against Mrs. Richardson's laptop.

The following day, Jeanne met Lily in the handicapped stall of the ninth-floor bathroom of Higgins, Higgins, and Applebaum—their venerable (or as Lily would say, "venereal") employer. The restroom was the perfect meeting place on a floor that was nearly all male; it was the one place they could be sure their bosses wouldn't follow them.

"Well you're quite the actress," Jeanne said as Lily perched on top of the toilet seat in tangerine stilettos. "You almost had me fooled."

Lily's almond-shaped eyes widened and she shook her head, sending her long blue-black hair cascading down her back. In a nod to the law firm's stuffy dress code, Lily reserved the hot-pink hair extensions and eyebrow ring for nights and weekends. "I didn't do anything," she protested. "Except ask the questions, of course. Those divining rods moved of their own accord."

Jeanne sighed. She had heard of people who were convinced of the power of Ouija boards, but who were in fact subconsciously moving it themselves. But she didn't realize her friend was quite that deluded.

"By the way," Lily said as reached under her zebra-print blouse and extracted a folded sheet of paper from her bra, "did you see this?" She handed it to Jeanne. "I just printed this out from the *Sludge Report*'s website. Our clients are famous. Can't say it's the most flattering picture, though."

Lily was right. It was not the most flattering portrait. The congressman's fleshy lips were wide open, in an unflattering pucker, his silver mane wreathed in a cloud of smoke. Mrs. Richardson's chin was tilted upwards, so

41

that her nostrils filled the center of the slightly grainy image.

And she was smoking a joint.

"Christian Crusader Secret Pothead," the tabloid screamed.

"Oh, no," Jeanne groaned, slumping against the cool yellow plastic wall.

As if on cue, Jeanne's cell phone began to ring.

The voice on the other end of the line had lost its pleasant, slightly soporific, drawl and with it, the veneer of gentility and refinement. Now, it was just an angry, high-pitched screech. "What have you done?"

Chapter Six

What had she done, indeed. Like many of Jeanne's plans, it had backfired spectacularly. When Fergus had suggested that someone could be spying on Meaghan through her webcam—or perhaps the baby monitor, or their home security system—and using what they learned to torment her, Jeanne thought covering the cameras would be a good way to make the harassment stop. She had not counted on Meaghan's tormentor to be quite so vindictive.

The House was expected to be in session quite late the following evening—they were debating a budget bill to forestall yet another government shutdown—and so Meaghan was confident that her husband would be gone all night. She requested that Jeanne come alone, at eight. "Jorge will be out with his friends," she informed Jeanne icily, "and Grayson will be asleep by then. So we can discuss this in total privacy."

Which was exactly what Jeanne was afraid of. As Jeanne threaded her way through the deserted back streets of Georgetown that evening, she found herself half-hoping that Lily was right—that Lucinda was a very

43

real presence in the house, and a benevolent one at that. Jeanne might need protection from a very angry client.

As she trudged up the Richardsons' front walkway, she imagined all of the ways the night could end: tied to the Richardsons' four-poster bed, being tortured by Jorge's drug trafficker friends; about to be rammed with a red-hot fire poker when suddenly saved by a mysterious supernatural presence; or clinking champagne glasses with Meaghan, laughing over this little mishap.

Jeanne was just about to rap on the door with the big brass knocker when the door swung open to reveal a shockingly disheveled Mrs. Richardson. Her face resembled some misshapen planet, a pale swollen mass of deep craters and red blotches, mascara-tinted tears streaking down her face like silt-clogged creeks. Her eyes, normally a clear celestial blue, were bloodshot and dull. Oily strands of hair hung limply against her temples.

Meaghan did not appear angry—just sad, weary, and defeated. "I did everything he asked," she said simply. "Everything."

Jeanne swallowed. "Who's he?"

"That's what I want you to find out, Imogene." For a moment, her client's eyes flashed with the anger Jeanne expected. "Or shall I call you Jeanne?"

"We beauty queens are not all stupid, you know," Meaghan said as she poured the tea into two tiny bone china cups.

"Of course not," Jeanne said quickly. She sat on the very edge of the divan, and tapped her foot lightly on the floor. It unnerved her that Meaghan knew her real name.

"Nor are we naïve," Meaghan continued as she took a sip. Jeanne noticed that she held her pinkie aloft, as though she were in a Jane Austen miniseries on BBC. The product of finishing school, Jeanne surmised. "I don't actually believe in ghosts, you know."

"No?" Jeanne's voice came out as a squeak.

Meaghan shook her head. "Nor do you. It didn't take me long to find out there was no Imogene Coakley—and that my husband had written a check to a Ms. Jeanne Pelletier."

Jeanne cleared her throat. "I apologize for the deception. Your husband hired me as something of an amateur private investigator. Since he believed that you believed in Lucinda, we thought it easiest to indulge your little fantasy."

"I don't blame you."

"But I still don't understand why you deceived your husband."

"What would you tell your husband if he found you stark naked, covered in black spots, and repeating gibberish?"

"The truth," Jeanne said, looking down at the sheet of paper that Meaghan had placed on the coffee table. "That I was being blackmailed."

"Have you ever been married?"

Jeanne felt the color rush to her cheeks. "No."

Meaghan tucked her legs underneath her and regarded Jeanne with the bemused look of an enlightened yogi. "I thought so."

Jeanne reached into her purse, pulled out a pair of thin gloves, and slid them on. "May I?" she asked, and Meaghan nodded.

Holding the paper aloft, Jeanne tilted it in the light. The chandelier sent beams of light dancing across it, but Jeanne detected no watermark. The paper was of the most ordinary sort, slightly off-white, the kind used in every office printer. Each letter had been cut out of a magazine—or rather, she suspected, several magazines—since the fonts did not match. "Have you dusted for fingerprints?" Jeanne asked.

"I bought a cheap hobbyist's kit." Meaghan sighed. "Nothing."

"The police might be able to pick up something you—"

Meaghan cut her off. "No police," she said. "Absolutely no police."

Jeanne considered this. "Well, in any case, there are probably no fingerprints to find. Whoever is doing this is quite clever. And even if there were, they probably wouldn't be in any database." She looked up from the note. "Where's the envelope this came in?"

Meaghan hopped up, crossed the room to the antique desk, and rummaged around until she extracted two envelopes. Jeanne could not help but be impressed by the way Meaghan practically glided across the room, as if she were on a runway.

When Meaghan rejoined Jeanne, she slid both envelopes, as well as another note across the coffee table.

A perfectly manicured fire engine red nail tapped the envelope on the left. "The first note came in this one, the second one came in that one."

Jeanne leaned forward and squinted at the postmarks. "Laurel, Maryland," she read aloud. "Do you know anyone there?"

"Not that I know of."

Jeanne picked up the first note and read it silently:

"You have taken my love
And for that you must pay
To your study you must repair each day
Disrobe, cover yourself in black spots and say:
I am a fat disgusting cow and no one will ever love me."

"I can't say I think much of his poetry skills," Jeanne said. "You have taken my love," she slowly repeated. "I can think of two possible interpretations. Either he"—she frowned—"or she—feels you were a rival for someone's affections and you won. Or they blame you for the death of a loved one. Was Congressman Richardson seeing anyone when you started dating him?"

"No. He was separated from his wife at the time, but there was no one else."

"His wife might not have seen it that way."

"There was also a little intern who was always following him around."

"Did they have an affair?"

"No." Meaghan's blue eyes flashed with indignation, but Jeanne was not sure she believed her.

"Name?"

"I don't remember. I paid no attention since I knew I had nothing to worry about."

Jeanne had her doubts. She scrutinized the second note, which had arrived earlier that day:

You have taken away my vision
Of your humiliation
Before 'twas private your painful incision
Now, you must face the nation
If you do not begin to behave
My slave, and honor our deal
As you know, there is much, much more
That I can—and will—reveal.

Jeanne tossed both sheets back on the table. "What else can he reveal?"

"How should I know?"

"What I mean, Meaghan, is what other activities do you"—she groped for a polite word—"engage in, that could be used as blackmail?"

Meaghan's face flushed, so that all of the white spaces between her crimson blotches disappeared. "I am under no obligation to tell you."

Jeanne lowered her head, not daring to make eye contact. "But there are other things?"

Meaghan's silence told Jeanne what she needed to know. She had other secrets—and whatever they were, they were much, much worse than pot smoking.

Jeanne busied herself by examining *The Sludge Report* photo again. She held it aloft, and turned slowly around until she located the background. The Richardsons must have been sitting in the leather settee by the back window when the picture was taken. At the edge of the photo she could just make out the enormous blown glass vase on the end table next to the settee. Today, it held a dozen red roses; the day the photo had been taken, the roses were yellow.

"Do you remember when you last had yellow roses in the vase on the end table?" Jeanne asked without taking her eyes off the vase. She aligned the photo so that she was looking at the settee from exactly the same angle as the photographer and then began to walk backwards.

"My sister brought those on my birthday. July 12th."

Jeanne walked twenty paces until she could go no further. If she had, she would have walked straight into a glass case filled with dozens of antique dolls. "A wall of eyes," Jeanne murmured, as a hundred pairs of unnaturally blue eyes stared back at her. She supposed they were collectibles, but she found the effect quite creepy, not the least because they all resembled Mrs. Richardson.

"Beautiful, aren't they?" Meaghan said and Jeanne detected a bit of wistfulness in her voice. Unlike her, they would be perfect, silent, fragile, raven-haired beauty queens forever. They would never get old or wrinkly. Kept under lock and key, they were safe from the outside world, from the prying eyes of others.

But Jeanne suspected that at least one of them did indeed have prying eyes.

She glanced again at the photo. Mrs. Richardson's unusually large nostrils suggested that the photo was taken from down below, so she scrutinized the bottom two rows. "I need the key."

Wordlessly, Meaghan went to the desk, located the key, and brought it to Jeanne.

Jeanne gently reached around and felt the back of each of the doll's heads.

"That's the outfit I wore in the 1998 Miss South Carolina swimsuit competition," Meaghan babbled as Jeanne inspected one wearing a blue gingham bikini. "And that's a replica of my evening gown from the 1997 Miss South Carolina pageant."

Jeanne froze. "Is each of these dolls wearing one of your outfits from a beauty pageant?"

Meaghan nodded happily and sighed. Jeanne turned around to conceal her disgust. She felt almost dirty, poking and prodding her way through this monument to Mrs. Richardson's ego.

She was about to give up when she felt a soft spot on the back of yet another head of black horsehair. She pushed aside the hair to reveal a small hole.

Jeanne held a finger to her lips, then pried apart the plastic. She pointed to the tiny camera lodged behind the doll's eye.

The only sound was the thud of Mrs. Richardson's body hitting the hardwood floor.

Chapter Seven

When Mrs. Richardson regained consciousness, Jeanne hustled her across the street. While Meaghan huddled beneath a streetlamp, smoking her first cigarette in fifteen years, Jeanne gave her strict instructions to carry on as if there were no cameras. "If he so much as suspects you're on to him," Jeanne warned, "there will probably be another *Sludge* report."

"Ten times worse," Meaghan said hollowly.

Jeanne found herself wondering yet again what else the Richardsons were hiding, but she bit her tongue. Instead, she asked, "Are those the only two letters you've ever received?"

"Yes."

"It seems odd that he doesn't want any money. Don't you think?"

Meaghan shrugged and flicked her cigarette butt, sending a flurry of embers raining down on the thick mat of golden ginkgo leaves underfoot. "Not really."

"Don't you find his demands to be rather specific, rather"—she fixed her best long, hard stare on Meaghan,

who quickly busied herself with her cigarette—
"personal?"

"What's personal about making someone paint
themselves like a cow?" Meaghan scoffed. "If you ask me,
he's just a pervert."

Jeanne could not imagine that the average pervert
would expend so much effort—and risk such a long jail
sentence—just to see a naked woman painted as a cow.
And even in a city full of people with odd sexual
proclivities, this one seemed particularly unusual. "There
are any number of crack whores along New York
Avenue," she observed, "who would be more than
willing to strip naked and cover themselves in spots for a
single hit."

For a moment Jeanne shivered, thinking of the first
time she had driven down New York Avenue. At its
eastern end, it was an endless succession of soulless
barbed-wire ringed hotels, fast food restaurants, and gas
stations. It smelled of French fry grease and chicken fat
and, in stark contrast to the glistening, power-hungry city
below, it teemed with people who wanted nothing more
to forget and to be forgotten. The prostitutes stumbled
along the road, weaving into oncoming traffic, eyes
vacant and unseeing. Their fishnet stockings were
ripped, their tube tops were stained. They wore no make-
up and no jewelry. There was not even the pretense of
elegance, or romance, or even lust pure and simple. They
were willing to do anything to anyone for any price.

Along this desolate stretch of highway, in a seedy
motel room with a world-weary hooker and a bag of
coke, Marion Barry—once hailed as Mayor for Life—had
met his demise.

No, Jeanne realized, this was not about sex. It was about humiliation. It was about revenge.

"Did you ever humiliate anyone publicly?" Jeanne asked. "A fellow historian, a member of the Charity League, another politician's wife?"

Meaghan shrugged. "My husband has beaten quite a few opponents. But I don't think any one of them would hate us that much."

"I'll need their names." Jeanne thought for a moment. "Fat cow," she repeated slowly. She had been called that a handful of times herself, even though she was technically, as her doctor would say, "overweight but not obese." But factual or not, the words always stung, as if someone had pierced her side with a coil of barbed wire, and the more she struggled to rid herself of the hateful words, the more and more damage she did.

No one, she thought bitterly, ever called a man a "fat bull." Obese men were "sturdy" or "massive" or "solid"—pillars of strength, intelligent and immovable, forces to be reckoned with. Powerful. But fat women were cows—dull-witted, slow-moving herd animals who were to be eventually ground up for hamburger.

"Have you ever called someone a 'fat cow'?" she asked. The phrase stuck in her throat and came out slightly garbled.

"I can't remember," Meaghan said airily.

"I bet they would." Jeanne tried to keep her tone light, but a slight edge crept into her voice.

A gust of wind swept down the street, sending the fallen leaves scattering along the sidewalk.

"I'm going to need your high school yearbooks," Jeanne said. "College yearbooks, any old photos or programs from past social activities. Any names of anyone you might have insulted."

And with that, Jeanne bid her goodnight.

Jeanne's real estate agent picked her up at nine the next morning.

"Hop in, toots," Roxy bellowed out the window of her enormous black Suburban as she pulled into the driveway. Her platinum blond hair was piled on top of her head like a bird's nest, and her lips were the color of Pepto-Bismol. "Today's your lucky day, hon. Have I got the place for you!"

Heaving open the heavy door, Jeanne slid into the passenger seat and gave Roxy a weak smile. A thrice-divorced former Vegas showgirl, Roxy had been a stripper in Penn Quarter before it was glitzed up in the nineties, and then parlayed her connections to the rich and powerful to launch an astonishingly successful real estate career. She was also an eternal optimist, and Jeanne had heard her say "have I got the place for you" more times than she could remember—and often right before catching sight of a rat scurrying behind the countertops. One "cozy place in an exciting neighborhood" had even had a bullet hole in the bedroom window.

"I see that look, hon," Roxy said as she waved a liver-spotted hand laden with sapphires, rubies, and emeralds. With the weight from all of those rings, Jeanne was amazed Roxy could even lift her hands. "And

I know what you're thinking. 'I bet old Roxy's got a real doozy picked out for me today,' but trust me, this one I've already seen. I showed it to a client last week who decided she wanted to be closer to Georgetown. But it's going to be perfect for you and Scarlett. A block from the dog park. Big closets. A decent nineties kitchen. No bugs, no rats, no mice. So clean you could eat off the floor."

So Jeanne was mildly optimistic as they drove up Massachusetts Avenue and pulled in front of a Y-shaped high rise surrounded by a beautiful green expanse of lawn. Her excitement built as they took the elevator to the ninth floor and headed to the corner unit. When they stepped inside, the first thing that Jeanne noticed was what was not present: mold. "It smells nice."

Roxy dumped her bulging lemon yellow purse on the floor and kicked off her leopard print heels. "Then you know you're home. That's how I used to feel about The Frisky Puss. The minute I walked in, I'd catch a whiff of cheap beer and male sweat and I'd think, yep, this is where I belong."

Jeanne couldn't imagine feeling at home in The Frisky Puss, so she nodded absentmindedly and was relieved when Roxy led her into the kitchen to extol the virtues of the pine cabinets, white appliances, and cute little breakfast nook by the window. There was not a hint of anything avocado-colored in sight.

Roxy sashayed into the living room, a spacious expanse of parquet floors leading to a wall of picture windows and a cute little balcony. Roxy tapped a tangerine nail on the window. "And check out the view, hon. Right now, it's a covered swimming pool, but come summer, you'll be able to ogle all the strapping young hunks running around half naked."

Jeanne smiled in spite of herself. "I have a boyfriend, Roxy. Remember?"

"It's not a crime to look."

The more Jeanne saw, the more she loved it. The den was lined with bookshelves; the bedroom had a large wall mirror perfect for practicing belly dance routines. "I'll take it," she blurted out in the middle of Roxy's rhapsody about the ample closet space. "Er, how much is the asking price?"

"Three forty-nine."

"And the condo fee?"

"Two seventy-five."

Jeanne did a few quick calculations. With the money she'd received from the Richardsons, she could make a fifteen percent down payment. The monthly mortgage payment would only be about two hundred dollars more than her rent. If she could negotiate a small raise, or pick up a couple of extra belly dancing—or sleuthing—gigs, she could easily cover the extra. Or she could just switch to eating Scarlett's dog food.

"I can do that," she said with more confidence than she felt.

Roxy slung an arm around her and squeezed, giving Jeanne an overpowering whiff of Chanel No. 9, cigarettes, and hairspray. "I have a good feeling about this one, hon. If we can get an offer in by the end of the day, I think it's yours."

****

By the following evening, Jeanne had an accepted offer and a closing date five weeks away. She made Scarlett some doggie ice cream—frozen yogurt, honey, and peanut butter—to celebrate, and they curled up on the couch, slurping their respective ice cream and watching a thunderstorm roll over the National Cathedral. "I am going to miss this view, though," she sighed.

And Jerry, she thought with a sudden pang, and then she chuckled. If anyone had told her a year ago that she would be sad to move away from Jerry—her rude, crude, irascible neighbor who drank like a fish, smoked like a chimney, and blared his TV at all hours of the night—she would have laughed in their face. But now she counted Jerry as one of her best friends. He was almost like a brother to her.

"But don't worry, Scar," she whispered as she scratched behind her pooch's ears. "I'm taking you with me. And it's near the dog park."

As if she understood and was very pleased, Scarlett snuggled even closer to her. Jeanne was glad that Scarlett was pleased. Now she just hoped Fergus would be too.

When Fergus knocked on her door later that evening, she quickly pulled him inside, pressed him against the sink, and gave him a searing kiss.

Fergus came up for air just long enough to murmur, "Are you making lasagna?"

"Yes," Jeanne whispered, and she felt his lips curl into a little smile. Lasagna was Fergus's favorite food (or at least his favorite food that didn't involve stuffing a sheep's intestine, which was where Jeanne drew the line).

She had left nothing to chance. Homemade lasagna was in the oven, a cold Guinness was in the fridge, and a *Monty Python* marathon was queued up in her DVD player. She'd even made some extra doggie ice cream for him to take home to Magnus.

His hot breath shot into her ear. "What's the special occasion?"

"I'll tell you the good news after dinner."

He moved his arms down to her waist and touched his forehead to hers. "You look like a cyclops."

"So do you."

"Tell me the good news now." He gave her an extra little squeeze. "I don't want to wait."

Jeanne bit her lip and then tried to smile. Why was she hesitating? He'd be happy for her, right? He had, of course, wanted to see the place before she put an offer on it. But the D.C. real estate market was red-hot and if she hadn't put in an offer, someone else would have snapped it up. Surely Fergus would understand that. She gripped the counter. "I bought a house today!"

His jaw tensed and he loosened his grip on her waist. Jeanne felt as though some sort of vital life force was ebbing away from her, and panic began to well up in her chest. "You're going to love it," she babbled, grabbing his hand and pressing it to her heart. It felt cold and limp in her hot, clammy grip. "Lots of natural light, hardwood floors—okay, they're parquet, but still—

an okay kitchen—nothing avocado—room for Scarlett and—"

"And me?" He shook his hand free and stuffed it in his pocket. His cloudy blue eyes flashed with indignation, and beneath his coppery stubble, his cheeks were beginning to turn bright red. "Is there room for me in this place? Is there room for me in your life, for that matter? Does my opinion count for anything?"

"Of course—"

He cut her off. "Of course not. You don't consult me about anything." He angrily wiped away a tear that was forming in the corner of his eye.

Jeanne's mouth hung open. "I wasn't thinking," she whispered, the tears splashing down her face and turning her shirt into a hot, salty mess. "You know how the real estate market is in D.C. If you don't snap something up—"

"Save it," he said, backing away from her. He had one hand on the doorknob already. "Save your bogus explanation for sad-sack Jerry or drama queen Lily. They'll probably eat it up. But please tell your shrink the real reason—that your mommy issues have so damaged you that you won't let anyone in."

For a moment, he took his hand off the doorknob, and Jeanne felt a flutter of hope. But instead of rushing towards her and scooping her into his arms—which is, of course, what would have happened in a movie—Fergus stomped though the kitchen, grabbed a sheet of paper off the dining room table, and brandished it like a weapon.

With a sinking heart, Jeanne caught a glimpse of the seal of Maine.

"You think I don't know about this?" he fumed. "I have been waiting patiently for you to bring this up. But do you? No! How can I be with someone who hides everything from me?"

Jeanne noticed that the more he ranted, the thicker his brogue got. She cleared her throat. "I was going to—"

"When?" he roared.

Then he dropped the sheet of paper and looked hopelessly about the room, as if this were the last time he would ever see it. "I just can't do this anymore." He strode right past her, without bothering to look up. "Have a nice life, Jeanne. I hope you find someone who really loves a mystery woman who tells him nothing and consults him about nothing."

The door slammed behind him with a finality that made Jeanne jump. "I love you," she whispered helplessly at the door. She would have repeated it a hundred times—a thousand times even—were it not for the sudden beeping of her fire alarm and the acrid smell that suddenly filled the air.

Her lasagna was on fire.

Chapter Eight

Jeanne was in a terrible funk. She sulked at home, shuffling between her futon and the kitchen in a ratty pink bathrobe. Scarlett kept eyeing her hopefully, but Jeanne was in no mood for a walk. "No more romps with Magnus the Great," Jeanne said crossly. Magnus was Fergus's Aunt Margaret's Labradoodle, and it seemed as though Fergus—who had come "across the pond," as he put it, to care for his elderly aunt—spent half of his life walking him. "If it hadn't been for that horndog being unable to keep his paws off you, I wouldn't have cut my knee. And if I hadn't cut my knee, I wouldn't have gone to Aunt Margaret's house to get it bandaged. And if I hadn't gone there"—Jeanne's voice cracked and a single tear streamed down her face and sloshed into her hot chocolate—"I wouldn't have fallen for Fergus."

Scarlett snorted, turned tail, and went back to the futon, where she stretched out regally, like a sphinx with just one forepaw.

Even my dog thinks I am full of shit, Jeanne thought, as she took a sip of hot chocolate. It warmed her throat, raw from days of intermittent crying, but she found it oddly tasteless. Everything, in fact, was less— food was less salty, less sweet, less satisfying; coffee was less caffeinated; the skies were less blue. When she dragged a chair to the rooftop of her building to enjoy the view of the National Cathedral, the sight of a wedding party provoked a bitterness that surprised even herself. "Naïve romantics," she muttered as she tried to busy herself in a stack of Meaghan's yearbooks. "They'll probably be divorced within a year."

Jeanne had the odd sensation of living in one of those optical illusion paintings, where you can either see two ugly old women or a beautiful vase. Everything she saw resembled the ugly old women, and everything everyone else saw resembled the vase.

"You're scaring me, Jeanne," Lily said as they practiced their troupe's latest belly dance routine, a cane dance, in the basement of Lily's communal living experiment. Every so often, a roommate wandered in to look for a ukulele, a hookah, or Gloria, Lily's pet snake. "You sound a lot like Jerry right now. Bitter at the world."

"Why not? Maybe the world deserves it."

Lily sighed. "Why didn't you consult Fergus about the condo?"

"You know how fast things are snapped up in D.C."

"So fast you can't whip out a cell phone and ask him to come right over and see it?"

"Well, it is my house," Jeanne grumbled.

"Well, then," Lily said with the self-satisfying tone of one adept at reverse psychology, "you shouldn't be upset."

Here it comes, Jeanne thought, as she found herself speeding up. Her taps were a millisecond before Lily's and together they beat a jarring syncopation across the linoleum floor.

Lily waited until the turn to lower the boom. "After all," she said, "now you most certainly will have the place all to yourself."

Jeanne couldn't argue with Lily's logic, but it irked her nonetheless—and it continued to irk her the entire bus ride home. *You sound just like Jerry.* Lily's words echoed inside her, growing louder and louder, until she was sure the other passengers could hear it.

And so, after taking Scarlett outside for a quick pee, she gathered every scrap of paper and every inch of videotape chronicling Meaghan's existence at the pinnacle of the social pyramid and trooped off down the hallway, to a familiar place that reeked of smoke and strong coffee. Through the door, she could hear Bob Dylan's nasal, high-pitched voice lamenting something, and Jeanne couldn't help but be perversely pleased. The odds of Jerry's mood matching hers were high.

A moment later, the door flung open. "Twinkletoes," Jerry grunted with just a hint of a smile on his lips.

"Hi, Jerry." Grateful to be able to skip all of the normal neighborly pleasantries, Jeanne barged through the narrow galley kitchen—filthy, as usual, she noted approvingly—and dumped the stack of yearbooks and videotapes on Jerry's coffee table with a thud. The table wobbled slightly, sending the overflowing ashtrays skittering across the surface and blanketing the table in a thin film of ash.

"My new client Meaghan's whole life," she said by way of explanation.

"And how's *your* life?" Jerry called from the kitchen as the apartment door swung shut.

"I think today is the day I'll try Turkish coffee."

"That bad, huh?"

It was a rhetorical question. As Jeanne heard the familiar whirl of the coffee grinder, she settled into the smaller of two dips in the couch. The larger was a veritable crater, a glacial depression worn down by a decade of accommodating Jerry's considerable girth, not to mention his inimitable way of diving onto the sofa with all of the force of a torpedo hitting its target. The smaller of the two craters had been worn away by Jeanne's posterior which, she suddenly realized, had spent quite a few hours on this couch. She wondered if, in fact, she was the only other person that had ever sat on this couch.

Jeanne put her feet up on the table without bothering to remove her Mickey Mouse slippers. The head of the left one had been practically chewed off by Scarlett during her teething phase.

In spite of her vile mood, she had to smile at the irony as she flipped through Meaghan's college yearbook. Perfect Meaghan of the shiny long black hair and long eyelashes, some football or lacrosse player staring adoringly at her in every photo, was now at the mercy of Jeanne—she of the ratty bathrobe, half-chewed slippers, execrable manners (witness the feet on the table), questionable friends, and disastrous love life—to identify her blackmailer.

A few minutes later, Jerry brought her a chipped yellow mug that said "It's Five O'Clock Somewhere." Thousands of granules floated across the surface of the inky black liquid, forming little eddies and whirls. It looked as though Jerry had dipped the mug into a silt-swollen river during a one-hundred-year flood, but to Jeanne it seemed like truth serum.

She steadied herself and took a sip. "Not bad," she said, as much to her surprise as Jerry's.

"Not too strong?"

"No."

Jerry shook his head slowly and lowered himself into the crater. The sofa groaned under the added weight, and Jerry patted the armrest, almost as if to comfort it.

"Then it's bad," he said slowly, reaching for a cigarette and pulling an ashtray onto his lap.

In a well-rehearsed ritual, Jeanne hopped up and opened a window.

"Braveheart?" he asked as he lit a match.

Jeanne tried her best to shrug noncommittally as she sat back down. "It's not so bad being single, right?"

Jerry laughed and turned his sad liquid brown eyes towards her. "You're asking me? Listen, Twinkletoes, everyone has some kind of relationship, even single people. Mine just happens to be with Jim Bean and the Marlboro Man. And I'd say your relationship with Braveheart is" -he peered closely at her, and she flinched slightly—"or was, at least, a lot healthier than that."

She looked out the window to avoid his gaze. Jerry had a partially obstructed view of the cathedral, and she could see the fog swirling, dark and ominous, around the left spire. "Well look at my family's track record," she said. "Things didn't work out so well for Vivienne. Or my poor dad."

"Well to state the obvious, Jeanne, you're not your dad or your mom or Vivienne." He laughed, which turned into a coughing fit. When he recovered, he added, "For one thing, you're not as hot."

Which was Jeanne's cue to slug him and change subjects. She loved that about Jerry—he had that ability to know when to deliver advice, and when to change the subject. In a strange way, he was a master of human psychology—as only the truly damaged can be—and, at times like these, Jeanne could understand why—before the *incident*, as he called it, before the PTSD, before his torrid affair with alcohol—he had once been a successful CIA agent.

Fortified by Jerry's Turkish coffee, they spent the next two hours poring over Meaghan's yearbooks. Jerry scrutinized every photo that included Meaghan, searching for a frown, a wince, a sad gaze, anyone who stood slightly apart. When he found one, Jeanne googled the name on his laptop.

"It's interesting," Jeanne mused. "Some of these outcasts are wildly successful now. So far, we've got two doctors, three lawyers, a college professor, and a stay-at-home mom with eight children."

Jerry chuckled. "Well I'd call that success...unless one of the metrics is effective use of birth control." He took a long drag on his cigarette. "Seriously, though, it doesn't surprise me that much. Most people who were introverts in high school study hard and do well; it's the 'in' crowd that flames out. They look so smug in these photos. If only they knew that high school would be the best time of their lives. It's all downhill for them from there."

"What kind were you?"

He patted his gut, which spilled over his waistband. "Captain of the football team, can't you tell?" He gave her a conspiratorial, sardonic little smile. "You?"

"Middle of the pack, honestly. Not an outcast, not a popular kid." She took a sip. "Until, of course, my mom ran over and killed half of the popular kids."

"But you didn't stick around to see if they actually blamed you."

"I blamed me."

Jeanne wanted to add that if only she had listened to that pesky voice in her head and stayed home from Prom—if only she had hidden the keys from her mother, if only she had lent a sympathetic ear to her mother's pathetic retelling of her crowning as Prom Queen—her classmates would still be alive.

And her little sister Annie.

If only, if only, if only.

But Jeanne held her tongue; Jerry's response would be the same as always: "woulda, coulda, shoulda. Stop blaming yourself, Twinkletoes."

As if reading her mind, Jerry said, "We're always harder on ourselves than other people are."

Jeanne looked out the window again. The fog had completely obscured the spire, transforming the cathedral from a soaring Gothic edifice to a squat stone rectangle. "I've got a chance to find out, though," she said. "My high school reunion is in three weeks."

"Maybe it's time to make up with Braveheart," Jerry said. His voice was serious, although it seemed to Jeanne that he was trying to inject some levity. "It's always nice to make an appearance with an attractive significant other on your arm."

"Fat chance." Jeanne turned back to look at Jerry. "And I can make it a two-fer. My mom's parole hearing is the next day."

Jerry nodded sagely. "Are you going?"

"To which one?"

"You tell me."

"Maybe." She took another sip. "What was that last name? The one who rushed Meaghan's sorority her junior year?"

"Edith Sawyer."

"Edith," Jeanne repeated as she typed the name in. "With a name like that, I can see why she was unpopular."

Jeanne sucked in her breath. "Well, here's one that was not that successful. Or not that lucky anyway."

She turned the screen so that Jerry could read the *Baltimore Sun* obituary with her.

"And look at the date—three weeks before Meaghan got the first letter."

Chapter Nine

It was not terribly hard to guess Edith's cause of death. As Jeanne devoured every last online trace of the woman, she was struck by the contrast between the slightly pudgy, round-faced girl in the yearbook picture and the scraggly hair, toothpick arms, and protruding collarbones that jutted out of Edith's recent LinkedIn photo. If it weren't for Edith's slightly off-kilter beak nose and intense expression, Jeanne would have sworn it was a different person.

Jeanne felt a sharp pang of sympathy as she typed "Robert and Anna Sawyer" into whitepages.com. She could only imagine how awful it would be to watch your daughter waste away.

Running her fingers absentmindedly through Scarlett's fur, she scrolled through the results. There were six couples in Baltimore with those names, but only two that were in the right age range. She typed both addresses into Google Maps, and immediately knew which number to call. The other couple was in gritty east Baltimore and almost certain to be African-American.

The voice that answered was high-pitched and brittle. "Yes?"

"I'm an old friend of Edith's," Jeanne said. "I'm in town for a conference and I was hoping to come by and offer my condolences. Unfortunately, I just couldn't get away for the funeral."

"You must know her from Whistling Springs."

Jeanne's heart sank. There went her backstory about being Edith's lab partner. She had no idea what Whistling Springs was, so all she could do was play along. "How did you know?"

"Those are the only people who call her Edith. Everyone else calls"—her voice broke as she switched to past tense—"er, called, her Edie."

Mrs. Sawyer was silent for a moment. Then, in a voice so low Jeanne could barely hear her, she said, "Come by at four."

An hour and a half later, Jeanne slid into a seat on a sleek Acela train—expense accounts were a wonderful thing—next to a gray-haired man in a double-breasted black suit. He smiled at her, his silvery stubble glinting in the sunlight. "Going to New York?"

"Baltimore."

"Ah." He shifted in his seat and stretched out his legs. "Me too. I'm speaking at a gastrointestinal health conference."

Jeanne tried to make some polite noises of delight and admiration, but she found it difficult to get too excited about her seatmate's expertise in irritable bowel syndrome. Disappointed, he crouched over his tray table, making the occasional edit to his speech, while Jeanne closed her eyes and pretended to sleep. She silently reviewed everything she had crammed into her head about Whistling Springs, "an award-winning, patient-centered residential treatment facility for women with eating disorders."

Thirty minutes later, thanks to the magic of high-speed rail, they were in Baltimore, and one hour, a bus ride, and a water taxi after that, Jeanne was lifting the brass knocker on the front door of an expensive, three-story rowhouse in Fells Point.

She knocked three times before she heard the slow, deliberate footsteps, the click-clack of a solid heel on hardwood floors. A pale, bird-like woman opened the door, blinking into the harsh afternoon sun like a bear just emerging from a winter's hibernation. Her eyes were a pale, watery, robin's egg blue, heavily lidded and almost devoid of eyelashes. She peered out at Jeanne from beneath a very pronounced brow. "Come in," she said and ushered Jeanne into the house without even bothering to ask her name.

Jeanne followed her down a dark hallway and into a large sitting room. Other than the drawn shades, it reminded her of a set for a Martha Stewart special, all floral pastels and doilies. Mrs. Sawyer settled into a pink chintz couch, crossing one shimmery nylon-sheathed leg over the other in a most ladylike fashion. Jeanne marveled that anyone still wore nylons, especially at home.

Mrs. Sawyer tugged at the hem of her knee-length black skirt and then, almost as if it possessed some talismanic properties, ran a pale, bony finger over the silver frame of an 8x10 photo on the end table next to her. The photo had been taken some time between Edith's pudgy college days and her later emaciated phase. She was surprisingly, arrestingly beautiful—luminous even in the gloom.

Edith's mom flushed slightly and turned towards Jeanne, who was perched uncomfortably on a matching loveseat. Unlike Jerry's couch, it did not have the slightest give; she felt like a beached whale.

And evidently Mrs. Sawyer thought she looked like one. "I see you've made a nice recovery," she said as she zeroed in on Jeanne's slightly protruding tummy.

"Oh, yes," Jeanne said weakly and then confidently she added, "The program at Whistling Springs worked very well for me. Maybe too well." She patted her belly and attempted a laugh.

But Mrs. Sawyer was not laughing. "I wish it had worked that well for Edie. If it had—"

She didn't finish the sentence, but, then, she didn't need to. Jeanne silently finished it for her. If it had worked, Edie would still be with them.

Jeanne offered a string of vaguely comforting platitudes and some relatively generic tales about their exploits at Whistling Springs. She tried to avoid anything too specific. Details were dangerous.

Twenty minutes into their conversation, Mrs. Sawyer sighed. "Honestly, dear, I don't remember you." She shook her head. "I guess it's just old age."

"I'm sure you were just too preoccupied with Edith. She always said how much she enjoyed your visits. She was one of the lucky ones, to have such supportive parents."

"Did she say that?" Mrs. Sawyer's eyes filled with tears for a moment, and then she shook them away. Jeanne felt a small measure of satisfaction at being able to at least give her some comfort. "Well, that's all in the past." The older woman sighed. "Now what conference did you say you were in town for?"

"The American Association of Gastrointestinal Specialists," Jeanne said without missing a beat.

To Jeanne's horror, Mrs. Sawyer suddenly brightened. "What a coincidence! I was just thinking about seeing someone. I suspect I may have irritable bowel syndrome and all of this stress is aggravating my condition..."

Jeanne felt her hands go clammy and her throat go dry. The room began to spin. And as it began to spin, she caught a glimpse of another framed photograph across the room, on top of the grand piano. Edith was smiling, but her cheekbones were hollow and her hair had lost its sheen. One skinny arm was slung around a stocky, dark-haired young man with a full beard.

"...at first I thought it was a gluten allergy," Mrs. Sawyer was saying, and Jeanne tried nod along.

"Yes, the two are often confused," Jeanne mumbled, hoping that was true. She reached into her pocket, hoping to find a tissue to wipe the bead of sweat that was slowly tricking down her forehead, and her fingers brushed the edges of a small rectangular card. With a sigh of relief, she pressed the doctor's business card into

Mrs. Sawyer's hand. "My colleague," she said. "He's the very best. You should give him a call."

Jeanne smiled at Mrs. Sawyer, her heartbeat starting to return to normal. "I really need to be getting back to the conference." She rose and went to the piano. "But before I go, I just wanted to ask about her boyfriend." She gestured towards the photo. "What was his name again?"

"Brian."

Jeanne snapped her fingers. "That's it! Brian. Brian...O'Rourke, O'Malley, something like that?"

Mrs. Sawyer gave her a funny look. "Schwartz."

"Huh. Well I remembered it was some kind of ethnic name. Irish, German, something like that."

"I didn't think they were dating when she was at Whistling Springs."

"They weren't," Jeanne said quickly. "I met him just once when I was in town. Seemed like a real nice guy. Treated her like a queen."

"Yes, he did." Mrs. Sawyer's expression softened. "A real sweetie, and very smart. He was always fixing our computer. A real whiz kid."

"How wonderful. Did he work in IT?"

"That was my impression. He worked for the government, I know. But in this area"—a hint of a smile played on her lips—"I know not to ask too many questions."

Jeanne thanked her for her time, gave Mrs. Sawyer an awkward hug, and walked back out into the blinding sunshine. Closing her eyes, she turned her face to the sun and the warmth suffused her face. She was happy to be out of the gloom. She was happy to be alive.

And, for once, she felt happy—ecstatically happy—about her body. Curves, bulges—she loved it all. She would rather be nine hundred pounds and evacuated from her home on a whale sling than suffer the way Edith had.

There was only one thing to do. She made her way to Vaccaro's in Little Italy, ordered an overflowing chocolate cannoli, and as she cheerfully licked the last bits of chocolatey, cheesy goodness from her fingertips, gave her client a call.

"Mmmm. Hello?" Meaghan's drawl was more soporific than usual, and she sounded a bit sleepy. Jeanne suspected she was being pampered in a tony Georgetown spa.

"Ever heard of a Brian Schwartz?"

There was a rustle of sheets, as if Meaghan were adjusting to a seated position. Jeanne could hear Meaghan inhale sharply. Good. She had her client's attention.

"He went to high school with me."

"Small world." Jeanne picked up a stray chocolate chip and popped it into her mouth. "He later dated Edith Sawyer."

"Who?" Meaghan sounded annoyed.

"Edith Sawyer. She rushed your sorority."

"Oh." There was a pause, and Jeanne could almost see Meaghan scrunching her perfectly arched dark eyebrows. "Kind of a fat, forgettable girl, was she?"

The words cut Jeanne like a knife. Edith was not all that fat, and she certainly wasn't forgettable. Not to Brian. Not to her mom. With a sudden shudder of revulsion, Jeanne pushed the phone away from her ear, as if just touching it would contaminate her with Meaghan's pettiness. Then she took a deep breath and reminded herself that this was a purely business relationship. She didn't have to like her client.

"Jeanne, are you still there?"

She moved the phone back to her ear. "Edith's not fat anymore, Meaghan. She's thin—anorexic actually—and she's dead." In spite of her best efforts, her voice came out icy, so hard she suspected it could have cut through Meaghan's diamond necklace, a replica of which was sparkling away in her client's creepy cabinet of mini-Meaghans. "According to Edith's mom, Brian is a computer whiz with some sort of top secret government job."

There was another rustle of sheets. "So what are you saying?"

Jeanne swallowed, choosing her words carefully. "If—rightly or wrongly—he thought you had anything to do with her anorexia, he might have held you responsible for her death. So he's got a motive. And he's a computer guy, so he's got the means."

Jeanne went to the cash register and fished a ten-dollar bill out of her pocket. "Plus, you've got to admit, the whole cow thing smacks of body shaming."

"Huh."

Jeanne couldn't tell if Meaghan was convinced or not.

"So do you want me to pursue this further? Should I go talk to him?"

To her surprise, Meaghan declined. "I'll talk to the congressman," she said. "Then we'll decide on next steps."

Jeanne hung up and slipped her phone in her pocket. How odd, she thought. Meaghan referred to her husband as "the congressman." She tried to imagine referring to Fergus as the "cybersecurity professional" or the "Scottish gentleman," and for a moment she almost laughed. But then she remembered that she might never have the chance. He might be out of her life for good.

Jeanne forced herself to put Fergus out of her mind, carefully folded her receipt, and stuck it in her pocket. She was definitely expensing the cannoli.

Chapter Ten

Jeanne did not hear from her client for the entire rest of the week. "Do you think she's mad at me?" she asked Lily as she rehearsed for her performance at the Charity League Halloween party.

"As long as the check clears, who cares?"

Lily had a good point, but Jeanne still found herself caring. "I don't want it to be awkward when we run into each other at the party," Jeanne said as she balanced a tray of illuminated plastic skulls on her head. The venue wouldn't allow her to use actual candles—something about fire code violations—and so she thought the skulls were a nice, safe, occasion-appropriate alternative.

"That's her problem," Lily snorted. "You have no reason to feel embarrassed. She's the one who harassed poor Edith until she literally starved to death."

"We don't know that. That may be what Brian thought, but that doesn't mean it's true. And"—she reached up and added a few more skulls to the tray—"we don't even really know it was Brian. Motive, means, and opportunity don't always equal perpetrator."

Lily harrumphed.

But Jeanne needn't have worried. Meaghan was polite, but distant, when they crossed paths by the snack table, Meaghan nibbling on some fruit while Jeanne scarfed down a lava fudge cupcake. To her surprise, Meaghan suddenly grabbed a cupcake off the table and devoured it. Maybe the stress was getting to her. And, Jeanne thought with regrettably enjoyable malice, Meaghan looked slightly plumper than she had the week before.

"Your dance was lovely," her client said. "I especially liked it when you danced with those big wings."

"Isis wings," Jeanne corrected her. "Like the Egyptian goddess, not the terrorist group. Everybody loves them." She snatched another lava fudge cake off the tray before moving closer and lowering her voice. "Have you decided what you want me to do next?"

Meaghan shook her head, picked up her wine glass, and swilled the deep red liquid. Jeanne noticed that her fingernails matched her beverage. "Not yet."

A moment later, Meaghan was off, fluttering through the crowd—a wave here, a wink there—like a bumblebee with too many flowers to choose from. Jeanne tried to catch Congressman Richardson's eye, but to no avail. He seemed to be occupied with an endless stream of well-wishers and hangers-on who pumped his hand vigorously, as if hoping some of his power would rub off. Rather than join the line, Jeanne decided to call him later in the week.

It was after two o'clock when Jeanne staggered into Vivienne's station wagon, exhausted. There were still quite a few revelers stumbling down M Street, wigs askance, costumes beginning to unravel, but the back streets were deserted.

"Have you given any thought to attending Mom's thing?" Vivienne asked. Jeanne noticed that, in a classic Vivienne move, her sister kept her eyes on the road. Vivienne always waited until they were in the car to have difficult conversations.

"You make it sound like a garden party," Jeanne fumed. "Just say it. Parole hearing. Are you going to Mom's parole hearing?"

"Okay, are you going to Mom's parole hearing?"

"I haven't decided yet."

"Well decide already. It's in two weeks. I know you're saving for a condo, so if you're worried about the money, I could—"

Jeanne cut her off. "It's not the money."

Vivienne swung onto Wisconsin Avenue and pulled in front of Jeanne's building. "Think about it," she said.

Without another word, Jeanne flung open the door, slammed it, and stomped up the steps, her silver coin belt jingle-jangling into the night.

Jeanne felt absolutely wretched the next morning. First, she had alienated Fergus. Now she'd been unpardonably rude to her sister. "About the only people who still like me are Jerry and Lily," she groused as she dipped a chocolate biscotti absentmindedly in a glass of milk.

As if on cue, Scarlett hobbled over and put her head in Jeanne's lap. "And you, of course," Jeanne said as she scratched behind her dog's ears. "At least you still like me. But then again, I feed you."

If only it were that easy with humans. She'd just send Fergus and Vivienne some treats—brownies or scones, perhaps—and they'd come scampering back, wagging their tails.

With a deep sigh, she picked up her phone and dialed Vivienne's number.

"Mea culpa," she said when her sister answered.

"For what?"

Jeanne rubbed her eyes. "What do you mean 'for what'? I was completely snotty to you last night. It's only natural for you to ask if I'm going to our murderous, hard-drinking mom's parole hearing."

"And it's normal for you to be upset."

Jeanne took a sharp breath. She could hear *Dora the Explorer* in the background and the sound of her nephew Everett's tower of blocks crashing to the floor. "Wow, you're a good sister."

"You're not so bad yourself."

Jeanne felt slightly let down. Vivienne had accepted her apology a little too willingly. She felt the need to grovel. She deserved to grovel. Finally, she said, "Well at least let me make it up to you by coming over and babysitting."

Vivienne's voice immediately brightened. "That would be terrific. Meaghan asked if I wanted to have lunch with her this afternoon, but of course I said I couldn't. But if you could stay with Everett…"

"No problem. I'll be over at eleven."

****

By noon, Jeanne and Everett had finger-painted (leaving only one small spot on the table, which Jeanne considered a success), constructed a space ship out of sofa cushions and an overturned sled, defeated an alien invasion, and raced Everett's fire engines around the living room.

"Would you like some lunch?" Jeanne asked wearily as Everett crashed his fire engine into a squad car.

Everett shook his head. With his dimples and his white-blond curls, he looked like he should be starring in a Cheerios commercial. "Not hungwy," he said, and Jeanne tried not to smile at his adorable lisp.

Jeanne looked out the window and sighed. It was a perfect fall day, clear and crisp, the sun illuminating the scarlet leaves of the Japanese maple tree in Vivienne's backyard. "Let's go for a walk, Everett," she said suddenly in her won't-this-be-fun voice. "We can go on patrol and see if there are any fires that need to be put out."

He looked slightly suspicious, but put up no resistance as she zippered up his jacket and coaxed him down the street. They headed down P Street, then up 29th past a block of modest (yet somehow still ridiculously expensive) pastel rowhouses, followed by a stretch of ivy-covered stone walls.

"No fires," Everett said dolefully as Jeanne clutched his hand and guided him gingerly across R Street and up to the imposing metal gates of Jeanne's favorite cemetery, Oak Hill.

In Jeanne's opinion, Oak Hill was one of D.C.'s most underrated sights, a great green expanse of topsy-turvy hills that dropped precipitously down to Rock Creek, dotted with sun-dappled monuments to some of the city's most prominent—and occasionally notorious—citizens. The cemetery was a park, a sculpture garden, and a history lesson all rolled into one—and she nearly always had the place to herself.

Once past the gate, she led Everett to the right. After pausing to admire the exquisite little Renwick Chapel, which was designed by the architect of the Smithsonian Castle, they strolled past the mausoleums of Philip Graham, founder of *The Washington Post*; Dean Acheson, Truman's Secretary of State; and Colonel Orton Williams, a descendent of Martha Washington's who lived at nearby Tudor Place and was hanged as a Confederate spy. From there, Jeanne and Everett followed a long, tree-lined avenue that hugged the contours of the hill before slipping down amidst a forest of mossy granite spires with the odd stone angel keeping a mournful watch.

To her surprise, Everett did not seem the least bit spooked as they trudged past the tombs of countless Civil War generals, spies, philanthropists, and cabinet secretaries. Everett was most impressed by the Corcoran mausoleum, an octagonal rotunda nestled in a grove of trees. "It looks like the Capitol, doesn't it?" Jeanne said, and Everett looked at her as though she were from outer space. Jeanne decided to skip the lecture about how it was designed by the architect of the Capitol. Sometimes she forgot that he was only three.

They skipped back up the crest of the hill, scanning the horizon for spaceships or—even better—spaceships that had crashed, were on fire, and in desperate need of

Everett's crew of crack firemen. Finding none, they instead pretended that the graceful, long-necked statue in the Heron Fountain was a pterodactyl and proceeded to hunt through the bushes for dinosaur eggs.

"Do you want dinosaur eggs for lunch, Everett?"

He shook his head. "Peanut buttah and jelly. No cwusts." Then he remembered his manners and shot her a toothy grin. "Puh-leeze."

"Are you hungry now?"

"Uh-huh."

She took his hand and they raced up to the top of Reno Hill, within sight of the exit.

And suddenly she realized that they were no longer alone.

At first, she thought it was a bird. But then she realized that the sound coming from her left was distinctly human, something between a strangled cry and a gasp. She jerked her head just in time to see a long, gray, grizzled ponytail that snaked down the back of a filthy pea green army jacket. Two stout, stubby legs charged unsteadily though the trees, kicking up a cloud of dust.

She felt a little tug on her sleeve. "Auntie Jeanne, wook." Everett spoke in a quavering whisper.

Whipping around, she saw a man twenty feet to her right, lying face up in the grass and clutching a bouquet of red roses. "Don't go near that man," she admonished Everett, "and stay right here. I mean *right* here."

Jeanne took off running after the man in the pea green coat. Despite his odd gait, which reminded her of a rampaging bull, he was surprisingly fast as he wended his way through the gravestones.

"I just want to talk to you!" she shouted as they approached the fence, which was at least twelve feet high.

At last, she was gaining on him and could hear his short, puffy gasps for breath. He stumbled, and she closed the gap to within a few paces as he lunged ferociously at the fence and Jeanne fumbled in her pockets for her phone. There was no way she was going to chase him over the fence and leave Everett alone with a man who was either unconscious, drug-addled, or dead, but she could at least try to get a picture.

She steadied her hand and tugged at his sleeve. He turned for just a second, but it was long enough for her to snap a photo of his face in three-quarter profile.

And then he was gone.

Chapter Eleven

Jeanne raced back to the crest of the little hill, perhaps twenty yards away, tears springing in her eyes. How long had she been gone? Two minutes? Or was it five?

She would never forgive herself if anything had happened to her nephew.

"Everett! Everett!" she called, dry autumn leaves crunching underneath her, spindly tree branches brushing her face. She spun around frantically, her eyes scanning the horizon for a wisp of curly blond hair or a red fire truck. But all she saw was the same dark-haired man clutching the bouquet of roses. As far as she could tell, he hadn't moved an inch.

"Everett. Ev—"

"Auntie Jeanne!"

She breathed a sigh of relief as she heard the familiar high-pitched voice waft through the air from somewhere far down below.

She began running in the direction of the voice. "Everett, where are you?"

"I found dinosaur eggs, Auntie Jeanne!"

She abandoned the slow, meandering path and stumbled down a steep embankment and suddenly, just below, she could make out the top of his head. To her surprise, he was crouched in the middle of a crumbling family tomb.

She took a long leap and landed on a little gravel path that ran alongside a row of family mausoleums. Below, the land fell away precipitously to a fringe of dark woods and, beyond that, to the swift-moving Rock Creek. She silently uttered a prayer of thanks that Everett had gone no further.

Everett looked up and grinned. "Look, dinosaur eggs," he announced as he poked something blue at the back of the tomb. Crouching down, Jeanne ducked under the entryway and knelt in the sunlit space. The roof had long since collapsed, leaving a few slabs of granite in the tomb like so many shards of glass.

As she turned to get a closer view of the egg, she gasped. There, illuminated by a shaft of sunlight, was engraved the name of Thomas Hardwick and below it, a few faded scratch marks. For a moment, she was confused. Hadn't he been buried at Holmead's? But then she remembered that the city had condemned the cemetery in the 1880s, when even a light drizzle was enough to send decomposing bodies floating down Florida Avenue. Being people of means and prestige, the Hardwicks must have moved the tomb here.

She may not have been standing on the exact spot where Lucinda Cartwright saw the white rabbit, but she was standing on the same granite floor.

And this tomb was now home, apparently, to a dinosaur egg. Which, to Jeanne's untrained eye, bore a suspicious resemblance to a robin's egg.

"It is a dinosaur egg," Jeanne said approvingly. She cast her eyes upwards and could just make out a nest in a tree a few feet above them on a hillside. Poor mother, she thought. "You are a very good hunter, Everett. But remember, the most important rule in dinosaur egg hunting is to stick with your partner. It's dangerous to go off on your own. There might be a dinosaur mommy nearby, and she might get very angry if she sees you messing with her eggs."

Everett's eyes got very wide. "Oooooh."

"Now," she said, taking his chubby hand in hers, "let's leave this dinosaur egg alone so his mommy can take care of him. I have a special surprise for you."

"You do?"

"Yes. I have a feeling you are going to meet some real police."

They trudged back up the hill and this time, Jeanne resolved not to let Everett out of her sight.

"Is he dead?" Everettt whispered as they approached the body.

"No, just hurt," Jeanne lied as she noted the bluish cast of his hand. His fingernails, in contrast, were as white as snow. The tendons on his hand were hard ridges, and the cellophane encasing the roses fluttered in the wind, tapping out a strangely soothing rhythm against a gray granite monolith. The name on the gravestone was Antonia Ford Willard, and next to it was the monument to Major Joseph Willard. She wondered if they were from the same family that had founded the Willard Hotel.

"Look. Ja-wee beans." Everett pointed to an area in the grass, near the man's feet.

Jeanne squinted and rubbed her eyes. Everett was right. A trail of yellow jelly beans started beneath the man's work boots and wound around the gravestone and down the hill for about five feet.

A single rose petal wiggled loose and flew across the gravesite, down the hill, in the direction of the tragic Thomas Hardwick and Everett's prized blue dinosaur egg. She squeezed Everett's hand harder, and a lump came to her throat. Life was fleeting.

"I love you, Everett," she said softly and silently added Fergus's name as well.

"I wuv you, Auntie Jeanne." Her nephew's little voice quavered with emotion, as if he somehow sensed the solemnity of the moment.

She clutched her phone and was about to call 9-1-1. But something made her step closer to examine the dead man's face. Before, it had just been a blur of indistinct features. She hadn't really wanted to stare into the face of death.

But now, the full dark beard and chubby cheeks came into view. The lips, while bloodless, retained that same fleshy sensuality. His left temple was bruised and swollen, and a gash ran down his forehead, ending in a dried pool of blood by his left eye.

The slightly almond-shaped brown eyes, now sunken into the skull, regarded her with glassy reproach. You know me, the corpse seemed to say.

And, unfortunately, she did.

While she waited for the cops, Jeanne walked over to the gatehouse to alert the gatekeeper, a fifty-something matron with flaming red hair named Mary Sue. "I'm not sure if this is good or bad for business," Mary Sue joked, and her ample belly shook. "What gravesite did you say the body is at?"

"The Willards."

The gatekeeper's eyes narrowed. "Which Willards?"

"Antonia Ford and Major Joseph."

"Ah-hah," she said, nodding her double chin as though this were very significant.

"Are they the Willards of the Willard Hotel?"

"That's right, hon." She lifted Everett onto her lap, twirled him in her swivel chair, and took a bite of a chocolate chip cookie. "But what's much more interesting about them is that he was a Union officer and she was a Confederate spy. He arrested her, they fell in love on the way to the Fairfax Courthouse prison, and they later married." She brushed a few crumbs off her bosom and onto the floor. "Mmmm-hmmm. I'm a sucker for a good romance," she said and then smiled mischievously. "And a good mystery."

Mary Sue offered to watch Everett and treat him to a few of her chocolate chip cookies while Jeanne returned to the gravesite to wait for the police.

She had just enough time to snap a few photos of Brian Schwartz's corpse before the detectives showed up.

Detectives McKinney and Villanueva interviewed Jeanne for half an hour. They asked a lot of questions, and she answered, for the most part, truthfully. She admitted that she had delayed calling the police for about ten minutes while looking for Everett, and she showed them the picture of the man who had fled the crime scene.

When they asked if she knew the victim, she shook her head no. Technically, this was true. She had never met Brian. She had only seen a picture of him and gleaned his name from Edith's mother under false pretenses.

She felt a little guilty as she plodded back to the gatehouse to retrieve Everett. She hadn't lied when she said she didn't know him, but she could have offered that she recognized him. But she shuddered to think of the consequences. At best, she would have to betray the Richardsons' confidence. At worst, she might embroil her clients in a murder investigation.

She swung open the screen door and was greeted by a chocolate-stained Everett, who rushed to embrace her. "Wook, Auntie Jeanne!" he shouted proudly, shoving a piece of paper into her hand.

Mary Sue clucked approvingly as Jeanne looked down at an almost illegible signature and a small chocolate handprint. "It's an autograph from one of the cops."

"Neat," Jeanne said with as much enthusiasm as she could muster. Her heart was racing, and her palms were sweaty. Could her client have been involved somehow? They certainly had a motive. But, she chided herself, they also had a rock-solid alibi. She herself had seen them at the benefit the night before. And her guess was that the body had been there a while.

Plus, how could they possibly have lured Brian Schwartz to an assignation in the cemetery?

And was that what it was? Were the flowers meant for the living, or for the dead?

A leathery hand brushed Jeanne's wrist, causing her to start. "Are you okay, hon?" Mary Sue's big hazel eyes were trained intently on her, full of concern.

"Huh?"

"You've been staring at a spot on the rug for a full minute. But then it's not every day that you stare death in the face like that." Mary Sue hobbled over to her desk, grabbed four chocolate chip cookies, and dropped them in a Ziploc bag. She handed them to Jeanne and winked. "Take these for later. If he's good."

Jeanne smiled weakly and slid the bag in her pocket.

Mary Sue took Jeanne by the elbow, took Everett's hand, and slowly led them to the door. When her hand was on the screen door, she paused suddenly. "The weird thing," she mused, "is that this happens every Halloween."

Jeanne gulped. "A murder in Oak Hill Cemetery?"

"Oh, heavens no." Mary Sue waved a thick, leathery hand and laughed. "But every year, someone leaves a dozen red roses on the graves of the Willards. I always thought it was romantic." She sighed. "Until now."

Chapter Twelve

Jeanne and Everett made a brief detour to Vivienne's to make a crustless peanut butter and jelly sandwich. After cutting it into quarters, Jeanne stuffed it into a plastic bag, grabbed a few napkins off the counter, and hustled Everett back out the door.

Everett scrunched up his little face. "But my samwidge..."

"You can eat and walk. That's what the police do when they're chasing bad guys—or fighting aliens. Do you think they eat their doughnuts first and then go save people?"

Everett looked confused.

"Nooooo. Otherwise the bad guys would already have gotten away."

He seemed to accept this explanation, because he reached out and accepted a quarter sandwich from Jeanne and munched it happily as they walked briskly down the street.

Twenty-five minutes later, Jeanne and Everett were standing in front of the staircase that led down into the sun-dappled courtyard of Café Mozart. She fished a napkin out of her pocket and wiped the peanut butter off Everett's face. Taking Everett's chubby little hand in her own, they walked slowly down the steps.

Vivienne's red-gold hair, brilliant in the October sunshine, came into view halfway down. Her back was to Jeanne, but Meaghan faced the staircase. For a second, Jeanne thought she saw a shadow pass over Meaghan's face, but then Meaghan was on her feet, all smiles, giving her beauty pageant wave. "What a nice surprise!" she enthused.

Not as nice as a surprise as I'm about to deliver, Jeanne thought grimly, as she approached their table.

Vivienne craned her neck around. "Jeanne, what are you doing here?"

"Oh, I just thought I'd take Everett to play in the magic fountains," she said. The fountains were the city's latest attempt to spruce up Georgetown's waterfront, a long-neglected bend in the Potomac facing Roosevelt Island, and they were just two blocks away from Café Mozart. "It's a nice day."

"For November," Vivienne said, eyeing her sister suspiciously. "It's not exactly the kind of day to get drenched in the fountains. Besides, I think they've turned them off for the season."

"Huh. Vivienne, would you mind taking Everett inside to look at the cakes for a minute?"

With a resigned shrug and an eye roll, Vivienne trudged inside with her son. Jeanne slid into Vivienne's seat and squinted at Meaghan. "Your problems are solved. Brian Schwartz is dead."

"Brian—?" Meaghan started, then a flicker of recognition suffused her features. Her fork fell out of her red, raw fingertips and landed with a clatter on her plate. "Oh, that Brian."

"That Brian."

"How did he die?"

"I'm not quite sure, but I suspect some sort of blunt force trauma to the head."

Meaghan's hand shook slightly. "In other words, murder."

"Almost certainly."

"And how do you know this?"

"I just found the body." Jeanne kept her eyes fixed on Meaghan's face, which had drained of all color. "In Oak Hill Cemetery."

She didn't need to say the rest of what she was thinking. Her client knew as well as she did that Oak Hill was less than a five-minute walk from Meaghan's house.

Jeanne flipped to the picture on her phone. "You recognize this guy?"

Meaghan shook her head. "Should I?"

"No." Jeanne shrugged. "Well maybe. He was running away from the body. Since you know Brian, I thought you might know him." She frowned. "Although he's too old to be another high school classmate of yours."

Pushing away her salad, Meaghan sighed. "Well this is going to be the talk of the reunion."

"Which is when?"

"Next weekend. Our twentieth. Unfortunately, I can't go. We've got to be back in South Carolina for some fundraiser." She grimaced. "And, of course, the trophy wife's got to be there."

Jeanne was momentarily taken aback by Meaghan's tone. She had never gotten the slightest impression that Meaghan resented her role. In fact, it seemed tailor-made for a former beauty queen. But before Jeanne could ask Meaghan for any details about the reunion, Vivienne and Everett rejoined them, Everett beaming as he clutched a plastic clamshell filled with a strawberry mousse tart.

"Well, enjoy your lunch," Jeanne said brightly as she took Everett's hand in her own. "If the fountains aren't on, I guess Everett and I will head to the playground."

As she turned away to trudge back up the stairs, she caught a glimpse of Meaghan's parting wave out of the corner of her eye. Suddenly, a flurry of images flooded her brain. Meaghan shaking her hand at their first meeting. Chatting with Meaghan at the snack table at the Charity League benefit, Meaghan clutching her wineglass.

She spun around suddenly. "What a lovely ring," she gushed, staring at Meaghan's hand. "I just caught a glimpse as you waved. How many carats?"

"Oh, more than it should be," Meaghan said modestly. "My husband knows I like jewelry."

"It's lovely," Jeanne said, taking note of the red, raw fingertips—the same red, raw fingertips she had always seen on Meaghan.

Except last night.

****

Jerry met them at the playground. Jeanne kept an eye on Everett as he careened down the slides, while Jerry punched things into his phone and grunted.

Jeanne was sufficiently attuned to Jerry's grunts to know which ones were truly significant. "Bingo," he said after one particularly deep grunt, "she's got a twin sister with a criminal record."

"What do her fingernails look like?"

"They're not in the mug shot." He looked up. "You know, Twinkletoes, I agree that it looks bad. It looks suspicious. But all you've got is a couple of coincidences. Her blackmailer was murdered on the same day she skipped out of a party."

"Those are some pretty convenient coincidences."

"But—and this is an important but—how could she have possibly known that Brian Schwartz, her blackmailer—"

"Possible blackmailer," Jeanne interjected, already mentally composing her testimony if charged as an accessory to murder. "I never said that he was definitely blackmailing her. I had no proof."

"Right," Jerry said dismissively. "How could she have known her alleged blackmailer Brian Schwartz was going to be at the Willards' gravesite last night?"

"Maybe she asked him to meet her there."

"He hated her guts. Why would he do that?"

Jerry had a good point, and Jeanne mulled it over as she helped Everett on the monkey bars. Meaghan had gone to high school with Brian, but claimed not to know him well. And even if she had known him better than she let on, Jeanne couldn't imagine how she could have lured him to the cemetery. And even if she had, Jeanne wasn't sure that Meaghan had the strength necessary to fell a man as large as Brian Schwartz.

When Everett went back to the little plastic slide, Jeanne rejoined Jerry on the park bench. "Maybe you're right," she said as she plopped down. "Maybe I'm letting my overactive imagination get the best of me. Maybe Meaghan just got a lucky break. Maybe Brian had a dozen other sworn enemies."

"Maybe the government offed him," Jerry said darkly. "Maybe he was another Snowden, but he hadn't opened his mouth yet."

Jeanne considered this for a moment. She often dismissed Jerry's conspiracy theories out of hand, but with all of the wild allegations surrounding Snowden, this one had the ring of credibility.

"Maybe he leaked something to a journalist, and she tipped off the feds."

Jerry frowned. "That doesn't sound like any journalist I know."

Jeanne sank lower into the bench and closed her eyes, the warm sunshine suffusing her face. "We may have a lot more questions than answers, but the first one I need to answer is: If my client wasn't at the benefit, where was she?"

"Well, normally, Twinkletoes, this is where Braveheart would come in."

Jeanne groaned. "Meaning?"

"Meaning I'm guessing that the cameras know exactly if Meaghan was home and when she was home, and your boyfriend—er, ex-boyfriend—is the cybersecurity expert. So if anyone could figure out how to hack into the camera feed from the Richardsons' home, it would be him."

"I'm not going to ask Fergus." Jeanne kicked stubbornly at a rock in the dirt. "That would ruin any chance of our getting back together. He'll just think I'm using him for his brain."

"There are worse things to use people for."

"Jerry," she said forcefully, a hint of warning in her voice, "I'm not going to ask him. I'm just not."

They sat in silence for a moment, Jeanne stewing, Jerry pondering.

"Do you have a picture of one of the cameras?" he suddenly asked.

Pulling out her phone, Jeanne swiped through a few photos and then shoved the clearest one under Jerry's nose.

"You didn't see any wires?" he asked.

She shook her head.

"Ever heard of an SDR? Software-defined radio?"

"No."

"They can monitor wireless transmissions, from security cameras, key fobs, you name it. And they're not hard to come by—you can get one on Amazon nowadays." He grinned. "Feeling up for a stakeout?"

"I'll bring the takeout."

The stakeout was brief and perfunctory, wrapped up before Jeanne had the chance to scrape the bottom of her kung pao chicken. "Got it," Jerry's friend Steve grunted, reclining in the passenger seat of Jerry's rusted-out station wagon.

"Got what?" Jeanne asked, her disposable chopsticks suspended in mid-air.

"Everything. I've got the frequency, I've got the camera brand and model."

Jeanne was impressed. "So you've got the footage?"

He grunted again. "Not so fast, toots. But I've got enough information that I should be able to hack in within a couple of hours. A day at most."

Steve craned his thick neck around and peered at her. He had one lazy eye, which was hazel; the other was bluish green and focused on Jeanne like a laser beam. His gaze unnerved her.

Tapping the SDR twice, Steve said, "This is a crime, you know."

Jeanne swallowed, hard. Out of the corner of her eye, she could see Jerry watching her in the rear-view mirror. "I know," she said. "But this is a matter of life and death."

"Ah," Steve said. "I know all about that."

Jeanne decided not to ask.

Steve was as good as his word. By the following evening, Jeanne and Jerry were sitting in their respective depressions on Jerry's couch, watching hour after hour of footage from the Richardsons' home on Jerry's 1970s TV, which he had rescued from the dump. "Man, I wish we'd made popcorn," he said as he gaped at the scene unfolding before him. "This is better than any movie."

While equally fascinated, Jeanne was more discomfited, especially as she watched her employer slither out of a skin-tight black dress and into the arms of a very naked, very aroused Jorge. "Apparently, he has other duties as assigned," she murmured.

But what truly took her breath away was when a rich, stentorian voice—a very familiar voice—suddenly cut in. "Are you two frisky kids at it again?" the man off-screen drawled.

Now the strange look that had passed between the congressman and his wife made sense. And yes, *The Sludge Report* could have published something much, much worse. Meaghan Richardson was having an affair with the Colombian household help—a man barely out of his teens—all with the congressman's knowledge and encouragement.

The tape showed Meaghan and Jorge bidding good-bye to the congressman and Meaghan's twin on Halloween—Meaghan re-arranging her twin's hair at the last minute to make it perfectly mirror her own—and then, once the door had closed, making love on the couch. But their whereabouts for the rest of the night could not be ascertained. They could have repaired to the bedroom, watched TV in the family room like an old married couple, gone clubbing...or walked to Oak Hill Cemetery, bashed Brian Schwartz's head in, and been back home in twenty minutes.

Chapter Thirteen

Jeanne spent the entire next day vacillating about whether she should confront her client. On the one hand, Meaghan might have a perfectly reasonable explanation like "I wanted to go on a date with my boy toy manny, and my sister wanted to go to the charity benefit" and be able to produce credit card receipts showing that they had dined at Café Milano and gone to a movie at the Georgetown Cinema. On the other hand, if Meaghan were a murderer and thought Jeanne was on to her, she might lure Jeanne to her house with Patisserie Poupon macarons, whip out a crème brûlée blowtorch from her perfect Martha Stewart kitchen, and slowly burn Jeanne to a crisp while taunting her about her extra baby fat.

For the tenth time that morning, as Jeanne absentmindedly followed the home inspector around the condo—nodding as he showed her the HVAC system and trying to avert her eyes from his ass crack as he bent down to look under the sink—she changed her mind.

"No," she said and then realized that she was talking out loud.

He squinted up at her and pushed his glasses up his nose. "You don't want me to look in the refrigerator?"

"Oh, no," she said hastily, "I do. Yes, please look at the fridge."

He stood up, shrugged, and started fiddling with the refrigerator settings.

No, she repeated silently to herself, I will not let Meaghan know that I know that she has no alibi. It was entirely too risky. She would do some sleuthing on her own and then see if there was any point in telling the police of her suspicions.

Her phone rang. "Excuse me," she shouted, entirely too loudly, and her heart began to beat wildly. Maybe it was Fergus. Maybe he was returning one of the seventeen voice messages she had left that week. Then she could apologize and—

But the caller ID told her it was not Fergus.

"Oh, hi, Carlos," she said as she looked down at the covered pool.

"Are you okay? You sound kind of *deprimida*."

They had once spoken only Spanish to each other, shortly after he was released from the jail where Jeanne had volunteered teaching English as a Second language, but as Carlos's English had improved, they had switched to Spanglish.

She sighed. "I've been better. Boy trouble."

She hadn't told Carlos too much about her relationship with Fergus and she wanted to keep it that way. Somehow it made her feel dirty—and more than a little guilty—to talk about her relationship with the only other man in her life who could get her pulse racing.

A man who was completely wrong for her, of course—in all the ways that Fergus was not.

"*Eres una rompecorazones*," Carlos teased. "How do you say that in English?"

"Heartbreaker. Yeah, something like that."

The home inspector was running the garbage disposal now, so she moved into the bedroom and shut the door. "How are things with you?" she asked to be polite.

"Actually, things are getting kind of hot right now. Tonio's getting out tomorrow." She heard him suck in a deep breath. "And I heard that he thinks *que yo sea un soplón*."

Jeanne whistled. She had never had the courage to ask Carlos if his relatively light sentence was in exchange for valuable information. But it didn't really matter if he was a snitch; it only mattered if the *mara* thought he was. "So you need to get out of town in a hurry."

The wheels were turning in her head. Was this some sort of sign from above? He needed to get out of town; she needed a way to sneak into Brian's high school reunion.

And Carlos was practically a dead ringer for Sergio Vargas, a smoldering Venezuelan exchange student she'd seen in Meaghan's class photo.

"Any interest in a trip to Middleburg?"

The home inspection wrapped up around noon, leaving Jeanne with a rare Friday afternoon off. She holed up in the back corner of Kramerbooks with a cappuccino, a slice of Goober Pie, a stack of Meaghan's old high school yearbooks, and her laptop, preparing a dossier for Carlos.

Jeanne started by making a list of all of Sergio's extracurricular activities: President of the Spanish Club, Treasurer of the Horseback Riding Club, the goalie on the championship soccer team, and a member of the National Honor Society, the Prom Planning Committee, the choir, the band, and the chess club. Jeanne sighed. Obviously, Sergio and Carlos were from two very different strata of Latin American society. She doubted Carlos had ever ridden a horse (or perhaps even seen one, except in the movies), and she shuddered to think what he would say if one of the chess club alumni tried to talk to him about the game. At least he could speak Spanish, dance, and play soccer.

Flipping to the back, her lips curled into a little smile when she saw that Sergio had been voted Middleburg High School's Class of 1995's Most Eligible Bachelor. Carlos would like that.

Two other names stood out on the list: Meaghan had been voted Best Legs, Most Dreamed About, and Most Popular.

Brian Schwartz had been named Biggest Geek.

Other than that, he made only two other appearances in the yearbook—as a mathlete and second trombone in the band.

Jeanne made a list of all of the trombone players that were neither in the horseback riding club nor the chess club and labeled the list 'MUST TALK TO.' She figured that these were the people most likely to remember both Brian and Sergio without incurring the risk that they would expect Carlos to know a rook from a queen or a thoroughbred from a mule.

Jeanne made a few more notes about the band (their third-place finish in the state competition, for example) and was scraping every last bit of peanut butter and chocolate ganache off her plate when Lily called. Hearing the hum of printers and copy machines in the background, she felt a bit smug that for once she was not at work.

Lily cracked her gum loudly. "How'd the home inspection go?"

"Surprisingly well, actually. The kitchen faucet drips and the garbage disposal needs to be replaced, but other than that, everything's in good shape."

"Well then we should celebrate."

"Sure. I'm up for anything. Just so I'm home fairly early. Carlos and I have a funeral and a high school reunion to hit tomorrow."

"Carlos, huh?"

Jeanne could hear the insinuation in Lily's voice. Lily had always carried a torch for Carlos, but had never made a move. Somehow, she sensed that he was the bad boy Jeanne kept on the back burner.

"He needs to get out of town and I need a way to get into the reunion. He looks like the guy least likely to show up at the reunion—Sergio Vargas, a Venezuelan exchange student."

"Are you sure he's still in Venezuela?"

"No."

Lily laughed. "Well I hope you have a Plan B. And who are you supposed to be?"

"Jennifer Walpole, his girlfriend. We met while snorkeling in Aruba and now live in Miami. I'm a lawyer—naturally—and he runs an import-export business."

"In what? Arms trafficking?"

"Flowers."

"Flowers? What does Carlos know about flowers?"

Jeanne sighed. Lily had a point. "So what do you suggest?"

"Keep it simple. Carlos works in a kitchen, right? Just make him a high-end personal chef. That way, no one can ask too many specific questions. He's a chef to the rich and famous. Has to be very discrete. You know the drill."

As Jeanne scratched out part of the dossier and wrote in the new personal chef background story, Lily gave her the details about the pub crawl she had just signed them up for. "I know you're not much of a drinker," she said in what must have been the understatement of the year, "but it's for a good cause. Autism research. My friend's the events co-chair. And we can always kill two birds with one stone. What better way to see if anyone saw Meaghan and Rodrigo in Georgetown on Halloween?"

By eleven o'clock, Jeanne's sensible black boots were sticking to the fourth beer-soaked floor of the night. Her feet were killing her, and her ears were throbbing. Lily, in contrast, looked as comfortable and serene as ever in

108

her skintight snakeskin pants, black stilettos, and teeny-weeny black halter top. She had already amassed six or seven telephone numbers and given out quite a few herself, including one scrawled in cherry red lipstick below a muscle-bound karate instructor's giant dragon tattoo.

"I just met a guy from the Swedish Embassy," she shouted in Jeanne's ear. "A real brainiac, kind of serious. You want me to introduce you?"

Jeanne shook her head. The thought of going on a date with anyone other than Fergus made her slightly nauseous.

"You and Fergus broke up, you know."

Jeanne winced. "All too well."

"Any luck so far?"

Jeanne shook her head. "I've been trying to get the bartender's attention for twenty minutes now."

"Here, leave it to me." Lily pulled her top down lower on her chest, dramatically swinging her long, silky black hair down her back. Jeanne felt Lily's fingers gently brush hers and take the grainy black-and-white photo out of her hands. It was a still from the video feed from Meaghan's house. Meaghan and Jorge's faces were clearly visible, if a little pixelated, except for a lock of hair that had fallen over Jorge's left eye. There were some better pictures on the video, but this was the best in which they were still wearing clothes.

In less than a minute, a ruddy-faced bartender was taking their order.

"Anything else for you ladies?" he asked hopefully.

Lily reached out and grabbed him by the wrist and gently stroked his hand. His face went from pink to bright red.

"Actually," she cooed, "I'm hoping you could tell us whether you've seen this couple in here." She waved the photos in his face. "My friend here" -she nudged Jeanne -"suspects that her boyfriend is cheating with this little tramp and, as you can see, she's a mess."

Under other circumstances, Jeanne might have taken umbrage at being described as a mess—she thought she looked nice, if a little staid, in a pink cardigan and black pencil skirt—but she was grateful Lily had at least caught the bartender's eye. Sticking out her bottom lip in what she hoped was a pout, Jeanne tried to look appropriately anguished.

The bartender took the photo in one hand, brought it close to his face, and squinted. He nodded as he handed it back to Lily. "Halloween night. Hard to forget them. She's kind of a cougar, isn't she?"

"I guess the bastard likes older women." Jeanne bit her lip. "What do you mean by 'hard to forget'?"

"Well, for starters, she was already pretty smashed. He was kind of propping her up. And then she was going on about how this was 'their' dive bar, a place where her uppity husband wouldn't be seen dead. But she didn't seem like a dive bar chick. Real imperious. Kind of snapping her fingers at me. Plus, she looked like she had covered herself in glue and walked through a diamond mine. She was sparkling so much, it almost hurt by eyes."

"Do you know where they went afterwards?"

"No idea. But I did see them hail a cab. She tripped on the curb and would have face-planted in the street if he hadn't been holding her up."

"And what time was that?"

"Right after last call."

"And how long were they here?"

He shrugged. "It's hard to say. But at least forty-five minutes, maybe an hour."

Jeanne and Lily thanked him, left a generous tip, and headed outside to huddle beneath a lamppost. It was just too loud inside to talk.

"What time did Brian die?" Lily asked through chattering teeth. It was the first truly cold night of the season, but Lily hadn't let that stand in the way of wearing a halter top.

Jeanne sighed. "I don't know. I'm not exactly a forensic expert. By the time I found him around twelve-thirty in the afternoon, rigor mortis had definitely set in, but all that means is that he'd been dead anywhere from a few hours to a day."

"What does the *Post* say?"

"That he was killed either late on Halloween or early on November 1st."

"So probably between ten p.m. and three a.m."

"Something like that. Which still leaves plenty of time for my client—or her lover—to kill Brian Schwartz. All I can confirm about her whereabouts that evening is that she was still at home until at least ten-thirty—the last time she's seen on the surveillance tape—and she was in this bar, drunk—"

"Or pretending to be drunk—"

"—and dressed to the nines by around two. But given the relatively short distances involved, she could have been in the cemetery as late as one-fifteen, run five minutes home, changed out of her bloody clothes, put on a designer dress, covered herself in diamonds, called a cab and been here by two."

"Or the cab they hailed at two forty-five could have dropped them off by the cemetery. In less than twenty minutes, they could have snuck in, killed Brian, and been back home washing off the blood."

"Less likely. The senator would have been home by then. I'd say he left the benefit around one-thirty."

Lily tossed her hair and arched an eyebrow. "Well maybe he was in on it. After all, he apparently knows about Meaghan and Jorge's affair. Maybe he knows they're murderers, too."

Jeanne pondered this for a minute. "But if she wasn't acting, and she really was drunk, it would have been hard for her to kill Brian after she left the bar. Her coordination would have been terrible. And in order to be as drunk as the bartender claims, she would have had to start drinking a few hours before she arrived here, leaving a relatively short window of time just after ten-thirty to commit the murder."

"Well, you're overlooking a key detail. Jorge was sober—or at least relatively so—when he left here. He was probably sober all night. She might have just sat at home, all dressed up and ready to go, knocking back glass after glass of expensive red wine, while her dutiful lover killed Brian, and then came back to escort her on a victory lap through Georgetown." She shot Jeanne a meaningful look. "It seems to me that you're working overtime to convince yourself that your client didn't kill Brian Schwartz—even though she had a very strong motive and you have proof that she manufactured an alibi."

Through clenched teeth, Jeanne said, "I just don't want to falsely accuse her. Or Jorge. I'm sure there are a dozen other people who might have wanted Brian—"

She broke off suddenly as a familiar deep rumbling made her turn and squint into the darkness. Her mouth suddenly went dry. She steadied herself against the lamppost and took a deep breath.

Lily's dark eyes flashed. "What?"

"Incoming," Jeanne muttered without moving her lips, a weak smile plastered on her face. "Braveheart."

Lily spun around so that both of them were silhouetted in the glare of the lamp light, as Fergus and a petite brunette loomed ever closer. He did not notice them at first, absorbed in his conversation with his companion, who gazed up at him admiringly.

Jeanne felt a full-blown panic well up in her chest. She couldn't quite catch what they were saying—sweet nothings, she supposed—but the woman's voice had a sweet, sing-songy lilt. Could this be Fergus's ex-girlfriend Pamela? The Pamela that he dated all through college and then for several years afterwards? The one his parents adored? The one he was once engaged to?

Jeanne didn't know what would be worse—to run away ignominiously and miss her opportunity to size up her rival or to stand stupidly rooted to the spot, hugging the lamppost like a sloppy drunk college girl trying to decide whether or not to vomit in the curb.

Maybe she should let go of the lamppost.

But then what? Just stand in the middle of the sidewalk?

She bent over and removed her left boot and pretended to examine it, presumably to remove a rock. Unfortunately, at that exact moment, a skinny blonde in a shiny red tube dress flung open the bar door and lurched towards the curb, barreling over Jeanne in the process. The last thing that Jeanne saw before landing with a thud was a blur of pavement and a cute pair of black Mary Janes.

Wincing in pain, she slowly looked up and, to her horror, discovered that those Mary Janes were connected to a pair of petite, perfectly toned legs, and the legs were connected to a perky little body in a long-sleeved emerald green dress.

And the body was connected to the very concerned face of Fergus's companion.

"You poor dear," she said, scrunching up her little button nose and giving her perfect brown bob a little shake. She had big dark eyes, perfect white teeth (wasn't Britain supposed to be an island full of snaggle-toothed women?), and a smattering of freckles across her nose. "Are you all right?"

Jeanne sucked in a deep breath and, with as much dignity as she could muster, struggled to her feet. She quickly crossed her right knee over her left, which was badly skinned and beginning to ooze blood over her tights. The blonde retched loudly behind her.

"Fine," she lied as she felt a throbbing pain course through her. "Par for the course for a night out in Georgetown."

"Hullo, Jeanne," Fergus said stiffly.

Huh, she thought. So that's how he wants to play it. All stiff upper lip, very British.

He was less than a foot from her. She could smell his cologne and found herself fighting a sudden urge to reach out and caress his stubble. He was also wearing her favorite shirt, the green and blue plaid button-down that he had been wearing the day they met.

Jeanne decided to respond in kind. Two could play this game. "Fergus," she acknowledged him curtly.

The brunette looked from one to the other. "You two know each other?"

"Used to," Jeanne said cryptically. "We met at the dog park."

Fergus rubbed the back of his neck in what Jeanne knew to be a sign of nervousness "Well, you see," he explained, the color creeping up his neck and spreading across his face, "Magnus had a sudden urge to shag her dog, Scarlett; she tried to protect her dog's womanly virtue and was injured in the ensuing scuffle. So I took her back to Aunt Margaret's and bandaged her up like any Good Samaritan would."

While perhaps technically true, he left out the fact that his motives were not strictly altruistic. Jeanne caught his eye for a moment. You forgot to mention, she wanted to say, that you asked me out for the first time in Aunt Margaret's frilly pink bathroom, Ace bandage in hand. She could tell he was thinking the same thing, because he glanced away guiltily.

The brunette scrunched up her eyebrows. "Huh. That's an interesting way to meet. Well aren't you going to introduce us?"

"Aye, of course," he stammered. "These are my old friends Jeanne and Lily."

Jeanne felt a lump in her throat as he said the word "friends." It was better than "acquaintance," she supposed, but it had a finality to it that caused her to tremble.

"And this" -his eyes, now steel gray in the half-shadows, locked on Jeanne's for a moment—"is Pamela."

Chapter Fourteen

The weather was perfect, in a portentous, Shakespearean kind of way. An incessant, driving rain pounded the roof of Lily's Crown Vic, while a howling north wind lashed the tall, spindly trees along I-66, sending a torrent of slick yellow leaves crashing against the windshield.

Jeanne drummed her fingers on the steering wheel and hummed an angry tune off key. She was on her way to a funeral for the murdered blackmailer of her preening, ice queen client, and if she had harbored any hopes of getting back together with Fergus, they were now dashed. Perky Pamela—she of the sunny disposition, adoring gaze, and perfect petite little body—was back in the picture, and there was no way Jeanne could hope to compete. An awkward five-minute conversation on the street corner, followed by a two-hour de-brief with Lily, had confirmed what Jeanne had feared: Pamela was Jeanne 2.0, a vastly upgraded, much more user-friendly model with all of the kinks worked out. Fergus liked dark-eyed brunettes, apparently, but Jeanne was the Camry and Pamela was the Lexus of that category.

Pamela had shinier, silkier, more malleable hair; better skin; a better smile; and a much better body. She actually made Fergus look tall. And if that weren't enough, their brief conversation revealed that Pamela deferred to Fergus's judgment on absolutely everything. She gushed about his services as a tour guide and host. Before offering an opinion, she asked what he thought. "But what do you think, Fergus?" she had simpered at least three times, batting her long eyelashes in his direction, to Jeanne's irritation.

Pamela, Jeanne could tell, would never conceal anything from Fergus. Not a family member's parole hearing. Not a home purchase.

She'd probably consult him before getting a ten-dollar manicure.

Jeanne let out a demented little laugh, picturing a bewildered Fergus being asked to choose between Come to Bed Red and Killer Crimson (two of Lily's favorites), before remembering with a start that she wasn't actually alone.

Out of the corner of her eye, she caught Carlos staring at her. He let out a long, slow whistle. "You're in a strange mood today."

"Sorry," she mumbled.

Carlos sighed and leaned against the window, tracing a raindrop as it made its way down the pane and then out of sight. "*Dime todo.*"

Even though she had resolved not to confide in Carlos—even though she had repeated that to herself in the mirror that morning and later to Scarlett over five chocolate-drenched biscotti and a steaming mug of hot chocolate—she now found herself craving a sympathetic ear. Besides, she rationalized, it wouldn't hurt to get a male perspective.

He listened attentively for nearly half an hour as they sped through the ugly urban sprawl that ringed the city. "Are you done?" he asked as she finally fell silent.

"Yes."

"Well here's what I think. You're 2.0—not her. He dated her first, rejected her, and then—how do you say?—improved—"

"Upgraded."

He snapped his fingers. "Yes—upgraded to you. You're 2.0."

They were silent for a moment. The rain was coming down even harder, and she turned the windshield wipers to their maximum setting. Carlos yawned and sank down into the deep leather seat. It was warm, bordering on stifling, in the Crown Vic. With Lily's car, the heat was either all or nothing.

"She sounds boring," he added. "I don't know how British men are, but Latinos like a little mystery. It keeps things interesting."

They had reached the Middleburg exit. Jeanne maneuvered into the right lane, veered off the interstate, and turned onto a bucolic country lane. Forty miles from D.C., just past the unsightly cookie-cutter subdivisions and strip malls, it was a genteel, colonial-era town—"very posh," as Fergus would say—chock-a-block with stately limestone edifices, its main street lined with smart cafés, pricey boutiques, and antique stores whose displays dripped with gold and silver. Nestled in the rolling green hills of Virginia's horse and hunt country, the surrounding countryside was dotted with vineyards, old plantations, and white picket fences corralling prized thoroughbreds. The state's largest horse race, the Virginia Gold Cup steeple chasing classic, took place at nearby Great Meadow, and—bizarrely, Jeanne thought— female spectators were expected to wear hats. Jackie Kennedy had kept her horses in the area.

She could feel Carlos's liquid brown eyes boring into her as they approached the city limits. Jeanne glanced over at him, and he crossed his arms over his chest. "I don't know about Fergus," he said slowly, "but I find you very attractive. And if he doesn't think so, he's an *idiota*. And why would you want to be with an *idiota*?"

His rhetorical question hung heavily in the air. She had felt the electricity between them a handful of times before, but it had always gone unsaid. And ever since she had begun seeing Fergus, she had been even more circumspect than usual where Carlos was concerned.

But now, blabbing about her love life, she had given him the perfect opening.

"Read me the obituary again," she said to change the subject.

" 'Brian Schwartz, 38, of Elkridge, Maryland, passed away in the early hours of November 1st. A graduate of St. Agatha's Academy and Rutgers University, he was a longtime employee of the National Security Agency. He also served as President of the Pennsylvania 16th Reserve Volunteers from 2010 to 2012. Survivors include his mother, Mary Katherine Schwartz, and brother, Sam Schwartz. The funeral will be held at Nardelli's Funeral Home in Middleburg, at 2 p.m. on Saturday, November 7th.'" He looked up. "How do you want to handle this?"

"You take the high school and college friends. I'll take the re-enactors and family members. And remember, you're Sergio Vargas."

He smiled. "The Class of 95's Most Eligible Bachelor."

Jeanne and Carlos had an hour to spare, which they spent at The Upper Crust devouring two chicken barbeque sandwiches and a half dozen cow puddle cookies while Carlos pored over Jeanne's dossier on Sergio. A few minutes before two o'clock, they pulled into the parking lot in front of Nardelli's Funeral Home. To her surprise, there were only ten other cars in the parking lot.

"Guess he wasn't very well liked," Carlos muttered as he chivalrously held the front door open for Jeanne.

They snuck into the back of a small chapel on the left, and Jeanne scanned the room while pretending to listen attentively to the pastor's dreadful sermon. He seemed hopelessly confused, rhapsodizing about Brian's career at NASA (and failing to correct himself when an elderly woman in the front row, presumably Brian's mother, launched into a coughing fit) and occasionally referring to him as "Brendan."

Jeanne wasn't surprised to see the back of Mrs. Sawyer's head. Her thinning, dishwater blond hair was carefully swept into a tight bun, and her pale hand, which trembled slightly, occasionally reached out to pat the arm of the woman Jeanne took to be Brian's mother.

Jeanne wondered if they'd been close for some time, or if the deaths of their children had brought them together.

Other than Mrs. Schwartz and Mrs. Sawyer, the only other mourners were two matronly older women in shapeless black dresses who occasionally whispered something in each other's ear (Brian's aunts, Jeanne surmised, or, if she were really lucky, the town gossips); five thirty- and forty-something men in dark suits huddled together by the door, their close-cropped hair and solemn, slightly uncomfortable demeanors suggestive of acquaintances who didn't particularly want to be there and were now forced to contemplate their own mortality; and a phalanx of bearded men in blue wool uniforms (fellow Civil War re-enactors, she presumed), interspersed with a few corseted women in hoop skirts. Each of them had a lace handkerchief in their laps, ready to be deployed at a moment's notice, but only one woman was actually using hers. Petite, with sandy brown hair, an upturned nose, and blue eyes that were a smidge too close together, she was hardly a beauty in ordinary circumstances. But today, she looked truly awful, all blotchy and swollen, with deep plum-colored circles under her eyes.

When the service concluded, Jeanne nudged Carlos in the direction of the re-enactors while she lingered by the guestbook, biting her lip as she held the pen just over the page.

Just as she had hoped, the more heavyset of the two older women trudged by just then, leaning on her cane. She peered intently at Jeanne as she pushed a pair of enormous tortoise-rimmed glasses further up the bridge of her nose. "It's hard to find something appropriately poetic to say, isn't it?"

"I'm just not any good at this," Jeanne confessed. "Are you one of his Civil War re-enacting friends?"

"Oh, no, sweetie. I've known Brian since he was a baby. He used to run across my lawn wearing nothing but a diaper. And he used to try to ride my Irish wolfhound Yeats like he was a horse." She held out a pale, doughy hand, with thick, veiny fingers. "I'm Maude, by the way."

"Jeanne." She found herself warming to Maude. Now here was a woman full of information. Leaning in, she touched Maude's arm sympathetically. "And whatever happened to his brother Sam?" she inquired. "I didn't see him here."

"Well I shouldn't say this." Maude lowered her voice, and Jeanne smiled encouragingly. "But they had an ugly falling out a few years back over some girl."

"Edith Sawyer?"

"Yes!" Maude brightened. "How did you know?"

"She and I were friends," Jeanne said, catching a glimpse of Mrs. Sawyer. They hadn't locked eyes yet, but Edith's mom was sure to recognize her eventually. And when she did, it would be better to have a consistent story. "That's how I met Brian."

"Oh, well you know the whole story then already, I'm sure."

Jeanne shook her head. "She alluded to some kind of love triangle, but I think it was too painful for her to talk about the details."

Maude sighed. "Well now they're both dead, so I suppose it doesn't matter if I tell you or not. Sam brought her home a few years ago and introduced her to all of the neighbors as his fiancée. She was a real pretty thing. Skinny, but pretty. But he was working all of the time for some consulting company, so whenever she asked him to take her anywhere, he suggested she go with his brother. At that time, Brian and Sam were only a few miles apart." Maude shrugged. "After a while, I suppose she wondered why she didn't just marry his brother instead."

Jeanne sucked in a breath. That certainly sounded like a motive for murder. No one appreciates having his fiancée stolen out from right under his nose. Especially by one's own brother.

On the other hand, why kill him after she's already dead?

"But they didn't actually get married," Jeanne observed.

"No. Some sort of newfangled nonsense about not needing a piece of paper. That's what Mary Katherine says anyway. I always wondered, though, if they were held back by some little niggling shred of guilt."

"Did they ever see each other again? The brothers, I mean."

Maude took out a compact and a tube of fuschia lipstick. She squinted into the little mirror, reapplied the lipstick slowly, and then dropped it back in her purse with a thud. "Just once, that I know of. They both attended their father's funeral last May. Poor Edith sat in the back, shaking like a wet leaf. Smart girl."

"Smart how?"

"The funeral was okay, but afterwards, in the parking lot, Sam overhead Brian introduce Edith to someone as his girlfriend, and Sam went crazy. It took all six of the other pallbearers to pull them apart. Sam's last words to Brian were 'the next time I see you, I'm gonna kill you.'"

"An unfortunate choice of words."

"Well...yes."

Maude shook Jeanne's hand and beat a hasty retreat, which freed up Jeanne to pour herself a cup of hot apple cider and go stand against the back wall next to a bored-looking young woman in a pink hoop skirt.

Jeanne let out a theatrical sigh. "Wow, first Edith, now Brian."

The young woman furrowed her brow and turned towards Jeanne. "You knew Edith?"

"A long time ago. We were at Whispering Springs together."

The young woman looked confused.

"An eating disorder treatment facility," Jeanne explained.

"Oh...that would explain a lot." She shifted slightly, and Jeanne got the impression that she was more than a little uncomfortable in her corset. "I liked her a lot. More than Brian, actually. I mean, he was nice enough, but she was so sweet. I couldn't quite see what she saw in him, although he did treat her really well."

Jeanne inclined her head towards the blotchy-faced woman, who was surrounded by three hoop-skirted companions proffering their handkerchiefs. "Who's the drama queen?"

"Chloe." She rolled her eyes. "She's been pining after Brian for years. She was always so desperate, so obvious. Right in front of Edith, even." Her eyes narrowed. "She even volunteered to play Antonia Ford."

Jeanne felt her pulse quicken. "The Confederate spy who married Major Joseph Willard?"

"That's the one. She thought if she could play his spouse in the reserve volunteers, maybe it would spill over from make-believe to the real world. As if. He was totally committed to Edith. Besides, they got married *after* the war. It wouldn't make any sense to have Antonia in a re-enactment." She sighed. "Of course, strictly speaking, Major Willard wasn't part of the Pennsylvania 16th Reserve Volunteers, either. But he was on the staff of Major General Irvin McDowell, and troops from Pennsylvania reserves were part of the I Corps that General McDowell commanded. And Brian was *so* adamant about playing Willard."

Jeanne took a deep breath. "Do you think Chloe might have killed him? You know, when she finally realized she couldn't have him."

The young woman stared at Jeanne, incredulous. "She wouldn't have harmed one hair on his head."

For a moment, Jeanne thought that the conversation was over, that she had wrung all she could get from the young re-enactor. But suddenly the woman leaned in, lowered her voice, and shuddered. "I wouldn't have been surprised if she had tried to kill Edith, though. And she probably would have if Edith hadn't beaten her to it by dying of anorexia. That girl is crazy. Absolutely crazy."

Chapter Fifteen

Jeanne took a deep breath as they approached the registration table. This was not her reunion, she reminded herself. Her mother had not killed any of these people's classmates. Tonight, she was just plain old Jennifer Walpole, whose name, she now realized, was fitting. She could be a wallflower if she wanted. After all, "Sergio" was the star tonight. He had gone to school with these people. He had wowed them with his athleticism, dark good looks, and sexy accent. All she had to do was play his mousy girlfriend. Sure, they would probably judge her. What was he thinking, they might murmur behind his back. But they would be criticizing Jennifer, not her, and it would all roll off her back.

"Sergio!"

A high-pitched shriek startled Jeanne out of her reverie. She looked up just in time to see a tall, big-boned brunette barrel towards them and wrap Carlos in a tight embrace.

"You're back from the dead," the woman said, finally drawing back. "I know, I'm sorry I've been out of touch," –he glanced discretely at her nametag while giving her an air kiss on each cheek–"Allison."

"Out of touch?" She squeezed his arm, and a cloud of perfume drifted in Jeanne's direction. "I heard you died in a plane crash on the way to Angel Falls to perform some sort of ecological survey for National Geographic."

Jeanne's heart sank. She had counted on Sergio not coming to the reunion, but not because he was dead. Obviously, her research had been subpar.

To her surprise, Carlos played it perfectly. Clasping Allison's hand, he leaned in and said in a low voice, "I'm sorry to hear you worried like that, Allison. You know how it is. Journalists like sensational stories. Another plane flew there, saw–how do you say?–*los restos*–"

"The wreckage?" she asked helpfully.

He snapped his fingers. "Yes, the wreckage, and they reported us as dead. But actually, everyone survived. We built a boat, went down the river, and six months later returned to civilization."

Allison's eyes narrowed. "You'd think the press would want to report that. They love survivor stories."

"Well I asked them–begged them–not to," Carlos said. "The government wanted to put me in jail because I wouldn't look the other way while their friends cut down *la selva*. So when I got back to civilization and realized I had been declared dead, I just went straight to Miami."

"Well this is like the Second Coming," Allison purred, wrapping a chestnut brown tendril around her pinkie and licking her bubble gum pink lips. "Only better. After all, I never hung out with Jesus under the bleachers. Which, by the way, I wouldn't mind—"

Not wanting to hear the rest of the sentence, Jeanne coughed loudly and elbowed Carlos.

"Allison, forgive me for interrupting, but I want to introduce my girlfriend, Jennifer."

The light immediately went out of Allison's eyes. Her gaze flitted from Carlos, to Jeanne, and back to Carlos. "Nice to meet you," she said coolly. "How did you two meet?"

"Snorkeling in Aruba."

"Ah. Must be nice. I'd love a vacation. A real vacation, I mean. My husband's idea of a get-away is to spend a week on the Jersey Shore with his parents."

And just like that, they had snapped back to reality. There would be no midnight tryst under the bleachers. Sergio may have been back from the dead, but even he— even the man who had slogged through the jungle and evaded powerful enemies—was now in a conventional relationship with a plain-looking woman with sensible shoes and a boring American accent. Jeanne wondered if Allison would have been happier if Sergio had just stayed dead.

From then on, Allison was all business. She fussed over the nametags, admonished them for not pre-registering, and got flustered when they insisted on paying in cash. "But it messes up my accounting," she pouted.

With a final apologetic wave, Carlos took Jeanne by the arm and led her past a laminated board crammed with photos. "In memory of those we have lost," read the beautiful calligraphy across the top, and Jeanne noted with satisfaction that Brian Schwartz was featured prominently.

Which meant that his murder would be on everyone's minds—and hopefully on their lips.

Jeanne followed Carlos past the restrooms and out into the winery's enormous tasting room. The view through the floor-to-ceiling windows nearly took her breath away—rolling blue-green hills criss-crossed with vines, their russet end-of-season leaves quaking in the wind, the mist curling up and over the distant ridgelines. A pond, flanked by a tiny white gazebo ringed with red rose bushes, glistened beneath the slate-gray sky.

Her class reunion venue—the Old Mill Restaurant, which was famous for just two things, the sawdust on the floor and the *poutine*—would be nowhere near as elegant. If, that is, she went. Which she probably, almost certainly, wouldn't.

"Beautiful," she murmured as a flock of Canadian geese landed on the pond, sending ripples to the shore.

"I was thinking the same thing."

Carlos's voice was warm in her ear, and she noticed that he was looking at her intently. He didn't seem to have noticed the geese at all.

Jeanne took him by the hand and dragged him towards a pot-bellied man with black-rimmed glasses and a soul patch. He was at least fifty pounds heavier than in his yearbook photo, but the strawberry mark that suffused his left temple was too distinctive to miss. "Time to circulate," she said. "See the guy with the birthmark? That's Gordon Althorpe. He was third trombone and ended up going to UVA with both Meaghan and Edith."

"Got it."

They reversed roles, and Carlos clasped Jeanne's hand in his and pulled her through the crowd. "Gordon!" he boomed. "*Amigo mio!*"

Spluttering, Gordon spit out a canapé onto a saucer. His eyebrows, thick as caterpillars, wiggled above his glasses. "I thought you were dead."

"No such luck."

Jeanne smiled. That was a phrase she had taught Carlos last summer, and he took every opportunity to use it.

"And I thought you hated me," Gordon exclaimed.

"Did I? If I was a *cabrón*, I apologize."

Gordon's shoulders and eyebrows sank back down, and he seemed to visibly relax. They exchanged five-minute life stories; Carlos had now embellished his to include an ill-fated union with Miss Venezuela and a six-month stint as a bush pilot surveying uncontacted tribes in the jungle, while Gordon puffed out his chest when explaining that he had just made partner at a white shoe law firm in Philadelphia. He had four perfect children—Jeanne and Carlos oohed and aahed over the obligatory cell phone photos—and each one was uniquely gifted in some way. One played viola in a prestigious youth orchestra, one was a chess champion, another had already mastered Chinese, and his oldest was an all-around genius who was about to graduate from high school at the tender age of thirteen. "Do you have children?" he inquired politely, peering at Carlos over his glasses.

"No. Not yet, anyway."

"Oh, what a pity." For a moment, Gordon looked genuinely grief-stricken and then his lips began to curl into a twisted smile. Covering his mouth, he tried to arrange his features into a more serious expression, but to no avail. The smile morphed into a smirk, then a snicker. Pretty soon, his entire pudgy little body was convulsed in laughter. "I'm so sorry," he said, clutching his stomach, "I shouldn't be laughing. But I just never imagined I'd ever have anything you didn't. I never imagined I'd feel sorry for you."

His laughter was contagious. Pretty soon, Carlos and Jeanne had joined in and the three of them were clutching each other in an attempt to remain upright.

When Jeanne was finally able to take a breath, she wiped the tears off her face. "Well in all seriousness," she said, "at least Sergio and I still have time. I'm afraid I can't say the same about Brian Schwartz."

The mention of Brian's name sobered Gordon right up. "Did you go to the funeral?"

"We just came from there."

"I should have been there, but it was just too depressing. And then" -he shook his head and lowered his voice—"to think he was murdered."

"What I can't understand," Jeanne said, "is who would want to murder him, and even if someone did, how they would know that he'd be alone in the cemetery at that time."

Gordon let out a nervous laugh and pushed his glasses further up the bridge of his nose. "Well that's because you didn't go to school with us. If you had...well, I'm sure Sergio can explain it to you."

Carlos cleared his throat and squeezed her hand. His palms were sweaty, and she could tell he was finally at a loss for words. "Unfortunately," he finally stammered, "I was too busy chasing girls to pay attention to poor Brian."

Gordon sucked in a breath and raised his eyebrows. "I guess that's what I get for always being the schmuck in the friend zone. All the girls wanted to study for finals with me, but that was about it. But between reviewing derivatives and conjugating French verbs, they told me how creeped out they were by Brian. They claimed he was a stalker. Once, as a joke, one girl—Sarah O'Brien— even agreed to go to Prom with him. He got so excited that he crowed about it on the morning announcements."

"He read the morning announcements?"

Gordon shook his head. "Unfortunately. He thought that was cool. But he would have been better off just fading into the background like the rest of us geeks. It made him the laughing stock of the school."

"So did he and Sarah go to the Prom together?"

He scoffed. "Of course not. When he showed up at her house, she was already at the Prom, dancing with Jordan Thompson."

She racked her brain for a moment, trying to recognize the name. Oh, that Jordan. The quarterback of the football team. "But Sergio told me Jordan was dating a girl named Meaghan."

"I'm not sure who he was dating, but Sarah and Meaghan were bitter rivals, that's for sure. Frenemies, I guess kids would say nowadays. Talk about mean girls." He sighed. "I wish I could say that I refused to help either Sarah or Meaghan with their studies, but that's not true. I was so blind."

"Was there anyone else who was especially cruel to Brian?"

"Oh, sure. Tabitha Edwards, Jessica Wallace, Caroline Beaulieu, Samantha Schall. People used to call them—and Sarah and Meaghan—the Sexy Six. They ruled the school and woe to anyone who got in their way."

Jeanne grabbed a shrimp cocktail off a tray that was floating past and popped it in her mouth. "But how could any of those women know he'd be in the cemetery at that time?"

Gordon smiled grimly. "The question is: who didn't know he'd be in the cemetery then?" He took a sip of wine. "Brian was obsessed with some Civil War ancestor of his. Maybe partly because he was a Union officer and that rankled people around here a bit. I think it appealed to Brian's contrarian nature." He smiled as he noticed Jeanne's confused expression. "Oh, yes, the Old South still rears its head from time to time here. We didn't learn about the Civil War, we learned about the War of Northern Aggression. Don't forget that we're just up the road from Bull Run—what you'd call Manassas—and we're not too far from James Madison's estate either. Home of the author of the Constitution—and a hundred slaves. Anyway, Brian was obsessed with this ancestor, who strangely enough married a Confederate spy after the war. Brian read a poem to them over the loudspeaker every year on their wedding anniversary, and he gave an hour-long presentation to our AP History class about them. But the weirdest part was that he would brag about sneaking into Oak Hill Cemetery on

Halloween and leaving flowers on their grave. I think he craved notoriety—kind of like the Poe Toaster."

"But the Poe Toaster was anonymous. He didn't brag about it."

Gordon shrugged. "I don't think Brian could help himself. Poor guy. I sure hope his life improved after high school." He swilled the wine in his glass and grimaced. "Well, until he was murdered, at least."

Jeanne could feel a headache coming on. Meaghan knew that Brian would be at Oak Hill on Halloween. Of that, she was sure. Of course, so did at least eight hundred other people.

The question was: how many of them wanted to kill him?

As a pair of raven-haired beauties approached Carlos, she whispered, "I'll be back in an hour." Then she slipped through the crowd and into the ladies' room. Ensconced in the handicapped stall, she lowered the toilet seat and crouched on it. She hoped she was not in for a long wait.

The minutes ticked by slowly. A petite woman swathed in periwinkle admitted to a friend that the tags were still on her dress and that she was going to return it to Nordstrom's in the morning; her husband's early midlife crisis, and subsequent switch to the non-profit sector, had left her cash-strapped. Two women compared their boob jobs. Several swapped cards for high-end tutors, personal trainers, dog groomers, and even divorce lawyers. One woman threw up in the stall next to her, and Jeanne counted at least three who downed several pills.

Perhaps Jeanne was not the only one terrified by the thought of attending her high school reunion.

Thirty minutes in, just when the wobbling in her calves was becoming unbearable, the heavy oak door swung open once more and Jeanne glimpsed a flash of curly red hair through the crack. This had to be Sarah. When Gordon had pointed her out, Sarah was holding court by the bar, and now, as parts of her willowy figure, plunging lavender silk neckline, and peaches-and-cream complexion came into view, Jeanne was sure she had her woman. It took Jeanne another minute to place her companion, who paced back and forth, giving Jeanne fleeting impressions of heavy gold jewelry, a bronzed and slightly wrinkled patch of cleavage (one too many trips to the tanning booth, perhaps), and a curtain of frizzy, honey-blond hair. Jeanne felt as though she were trying to make sense of a Cubist painting, all distended body parts and disorienting blocks of color, but at last the images clicked. This was Tabitha, one of Brian's other tormentors.

"I can't believe he's dead," Tabitha hissed.

"Relax." Sarah's voice was low and soothing, but it had an edge. Jeanne could only imagine how cutting a put-down from Sarah would have been in high school. She was one of those people whose voice—whose very bearing, in fact—dripped with authority. "This solves our problem."

"Our blackmail problem," Tabitha muttered, stressing the second word. "But it creates a whole new one, even worse. What if the police find out?"

"And how would they do that? These are the D.C. police, after all."

"Oh, I don't know. Go through his computers, say, look at any hand-written notes in his office. He worked for NSA, for God's sake. I hardly think they've got the B team on this. For all we know, the FBI's on it."

Now Sarah's profile came into view as she took a step towards Tabitha and put her hand on her hip. "And if they do—and that's a big if—we'll be the sympathetic victims. Does it give us a motive to murder him? Sure. But only" –she turned partly towards the mirror and re-applied her pale coral-colored lipstick—"if we knew his identity. But we didn't and we don't—"

"But Meaghan—"

"But Meaghan nothing. The fact that she called us three days before he was murdered means nothing. She was just letting us know that she wouldn't be able to make the reunion."

Jeanne steeled herself by clutching the bar on the side of the stall. Her knuckles had gone white. With her other hand, she covered her mouth. She didn't trust herself not to gasp. If Meaghan hadn't killed Brian, it was quite possible that one of these women had. And all because Jeanne had to go and open her mouth and accuse Brian of blackmailing Meaghan. Without any real proof, either.

"Who else did she call?" Tabitha asked.

"All of us. The whole Sexy Six. All people" –Jeanne could hear the smirk creep into Sarah's voice—"whom it would have been natural to call to let them know she couldn't make it." Sarah's voice came closer and soon there was a pair of strappy lavender heels in the stall next to Jeanne's. "Now don't go all squishy on me, Tabitha. Brian was a conniving, manipulative loser who invaded your privacy and threatened your marriage."

"Shhh. You never know who is going to walk in here." She lowered her voice. "Don't you ever think we brought this on ourselves? It's like karma or something." Jeanne could hear the sound of pantyhose snapping back into place, and she readied herself to move. By now, the pain was excruciating. A moment later, Sarah flushed and Jeanne took advantage of the loud swishing sound to shift into a cross-legged position. She stifled a sigh of relief.

"Oh, please. You wouldn't know karma if the Buddha bit you on the ass. Besides, if anyone got his comeuppance, it was Brian."

Sarah's stall door clanged open, and Jeanne caught a glimpse of Sarah surveying herself in the mirror. As much as she disliked the woman, Jeanne had to admit that she was stunning. Sarah bared her teeth in the mirror and, satisfied that no lipstick was besmirching her blindingly white teeth, snapped her lips shut again. "You always were a worrywart," she said to her companion. "That's why you were always a follower, never a leader. You lacked a certain imagination, a vision for just how far you could take your popularity. But I was Sarah the Barracuda, remember? I always get what I want. Eventually."

As the door swung shut behind them, Jeanne wondered if this included Brian's murder.

Chapter Sixteen

Five minutes later, as Jeanne was savoring the fresh air in the hallway and massaging her calves, her phone rang.

"Hello, this is Jeanne," she shouted above the din.

"Ms. Pelletier, this is Sergeant Villanueva. We need you to come down to the station and make an ID. We've got the man that you saw running from the scene in custody."

"I'm out of town at the moment. Can I come down tomorrow?"

"Fine. See you at ten a.m. sharp."

He hung up abruptly, and Jeanne headed off to find Carlos. He found her before she did. "*Baila conmigo.*" She felt his hand, soft and warm, cradling the small of her back.

The band was playing a Gloria Estefan song. He led her effortlessly in a rumba and, as they made their way across the room, the crowd began to part to make way for them. One by one, couples stopped dancing to just stand and gape.

"I hope Sergio was a good dancer," Jeanne murmured into his ear.

"Oh, the best," he reassured her. "Apparently he was good at everything. Including romance."

"Oh, I gathered that," Jeanne laughed, "from Allison's greeting."

As they executed a turn, he pulled her even closer to him—so close, in fact, that she could feel his heart beating—and whipped her in circles. The feel of his hand on her back was both reassuring and alarming. It was protective, yet it felt just a tad possessive too. It was nothing like Fergus's limp-wristed grip; Fergus tried, he really did, to humor Jeanne and learn how to dance, but it just wasn't his forte.

"So what did you find out?" he asked.

"That Brian was blackmailing quite a few people. That Meaghan told them that he was the blackmailer." Out of the corner of her eye, she spotted Sarah flirting brazenly with the husband of a miserable-looking, mousy blonde who was skulking resentfully in the corner. From the looks of it, Sarah hadn't lost her touch. "And that the mean girls in high school are still mean."

"Ready to make the mean girls jealous?"

She nodded. He released her, spun onto his knees, then sprang up twenty feet from her. She took a running start and leapt. For one glorious moment, she hovered above them all—the nerdy, the successful, the mean girls, and the repentant ones. This one's for Edith, she thought, as the room became a blur.

And then his strong arms were wrapped around her, bringing her back to earth. The crowd was whistling and clapping, but they sounded so far, far away to

Jeanne. She was face to face with Carlos, their lips a mere hair's breadth apart.

Time seemed to stand still. All kinds of images flashed before her eyes. Pamela's cute little button nose and sweet, docile expression. Fergus's guilty countenance. Carlos's searing gaze in the car earlier that day. She felt his liquid brown eyes boring into her, his smooth cheek against hers. Would this be what life with Carlos would be like? Smooth sailing over rough waters, one lark after another with a kindred spirit who didn't feel the need to plumb her dark, mysterious depths. She wouldn't have to change, to talk about her feelings, to try to be a better, more open and honest partner. She could be secure in the knowledge that he had a deep, dark past—even deeper and darker than her own. And they could each keep the past safely buried.

He lowered his head and his lips grazed hers just as she jerked her head to the side and kissed him on the cheek. Better to wait, she decided. If she did end up kissing him, she wanted to be clear that she was kissing Carlos—her former student with the rap sheet, the one who often smelled of chicken grease and onions at the end of a twelve-hour shift—and not Sergio the perfect.

He took it in stride, just the hint of a rueful smile playing on his lips before it was gone. He released his tight grip and held her at arm's length. The spell was broken.

"I got a call from the police," Jeanne shouted as they executed a fast turn. "They've got the guy from the cemetery in custody."

"What's his name?"

"I don't know. Why?"

Carlos shrugged. "Maybe I know him."

What was left unsaid was the implication that perhaps, just as Carlos had once been a frequent guest in lock-up, this guy was too.

Jeanne abruptly broke off their dance and led him back to the bar stool where she had left her purse. She fished out her phone and scrolled to the photo she had shared with the police. "Recognize him?"

Carlos held it up to the light. "Sure. That's Curtis. I don't know his last name, but what I can tell you is that he didn't do it. A stay in solitary at Red Onion destroyed his brain. Even if he wanted to kill someone, I doubt he could."

Jeanne sighed and slid her phone back in her purse. "Come on, let me take you to your 'safe house.'"

"Is that your apartment?"

"No, even better, I promise." And, she silently added, much safer than her house, in more ways than one. After that dance, she didn't trust herself to spend the night under the same roof as Carlos. "My real estate agent gave me the keys to one of her client's big, empty second homes. It's been on the market for nearly a year, the client moved to Montana and never visits, and it's all yours unless and until Roxy needs to show it."

Jeanne extracted a key ring, business card, and cell phone from her purse. "Here's a burner phone. Roxy will call you on it if you need to clear out in a hurry."

He looked at her with admiration. "You know, sometimes I think you'd make a great criminal."

"Sometimes I think the same thing. And it scares me."

****

142

The police had done a good job with the line-up. All of the men resembled each other. Wild-eyed African-American men in late middle age, they all bore the marks of hard living, had scraggly gray hair tied back in a messy ponytail, and wore a military-style jacket slung over their wasted frames. But there was no doubt in her mind that number three was the man she had seen.

Jeanne left the jail feeling dejected. Lately, everything seemed to be her fault. She had pushed Fergus away and practically flung him into Pamela's waiting arms. She had fingered Brian as Meaghan's blackmailer, Meaghan had blabbed to all of her friends, and now it seemed that one of them may have killed Brian. And she was the one who had snapped a photo of Curtis and put him on the police's radar.

Would she ever be able to make anything right again?

As she walked towards the bus stop, past block after block of tired-looking red-brick rowhouses, one word resounded in her head: Brown.

She was sure that they hadn't meant for her to hear, but one of the detectives had muttered it under her breath.

Ducking into a corner store, she slipped past the young Asian woman shielded behind bullet-proof glass, walked down an aisle brimming with potato chips and cheap liquor, and hovered by the tiny refrigerated case of fresh produce. Then she extracted her phone and searched for every Curtis Brown living in the District. There were eight Curtis Browns, but only four in the right age range.

On the third call, a quavering female voice answered the phone.

"Mrs. Brown?" Jeanne struggled to be heard over the hum of the refrigerator.

"Yes. Who is this?"

"My name is Jeanne Pelletier and I'm looking for the mother of a Curtis Brown who's currently being held in D.C. Jail."

There was silence on the end of the line, although Jeanne could hear the woman breathing. "Is your son the same Curtis Brown who spent time at Red Onion?" Jeanne prodded.

"Yes," the old woman said, and then added with sudden bitterness, "and it certainly didn't do him any favors."

"Could I come over and speak with you? I think I could be of help."

"Then come on over, dear."

Sunlight filtered through the makeshift kitchen curtains—two faded blue sheets dotted with daisies and strung up with twine—and danced across Mrs. Brown's sturdy kitchen table. Rubbing her hands together for warmth, Jeanne peered over Mrs. Brown's shoulder at the old photo album.

"The gas was shut off last week," Curtis's mother explained apologetically. Her mocha-colored fingers were gnarled and veiny, but they caressed each photo with incredible tenderness. "Here's Curtis's middle school graduation photo. I was so proud. I never thought he would make it." She traced a finger over his broad smile and cute chipmunk cheeks. Tears welled up in her big hazel eyes. "You see, my boy has an IQ of 75. His daddy ran off before he was even born, so I raised him on my own. I did the best I could, I really did, and he was the sweetest boy in the world."

"But others took advantage of his sweet, trusting nature, I take it."

Mrs. Brown nodded and pinched the bridge of her nose, squeezing her eyes shut. "He dropped out of school in tenth grade. Maybe I should have made him go, but I just didn't have the heart to set him up to fail day after day. The school just didn't know what to do with him, and I didn't want to send him away. But I had to keep working to support him."

"So he was alone all day."

"And lonely. Pretty soon some neighborhood low-lives were coming around, puffing him up, making him think they liked him. Giving him candy at first, then little jobs to do. Like being a look-out during their drug deals. He thought it was just a game. Like the cops and robbers five-year-olds play. He didn't understand that this was for real."

Mrs. Brown was very still for a moment, and Jeanne was afraid she wouldn't continue. "Sometimes they would give him money to hold too," she finally said. "One day, the cops mounted a sting operation and one of those hotheads shot a cop. A twenty-year veteran with a wife and three kids. My Curtis wasn't armed, but he was holding the money. And, being none too bright, he said a lot of things that didn't exactly help his case."

"How much time did he get?"

"Eight years."

"And they sent him to a supermax prison for that?"

Mrs. Brown harrumphed. "Well, not according to them. He was held in a medium security prison in Virginia at first, but prison didn't agree with him. He started having panic attacks and seizures. The noise bothered him. The lights were on all the time. He was terrified of the dogs. He had a hard time following the guards' directions; sometimes he just didn't understand what they wanted. Pretty soon he had been labeled as 'disorderly' and they were transferring him to Red Onion. You know where that is?"

Jeanne shook her head.

"On a mountaintop, on that little finger of land that juts into Kentucky. An eight-hour drive from here. I got no car, no way to get there. My baby was all alone in there. He was crying for his momma every day. And that got him put in solitary—twenty-three hours a day, seven days a week. For four years."

She let that sink in for a moment before continuing. "His panic attacks got worse. He started to hear voices. He got no treatment, other than some meds. But sometimes he didn't even get that. Whenever they were on lockdown, which was often, he wouldn't get his meds. Sometimes for days at a time. And if he got spooked and started yelling, they'd put him in five-point restraints. Once he was tied to the bed for forty-eight hours; the guards teased him mercilessly for defecating on himself, as if it was his fault. One day, a voice told him to kill himself, so he hung himself by a sheet. By the time they cut him down, he'd lost most of what little brain capacity he'd had."

Jeanne reached out and squeezed Mrs. Brown's hand. "I'm so sorry," she said. "One thing stands out to me, though. Based on what you're telling me, Curtis was never violent—at least to others—a day in his life."

"As God is my witness."

"So do you have any idea why he was in Oak Hill Cemetery on Halloween?"

"Honey, he rarely left home. If he went to the corner to buy some Doritos, it was a victory. My baby came home from prison a shell. Just a shell of a human being. He was afraid of everything—dogs, church bells, you name it. The sound of the mailman slamming the mailbox shut could send him diving under the couch."

"So what—or who—could have gotten him to go there?"

"Your guess is as good as mine."

Chapter Seventeen

Clutching her purse tightly, Jeanne hurried to the nearest Metro stop. A cold north wind howled through the parking lot, sending people scurrying into the bus shelters. A half dozen homeless people huddled by the entrance and even here—no less than at the Middleburg High School reunion—there was a pecking order. Those with the most seniority, or those that were the most conniving or intimidating, lay directly over the steaming metal grates, where the Metro station's hot, stale air was expelled. Tightly wrapped in shroud-like gray wool blankets, the homeless people reminded Jeanne of Egyptian mummies.

How many of them would end up in the D.C. Jail, or worse?

The station itself was a warm, reassuringly utilitarian expanse of hexagonal orange tiles, brown farecard machines, and bored station managers. Built in the practical, brutalist style of the 1970s and designed for maximum efficiency, the Metro had none of the romance or poetry of Paris's Metropolitan or the faded elegance of Moscow's subway stops. Sometimes the concrete block design made Jeanne wonder if the builders had meant for it to double as some sort of giant Cold War bomb shelter.

She descended into the bowels of the earth, hopped onto a sleek Italian-made train car, and in a matter of minutes was whisked from a nearly all-black island of poverty to a yuppie paradise. The stations all looked the same, as did the dark tunnels that whizzed past, but the color of the people crowding the train changed rapidly. She always found this disconcerting, but no one else seemed to notice.

When they reached Foggy Bottom, Jeanne trudged up the escalator and started the long trek home. Stopping briefly at Patisserie Poupon, she picked up two almond croissants, a tiramisu, and an exquisite little chocolate opera torte. Then, fortified with a perfectly frothed café au lait, she ran home, took Scarlett out to pee, and went and banged on Jerry's door.

One deep-set brown eye regarded her through the crack and then the door swung wide open. Eyeing the white pastry box in her arms, Jerry licked his lips. "What have you got for me today, Twinkletoes?"

"Enough sugar to keep you hyper until bedtime." She squeezed past his considerable girth, placed the box in the only free space on the kitchen countertop, and rooted around until she found two chipped plates. "And, yes, I'll take some Turkish coffee today."

"That kind of weekend, huh?"

"Well, to give you a brief recap, yesterday I was feeling sorry for myself because I've pushed Fergus into the arms of his charming, baggage-free ex—who, in some

149

sort of twisted impeccable timing, decided to just pop across the pond and visit Fergus right now—"

Jerry grunted. "Doesn't sound like a coincidence to me."

"And then, I took Carlos to Brian Schwartz's funeral and high school reunion—"

"Like a date?"

"It was intended to be just two buddies helping each other out. But it turned into kind of a date. Sort of. And" -in her agitation, she found herself combing through the freezer for some ice cream to top the pastries, as if any more sugar were needed—"I discovered a whole new bevy of suspects—Brian's brother, who reportedly shouted 'I'm going to kill you' at their father's funeral; unhinged, lovelorn little Chloe from Brian's re-enacting group; and a whole bunch of high school classmates that tormented Brian in high school and were being blackmailed by him."

By now, nearly the entire contents of Jerry's freezer were strewn over the counter. "The emergency Jeanne stash of New York Super Fudge Chunk is behind the frozen pot stickers," he said helpfully.

"Thanks." She took out a pint, grabbed the biggest spoon she could find, and shoveled the ice cream over the pastries. "Then this morning I'm hauled into the police station to ID the guy I saw running away from the crime scene—a guy that Carlos apparently knows and Carlos swears couldn't have done it. After that, I have a chat with his lovely mother, who tells me that he has an IQ of 75 and has lost his mind as a result of a four-year stint in solitary. So now I feel like a privileged little you-know-what. I was worrying about my love life while setting in motion the events that led to Brian's death and causing poor Mrs. Brown to worry that her mentally handicapped son is going to be incarcerated again for a crime he didn't commit."

Jerry sighed. "You don't know that."

"Which part?"

"Any of it. Just because Brian was blackmailing people doesn't mean they killed him. After all, you yourself admit there are other suspects. And you don't know that this guy Brown is going to be put away. After all, you saw him at what? Noon?"

"Twelve-thirty."

"Exactly. Probably hours and hours after the murder occurred. So unless they can put him at the scene at the time of death, and unless they can produce a weapon, they don't have much on him."

"That might be true if he were Joe Georgetown, with nary a parking ticket. But he was convicted as an accomplice to murder. Of a cop."

Jerry handed her a steaming little cup of inky black liquid and a plate overflowing with a precarious tower of pastries and ice cream. "Sit down and eat. If there's one thing I know about you, Twinkletoes, it's that you'll feel better the moment the sugar hits your bloodstream."

"You make it sound like heroin." But she obediently took the proffered goodies and went to lower herself into the Jeanne-sized depression in the couch.

Jerry joined her a moment later, launching himself onto the couch with a force that sent her coffee sloshing in the cup. "Red Onion, huh?" he asked without any sort of preamble.

"How'd you guess?"

"A couple of guys I served with in Iraq worked there. It's on a mountaintop surrounded by abandoned coal mines. The economy's in the toilet. About the only jobs there are at Walmart, 7-Eleven, or the prison. If you can believe it, the prison is considered the best job of all. Or, of course, you can join the military and go see the world. It's one of the places they always make their recruitment targets. It's almost like shooting fish in a barrel. Okay, bad analogy. It's more like we're scooping fish out of a festering cesspool, handing them a gun, and then putting them in a different cesspool. Only now they're the big kahuna. They're at the top of the food chain." He took a big bite of croissant. "The prison loves employing ex-military guys. They figure they're battle-hardened, tough, know how to use a weapon. What they don't realize—or then again, maybe they do—is that a lot of them also have acquired a taste for power. And when you give a guy with a power trip a weapon, it can be a very dangerous thing."

"Meaning?"

"Meaning they gave my friend a job, but they robbed him of his soul. He said it was like Abu Ghraib all over again—only instead of American guys—and women, let's not forget Lyndie England—lording it over a bunch of Iraqis, you've got a bunch of bubbas with guns, resentful that the American dream has passed them by, guarding a bunch of prisoners, some of whom have committed heinous crimes, many of whom are minorities, and almost all of whom are from far away."

"Aren't they all Virginians?"

Jerry laughed. "There are—or at least there were—lots of out-of-state prisoners. They're very proud of the fact that they earn $80 million a year for the taxpayers of Virginia by hosting out-of-state prisoners." He bit into a fudge chunk and smiled ruefully. "There's the military-industrial complex, and then the prison-industrial complex. And sometimes there's not much daylight between the two."

"Man, Jerry, I never pegged you as such a socialist."

"I'm not anything, Twinkletoes. Other than bitter."

Jeanne balanced her laptop on the wobbly coffee table and turned it on. "Well on that depressing note," she said, taking a sip of coffee, "let's get on with our research."

"Ah, I figured you wanted more than my philosophical musings of the day."

"As intriguing as they are, yes. What I want to know is how Brian was blackmailing Sarah, Tabitha, and the other popular girls in school and where they were on Halloween."

Two hours later, "Sergio" had an impressive Facebook profile, and Jeanne had managed to entice all six women of interest to "friend" him. Two of the six appeared to have iron-clad alibis. Samantha Schall was on a family vacation to Disney World and, given that a photo of her cherubic blond daughter was featured on the official Disney blog for October 31st, Jeanne doubted that her Facebook post was fabricated. Sarah the Barracuda (who opted to be listed under the much more prosaic Sarah Riordan O'Brien) appeared to have been recovering from liposuction in San Diego. Jeanne could not imagine why anyone would admit to that on Facebook (and underscore the point with a hideous picture of her sitting by the pool sporting an enormous bandage), but it did provide the perfect alibi. Her surgeon would be able to quickly confirm the date, which would rule her out.

So that left Caroline Beaulieu, Jessica Wallace, and Tabitha Edwards. And, of course, her client.

Caroline appeared to have been trick-or-treating with their children, but there was no indication of her whereabouts later in the evening. Tabitha had no posts for either October 31st or November 1st, but she had been tagged in Jessica's album. It appeared the two of them had gone drinking together in Georgetown, along with their husbands. Like so many women crowding the streets that night, they had opted for sexy over scary. Tabitha was dressed as Strawberry Shortcake—in a dress far shorter than the one Jeanne's childhood lunchbox icon actually wore—while Jessica was dressed, predictably given her buxom figure and long legs, as Jessica Rabbit. Jessica had written eight posts that night, and the accompanying photos chronicled the progression of the evening. At the start of the night, their make-up was perfect and their drinks were fluorescent orange and green cocktails misting over like bubbling cauldrons. By the last post, at one-thirty, Jessica's ears were drooping, their mascara was trailing down their cheeks, and they were clutching Coronas.

Jeanne took down the time of each post and then plotted each location on the wrinkled tourist map that she kept for out-of-town guests. The longest undocumented stretch was between 11:35 p.m., when they had been twelve blocks away from the cemetery, and 12:42 p.m., when they had been just six blocks away. It was more than enough time for them to have killed Brian. She didn't notice any blood on their clothes in any picture, but it was theoretically possible that they could have changed out of their costumes, done the deed, and changed back into their costumes.

She was so immersed in her research that a sudden grunt from Jerry startled her.

"Bingo!" he shouted, obviously very pleased with himself. "Listen to this. From a March 12, 2012, *Washington Post* article about prescription drug abuse: 'The U.S. Attorney's Office in Alexandria is reportedly investigating allegations that Leesburg physician Michael O'Brien, whom *The Washingtonian* named in 2011 as one of the area's top doctors, is running a pill mill, writing thousands of prescriptions a month for Oxycontin, Xanax, and Percocet without any basis in medical necessity. Dr. O'Brien's lawyer and spokesman, Doug Sinclair, denied the allegations.'"

Jeanne stretched out and put her feet on the coffee table. "But if that was already out in the open, that doesn't seem like a way for Brian to blackmail Sarah."

"Just wait, Twinkletoes, there's more. Less than six months later, the case against the good doctor is closed with no charges filed."

"So maybe there was nothing to the allegations."

"I might think that too, except for some very interesting coincidences. Dr. O'Brien happens to have been Congressman Murphy of Virginia's largest bundler of campaign contributions. He and Sarah the Barracuda seem to have hosted one fundraiser after another for him."

"So you think Congressman Murphy called the dogs off?"

"No, I think your client called the dogs off, as you put it."

She just stared at him. "My client?"

"Congressman Richardson is the chair of the House Judiciary Committee, which had oversight of the Department of Justice, and DOJ of course—"

"Oversees the U.S. attorneys."

"Exactly. Who are, of course, political appointees who tend to be extremely politically ambitious. And rumor has it that the U.S. attorney overseeing the pill mill case was angling for a Federal judgeship. So naturally it would be important for him to stay on the good side of the chair of the Judiciary Committee."

"But why would Congressman Richardson want to help Congressman Murphy?"

"Maybe the friendship between their wives was enough. Or maybe" –his lips curled into a malicious little grin—"there was a little quid pro quo. Two months after the charges are dropped, Congressman Murphy suddenly changes his position on the defense authorization bill and supports Congressman Richardson's amendment to expand naval operations in Charleston at the expense of operations in Virginia Beach. Technically, Congressman Murphy's district doesn't include Virginia Beach, but it still seems a little strange to buck the wishes of the Virginia delegation like that."

"And did it pass?"

"By one vote—Congressman Murphy's. Congressman Richardson is hailed as the savior of Charleston, completely quashing the hopes of the Tea Party candidate running against him."

"They found someone even more conservative to run against him?"

"Twinkletoes, the other guy was to the right of Attila the Hun."

Chapter Eighteen

Jeanne had never been a morning person, but after a long night of sleuthing with Jerry, she found it particularly hard to rise and shine on Monday. Bleary-eyed and cranky, she shuffled to the kitchen, snatched a few chocolate biscotti, and repaired to her futon. "I'll take you out to pee in a minute," she mumbled, scratching Scarlett behind the ears, as she fumbled with the remote control. Maybe the gloom and doom of the news would scare her wide awake.

To her surprise, her client was giving a press conference, and for once he wasn't shouting or raising his fist. Calm, cool, and collected—smiling, even—he was announcing his bid for re-election. When he walked away from the lectern amidst a flurry of flashing bulbs, the broadcast cut away to some inane political commentary. A very intense young woman who was billed as some sort of expert on the millennial generation could not stop proclaiming herself "flabbergasted."

"Everyone thought he was ready to call it quits," she pontificated. "He hadn't done any fundraising. He hadn't put any campaign staff in place. He'd given every impression that he wasn't running. And then he suddenly announces his re-election bid."

"Well what do you make of that, Hannah?" the anchorwoman asked. "According to your sources, what's behind this change of heart?"

"Well, he's very popular in South Carolina. For a while it looked like he had a serious Tea Party challenger, and maybe that's why he was leaning towards retiring. But his popularity has come roaring back, Elena, and maybe that spurred him to re-think his decision."

Jeanne turned off the TV in disgust. Now, Jeanne thought cynically. He's very popular now because he doesn't miss an opportunity to bash Snowden. The very same conservative voters who want the right to amass an arsenal to protect against government overreach would like to hang a man who had the audacity to point out that the very same government was spying on them.

Suddenly she heard three knocks on the wall and then Jerry's voice. "Are you going to need a ride to your closing later today, Twinkletoes?"

"That would be great, Jerry," she shouted back. "Two o'clock. In the meantime, I'm going to run down a hunch."

Slumped over in her chair, Maggie Cooper's dark eyes were downcast, seemingly fixated on her steaming bowl of Senate navy bean soup. She pushed the lentils around aimlessly before finally letting her spoon fall into the bowl with a loud clatter and pushing the soup away, uneaten. "How'd you find me?" she asked. Under other circumstances, her soft low country accent would have been charming, but Jeanne's line of questioning seemed to have sucked the life right out of her.

"A hunch," Jeanne said. "Not many people quit suddenly after six years of faithful service and a plumb position as deputy chief of staff to a powerful five-term Congressman and committee chair in order to take a position in a lowly junior Congressman's office."

"I was under a lot of stress," Maggie said defensively, her coffee-colored fingers hard at work shredding a paper napkin.

"And I can see that you still are. But something tells me that the stress has everything to do with something that you witnessed in Congressman Richardson's office."

Maggie looked up, her eyes flashing indignantly beneath perfectly curled lashes. In her left iris, a speck of yellow seemed to grow and pulsate until Jeanne felt as though she were in the crosshairs of an angry yellow spotlight. "I told you, my mother was ill at the time."

"I'm sure that was difficult," Jeanne murmured. "But she'd been sick for months already, and the Charleston African Methodist Episcopal Church's online newsletter reported that she was declared cancer-free one week after you quit."

"See?" Maggie glared at her. "Dedicating more time to my mom paid off."

"If you believe in miracles," Jeanne said, "perhaps that is so. If you believe in medical science, though, not so much. Cancer doesn't get cured in a week." Blowing on a steaming spoonful of soup, she decided to change tack. "You're an attractive young woman. Did Congressman Richardson ever make you feel uncomfortable? Ask you to stay late and work alone with him? That kind of thing?"

To Jeanne's surprise, Maggie struggled to suppress a giggle. "That's what you think? No, he didn't play on that team."

Jeanne sat back in her chair. Suddenly, things clicked into place. Congressman Richardson's lack of jealousy over Meaghan's affair with Jorge. The strange look that flitted between the Richardsons at the "séance." Their companionable, yet seemingly passionless, relationship.

Maggie stood up and pushed in her chair. "I think we're done here."

"Actually, we're not. I'm sorry to play hard ball, but I know there's more that you're not telling me."

"And why should I help you?"

"Because I suspect we've both been deceived by Congressman Richardson. And because, if you don't, I'll spread rumors that you've been talking out of turn about the congressman's affairs. Which, of course, is the kiss of death for a staffer's career."

"And who's going to believe you?"

"Not me. Thurston Huntsman." She tried to say the powerful—and very gossipy—staffer's name as casually as possible. "My best friend is dating him."

Here, she was stretching the truth. Lily had gone on a date with him last month, but nothing had come of it. But Maggie didn't need to know that.

"And if I help you?"

"I'll take your secret to my grave."

Almost immediately, Jeanne regretted her choice of words. Just how far would Brian Schwartz's killer—and anyone else in this sordid tangle of conspiracies—go to keep their secrets safe? She could tell Maggie was wondering the same thing; the young woman's arched eyebrow and grim expression gave her away.

"Fine," Maggie said in a low voice and sat back down. She leaned forward until her elbows were almost touching Jeanne's. "Between you and me, I've always suspected that the congressman's chief of staff, Scott Ferrer, handles the congressman's more, um, delicate assignments. Which has always suited me just fine. When you're unaware of something, it's easy to deny. But one day, Scott was late for an important meeting with a very well-connected constituent, so I went to go knock on his door. What I heard"—her hands trembled and she went back to shredding the napkin—"was troubling, to say the least. He was threatening a U.S. attorney if the attorney didn't quietly end his investigation into Dr. O'Brien. Over the years, I made my peace with the idea of dispensing political favors here and there—it's just the price of politics and, in the end, if you can do some good, it's all worth it—but this really crossed the line. So when a friend told me about a job opening over lunch the next day, I jumped."

"Does the congressman know why you left?"

"I have no idea."

Jeanne glanced at her watch. Her closing was in less than two hours. "How could I find out more about the investigation into Dr. O'Brien?"

Maggie shrugged. "Beats me."

"Would there be a way to get Scott to talk about it?"

"Sure, if you're a *Politico* reporter." Maggie laughed bitterly. "He loves setting up secret meetings with them, spilling the beans about this or that. He thinks he's like the James Bond of Congress. Makes him feel powerful or something."

A light went off in Jeanne's head. "Thank you for your time, Maggie," she said as she practically ran out of the cafeteria, past doddering old white men in dull gray suits and their twenty-something sycophants, bright and eager, with that Mr.-Smith-Goes-to-Washington gleam in their eyes. Oh, children, Jeanne thought, if only you knew.

Emerging into the blinding sunshine of a crisp November day, she ran down Pennsylvania Avenue until she found a newspaper stand. Jeanne scanned the racks for a *Politico*, thumbed through it until she found a list of the staff, and then dialed Congressman Richardson's office. "Scott Ferrer, please," she said in a voice slightly higher than her own, tinged with a mix of anxiety and proud self-importance.

When they put her through, she let loose a breathy torrent of words. "Mr. Ferrer? This is Olivia Van Sant. I'm an intern at *Politico*." She looked down at the paper and searched for the name of the editor. "Barry wanted to call you himself, but he's stuck at a hearing. But he said it's very important that I speak to you before we run a story about Congressman Richardson's surprising re-election bid. Could we meet this afternoon?"

She could hear a heavy door swing shut; presumably he didn't want to be overheard. "This afternoon's tough," Scott said. "But I could meet you in fifteen minutes at The Folger. I'd be able to speak to you for ten minutes before I'd have to head to the chamber."

"The Shakespeare library?"

"That's the one. In the exhibit hall."

Jeanne tried to hide her amusement. The Shakespeare library? Sure, it was conveniently located around the corner from the Capitol, but how cloak and dagger could one get?

"Fifteen minutes," she agreed and hung up.

Home to the world's largest Shakespeare collection, the Folger was a squat white marble building decorated with bas-reliefs depicting memorable scenes from the bard's oeuvre. Jeanne found the Art Deco façade quite ugly and, like the unfortunate WWII memorial, strangely reminiscent of the self-aggrandizing fascist architecture of Mussolini and Hitler.

But once inside, she felt immediately transported to Elizabethan England. Crowned by a vaulted ornamental plaster ceiling, the oak-paneled walls and mullioned windows provided a brilliant setting for the beautifully embroidered gowns, almost sculptural in form with their whalebone stays and wire bustles, of Shakespearean heroines and the gaudy doublets and hose worn by Shakespeare's male characters. Each magnificent costume was encased in glass and lined up in the center of the exhibit room; Shakespeare's first folio and other works were arranged in glass cases along the walls.

Jeanne extracted a notebook and a pen from her purse and fished her laminated press badge out of her purse. Casually perusing the displays, she kept one eye on the entrance.

Scott arrived a few minutes later, looking flushed and self-important. He wore the almost regulation navy blue suit of Hill staffers, but his expensive brown leather shoes, jaunty pink pocket square, and matching pink silk tie marked him as a rare fashionista.

He hurried up to her. "Olivia, I presume?"

"Nice to meet you, and thanks for coming." Jeanne flashed her badge at him, her thumb obscuring the words "Washington Post." "Could you tell me more about why Congressman Richardson changed his mind and decided to run for re-election? His colleagues all seemed to be under the impression that he was retiring."

Scott flushed with anger. "He changed his mind," he said curtly. "It's a free country."

"Yes, but why did he change his mind?"

"He decided he had more to accomplish. The crime bill, for example, is something he's been hard at work on."

"Might it have something to do with the fact that he twisted Congressman Murphy's arm to change his vote on the defense authorization bill and, as a result, the naval bases in Charleston will expand?"

"Well it certainly helps burnish his well-deserved reputation as a champion of our military and of military bases in South Carolina."

She led Scott over to an exhibit in the far corner of the hall and rested her elbows on the glass case. Casting a furtive glance around the room, she lowered her voice. "But how would voters react if they thought that the only reason Congressman Murphy changed his vote was because Congressman Richardson pressured a U.S. attorney to drop a case against Congressman Murphy's main campaign donation bundler?"

Scott blanched. "I don't know what you're talking about."

"Barry thinks you do," she said. "We've got a couple of sources that indicate that's the reason Congressman Murphy switched his vote. Can you confirm that?" She peered at him intently. "Off the record?"

"I don't do 'off the record.'"

"Of course you do. All the time."

"Says the intern."

"Says the intern who hears all of the office scuttlebutt. But, hey, Scott, that's okay. We can run the story without your information. And who knows?" She smiled maliciously. "Maybe Barry will let me investigate a story for the next edition about the role you played in arranging this quid pro quo."

"I didn't play any role," he said.

"Oh, so now you do admit that there was a quid pro quo?"

"I admit nothing of the kind," he snarled. "I didn't play a role because it never happened."

One of the three phones clipped to his belt began to ring. Scott shot Jeanne a contemptuous look as he glanced at the caller ID. "It's your boss," he said. "I'm sure he'll love to hear what his little intern is up to."

Jeanne's heart began to race. She had not counted on this.

"I'll be right back," she mumbled. "I've just got to pop into the restroom."

She caught snatches of Scott's diatribe as she walked briskly down the corridor. "What kind of nut jobs are you employing these days, Barry....that Olivia is some kind of unhinged conspiracy theorist...and she's not even hot...where are your standards, man?"

Jeanne was a few steps from the exit when she heard him shout, "You mean you didn't send Olivia to interview me?"

That was her cue to run. Sprinting down the steps, she hung a right on Second Street. Her heart beat wildly as she dodged traffic to cross East Capitol Street, then raced past the back of the Supreme Court. Scott was nipping at her heels. His suit jacket hung open, and his tie swung back and forth.

The sound of whistles and drums grew louder, and her heart soared as she realized there must be a protest in front of the Supreme Court. With a new spring in her step, she rounded the corner of Constitution Avenue and was soon happily swept up in a gay rights' march. Snatching up a discarded rainbow-colored wig, she shoved her hair underneath and followed the surging crowd to the Senate office buildings, then veered off down Delaware Avenue.

She didn't stop running until she reached Union Station. As she was catching her breath beneath the rotunda, Jerry called.

"Where are you?" he shouted.

"Union Station. I just accused Congressman Richardson's chief of staff of collusion in the quid pro quo involving O'Brien."

"Whatever for?"

"To see if he seemed rattled."

"Did he?"

"Well he chased me for several blocks in a really expensive suit so, yeah, I'd say so."

"Well, stop chasing Hill staffers," Jerry said, "and hurry home. We're supposed to be leaving for the closing now, remember?"

Chapter Nineteen

Jeanne mumbled her apologies to Jerry as they set off for the closing on the back of his Harley. She held on tight as Jerry expertly weaved through the traffic, catching an overpowering whiff of leather, cigarettes, and Febreze.

How could she have forgotten the closing? After all the years she scrimped and saved to put together a down payment and the weekends she spent trudging from one hellhole to another with Roxy, she would have thought that the closing was the one thing she would not—could not—forget.

And yet she had.

As they roared up Connecticut Avenue, tears welled up in her eyes. Stop it, she scolded herself. You should be ecstatic. The little girl who grew up in a miserable trailer—a place no one would ever mistake for a real home—would now have a condo of her own. She had made it.

But the problem was that, without Fergus, it didn't really seem like home. And living there would remind her, each and every day, of just how alone she was. She'd be without Fergus, and Jerry—and she'd even be a bit too far to walk to Vivienne's.

By the time they arrived at the neat little office near Chevy Chase Circle, Jeanne's face was wet with tears. She kept her head down, not wanting to look at Jerry, not wanting to answer his inevitable question: why?

She reached into the pocket of her fleece and fingered the cashier's check. It was warm to the touch, and she gulped as she recalled the amount written on it.

Sixty thousand dollars.

She thought of all the things that sixty thousand dollars could buy—things that could bring her, or someone else, so much more joy than an empty condo.

They entered the reception area. A door to an inner office was partly open, and Jeanne spotted a pleasantly plump middle-aged woman whom she took to be the seller. Had the woman been happy living there? She seemed to be alone. Was Jeanne destined to be her in thirty years' time, a lonely middle-aged woman ready to turn the keys over to a lonely young woman?

Roxy was seated on the couch, her long red nails furiously tapping out a text on her phone. She glanced up for just a second, long enough to spot Jeanne's tear-stained face. "Poor baby," she murmured, rushing over to Jeanne and enveloping her in a maternal embrace. "What's wrong?"

Everything, Jeanne wanted to say. But she only said, "I can't go through with this."

And then she ran out of the building, leaving Roxy's and Jerry's mouths hanging wide open.

She hailed a cab without knowing exactly where she wanted to go. All she knew is that she wanted to be somewhere, anywhere, other than the settlement office. She was not going to buy a condo today. Maybe she never would.

But when the driver asked her destination, she surprised herself by immediately answering "16th and K, please." It was as if her mouth were working faster than her brain.

Her hand flew instinctively to the cashier's check. It was still there, still burning a hole in her pocket.

When she alighted in front of the office building, she gave the driver a generous tip. Once through the revolving door, she studied the directory and then, with a trembling finger, pressed the button for the top floor.

She spoke so softly that at first the receptionist could not even hear her.

"What was that, miss?"

Jeanne cleared her throat. "Mitch Daniels," she said.

"Do you have an appointment?"

"No, but he'll see me. Tell him it's his ex-sister-in-law and it's urgent."

Her intuition proved correct. In just a few minutes, Mitch appeared with a furrowed brow and a frown. "Jeanne."

"Mitch."

"What brings you here?"

"Business."

He looked surprised.

"Do you have time for lunch?" Jeanne asked.

171

"It's three o'clock."

"Is it?" She looked at her watch. "Well, I haven't eaten yet. I've been too busy impersonating interns, being chased by corrupt Hill staffers, getting mixed up in a gay rights' parade, and skipping out on the closing for my condo. I'm exhausted and really, really hungry. Want a steak?"

"Lunch is on me," Mitch said gallantly as he led her to a table at the Capitol Grille, an old-school power-lunch spot famed for its dry-aged steaks. No one went there for chicken.

"Sure," Jeanne mumbled, too tired to argue.

"How's Vivienne?" Mitch tried to sound casual, but he didn't fool Jeanne. Little worry lines formed around his eyes and mouth.

"Fine, not that you'd care."

"I do care," he said. Then his voice softened. "But I know that's hard to believe after what I did."

"This isn't a family visit, Mitch."

The waiter came, recited the specials, and then nodded when Jeanne ordered the most expensive steak on the menu. When he had gone, Jeanne took the cashier's check out of her pocket, unfolded it, and slid it across the table.

Mitch whistled. "Now that's some moolah."

"It's every penny I've ever saved," Jeanne said, "and it's at your disposal. If, that is, you take my case."

He stared at her. "What case?"

"I want to hire you to defend Curtis Brown."

When her business deal with Mitch was concluded—and she recovered from the shock of having him accept the case pro bono—she waved down a taxi to take her home. There was nothing she wanted more than to curl up with Scarlett and a cup of hot chocolate and forget this day ever happened. She was about to ask the driver to step on it when her phone rang.

"Jeanne, it's me." Her sister's voice was a hoarse whisper, barely audible over the Ethiopian music blaring from the radio. Nearly all of D.C.'s cabbies were Ethiopian, and this was their soundtrack, which to Jeanne sounded like an angry, overly repetitive polka.

"Hold on, Viv." Jeanne tapped the driver on the shoulder. "Could you turn it down please?"

Wordlessly, he obliged.

"I can barely hear you," Jeanne shouted. "Where are you?"

"In the bathroom," Vivienne whispered, "of the community center where we're sorting the donations for the Charity League's annual toy drive."

"And that's top secret?" Jeanne joked.

"No, but this is. I was just sorting through a big cardboard box when I found a toy I recognized. It was a puzzle that Everett gave to Grayson at his last birthday party."

"You mean Meaghan's son?"

"Yes." Her sister sounded hesitant.

"So?"

For a minute, her sister did not answer. Jeanne could make out some muffled voice, a flushing sound, and then the whoosh of a heavy door slamming shut.

"So," Vivienne whispered, "there was also a baseball bat in the box. It caught my eye because it had been autographed by Bryce Harper, so I figured it was included by mistake. It would be way too valuable to give away. I mean, if they really didn't want it, the Charity League could auction it for thousands of dollars and have enough to buy a whole truckload of toys."

"So why don't you just do that?"

"You don't understand. When I looked closely, I found a reddish-brown residue. I think it might be...blood."

Jeanne could barely breathe. "Could you send me a photo right now?"

"Sure thing."

A moment later, her phone beeped. There, on her screen, was a bat, coated in what appeared to be blood.

"Bag it." They came to a stop in front of her apartment building, and Jeanne pulled a crumpled twenty-dollar bill out of her wallet and handed it to the cabbie. "But don't touch it. Put it aside, call the cops, and tell nobody until they arrive." Stepping onto the curb, she slammed the door behind her. "I think you've found the murder weapon."

Chapter Twenty

She was not surprised to hear from her former client less than an hour later.

"I assume you heard about the baseball bat," he said.

"Yes." It seemed pointless to deny it.

"I need your help, Jeanne." His drawl was as strong as ever, oozing his trademark buttery charm, tinged with just the right amount of pleading desperation. She could see why he was so successful as a politician. "I didn't do it."

"When you say you need my help—"

"I mean that I want to hire you again. As my PI. Or whatever you are. All-around smart, discrete person, I guess."

After all that she had learned, Jeanne couldn't imagine taking him on as a client. Now, no matter what she told herself, she would be a mere mercenary, in the employ of a man who, at the very least, had grossly deceived his constituents while posing as a rock-ribbed, family-values conservative and taken trading political favors to a whole new level.

But he didn't have to know that. Yet.

"Are there any big votes today?" she asked.

"Just the naming of a few post offices."

"Good. Then meet me in Dupont Circle, by the fountain, in an hour. And then," she added coyly, "we'll play Twenty Questions. After that, I'll decide whether I can take you on as a client."

Perched on the fountain's white marble edge, in the shadow cast by stone-faced Admiral Dupont and his mighty marble steed, Jeanne surveyed the scene. All in all, it was a relatively tame crowd today—two pink-haired teens strummed their guitars on a blanket emblazoned with a giant peace sign, a drum circle was beating a syncopated rhythm near the chess tables, a perky brunette in a T-shirt featuring a marijuana leaf was collecting signatures for a D.C. Statehood Party candidate to get on the ballot, and a homeless man was arguing loudly with a pigeon.

"That's just like you, Mother!" he shouted. "Pooping all over the place. Expecting everyone else to clean up after you."

The pigeon just flapped his wings, cocked his head, and let another one land with a splat.

"That's it," he growled. "I'm not sharing no bench with you no more." He struggled unsteadily to his feet, re-adjusted his blue stocking cap with exaggerated dignity, and staggered over to the fountain. To Jeanne's dismay, he plopped down next to her.

"Hello, Jeanne."

At the sound of her name, she started. How could he possibly know who she was? And, moreover, why would any homeless man care who she was?

The hairs on her head stood up as she turned to inspect him more closely. His voice just now had lost the growl. It had turned soft, almost genteel. The stench was just the right mixture of sweat, urine, and alcohol, and in the grimy work pants and scuffed work boots, he looked the part. But something was off—his hands, with nary a speck of dirt under the nails, were not those of a dumpster diver, and his face was clean-shaven.

And the voice. Something about the voice was unnervingly familiar.

And then it clicked.

"Congressman," she gasped.

"No names," he said in a low voice, and the growl was back. "You didn't think I'd show up in Gucci, did you?"

"No, but—"

"The police are at my house right now," he said, tugging at the frayed sleeve of his black winter coat. Jeanne caught a glimpse of his Rolex peeking out. "I can only assume the press is already on the story. And that they'd love to photograph me in the company of a young woman who's not my wife."

"Let me guess: there's a homeless guy on the Mall wearing your Gucci suit."

"Metro Center." He laughed. "It looks better on him than on me. Now ask me your questions."

Jeanne thought back to the primer Jerry had once given her on interrogation techniques. Start by asking the subject something you already know the answer to, he had said. Then, depending on whether they answer truthfully, you can get a sense of their expression when telling the truth or lying.

"Did you know your wife is having an affair with Jorge?"

"Yes."

He answered without the slightest hesitation or even, as far as Jeanne could tell, embarrassment.

"Are you gay?"

He looked up at her sharply. "Who told you that?"

"Just answer the question."

His shoulders slumped. "Yes, but I'll—"

"Deny it if I go to the press. Yes, I know. Next question: did you use your influence to get a case against a Dr. O'Brien dismissed?"

He shook his head vigorously. "No."

Jeanne studied his face and hands for the slightest indication that he was lying. She found none—no shaking hands, trembling Adam's apple, quivering lips, or twitchy gazes—but if this afternoon had proved anything to her, she had underestimated his resourcefulness and his acting skills.

"Then why would someone get that impression?"

"Did someone get that impression?"

"Yes."

"Who?"

"That's confidential."

He shoved his hands in the pockets of his coat. The shadows were lengthening and in the encroaching gloom, he looked as though he had aged ten years in the past few weeks. "I don't know."

Could Scott have been acting without the congressman's knowledge? And, if so, was he freelancing to enhance his own position, or did he and the congressman have an understanding that he was to act in the congressman's interest while giving him plausible deniability?

Congressman Richardson blinked, and she sensed that there was something that he wasn't telling her. Cross-examining another lawyer could be maddening. She sensed that he was parsing every question, giving her the bare minimum of correct information while withholding important details. The problem was that since she didn't know what she didn't know, she didn't know what to ask.

"Will the police find your fingerprints on the baseball bat?"

"I would expect so. It's not like I wiped it off after each trip to the batting cage."

"How did the bat end up being donated to the Charity League toy drive?"

"Damned if I know. Meaghan and I put together a box of things to give away—"

"And where was this box stored?"

"In the lower level of the coach house. We use the lower part for storage."

"And the upper level?"

"It's an apartment for guests. But there is no way to access the storage area from the apartment."

"So give me the timeline again," Jeanne said. "When was the box of give-away items assembled?"

"The weekend before Halloween."

"So would anyone—other than the two of you—have known that you were going to donate these things?"

"Well the box was labeled."

"Labeled?" she asked. "How?"

"Meaghan wrote 'Toys for Tots' on the box in black marker. That way, Ana Maria would know which box to drop off."

"And, as far as you know, did the box contain the baseball bat?"

"Most certainly not. Do you think I'd give away a bat autographed by Bryce Harper?"

"Not on purpose."

"Not on purpose, not by accident. And neither would Meaghan." His chin jutted forward defiantly and a touch of pride gleamed in his eyes. "You know, I paid five thousand for that at last year's Charity League auction."

"So who knew you had that bat?"

"Lots of folks," he said ruefully. "Everyone at the auction, everyone on my Facebook page. Hell, I think I even mentioned it at a meet-and-greet at a Little League game in Charleston."

Jeanne sighed. "And when was the last time you saw the box?"

"The weekend before Halloween."

"And where was the baseball bat at that time?"

"In a corner of the room. I was planning on buying a nice case to display it in. It was definitely not in the box."

Jeanne mulled this over for a moment. The drumming had built to a fever pitch, so she moved closer to the congressman and shouted directly in his ear. "So that leaves us with three possibilities. One, someone added the baseball bat to the box before the murder and either that person—or someone else—returned it to the box prior to Ana María dropping it off. Two, the murderer took the bat from the coach house and then put it in the box sometime after the murder. Or three, the murderer took your bat and never returned it to the coach house, but instead slipped the bat into the box after it arrived at the Toys for Tots drive."

He nodded slowly, and Jeanne got another whiff of stale sweat and alcohol.

"Which begs the question," -Jeanne coughed and scooted a few inches further away—"who had access to the box in the coach house, in transit to the toy drive, and at the toy drive? And who has a motive to frame you?"

His forehead wrinkled, and he rubbed the small of his back with his fist, as if it hurt. For a moment, she felt sorry for him. He looked much older and more vulnerable than his blustering alter ego on TV. His shoulders sagged with the knowledge that someone in his inner circle had betrayed him.

"Who doesn't?" he said glumly. "Every vote I take angers someone. And a lot of my rivals aren't happy I'm running for re-election."

"And your wife?" Jeanne probed gently.

"What are you suggesting?"

"That she didn't want you to run again. That she had a possible motive—wanting you out of public life, maybe wanting cover to ditch you and marry Jorge. That she had the means—after all, she certainly had access to your bat both before and after the murder—and the opportunity."

"Opportunity?"

"I know that the woman at the benefit was her twin," Jeanne said. She held up a hand. "Don't ask me how. Can you tell me that Meaghan has an alibi for every minute of the night?"

"No." He looked uncharacteristically defeated. It was hard to picture him commanding a Congressional hearing now. "But then, neither do I."

"But I saw you at the benefit," Jeanne stammered.

"Yes, but others there will attest to the fact that I received a call from one of the co-sponsors of my crime bill around midnight, and I excused myself for a good forty-five minutes."

"But surely you've got the phone records to back it up."

"Sure. But how do they know that I didn't talk to him on my way to the cemetery, bludgeon poor Brian with the phone on mute, then keep chatting on my way back to the party?"

"GPS. Based on the cell towers pinged, the phone company will know where you took the call from."

He sighed. "That's true, and might save me. But after the call, I spent maybe thirty minutes out back, smoking a cigarette, calming my nerves. Some backers had pulled their support, you see." He blushed guiltily. "Yes, I smoke. In secret. Old habits die hard."

"Your cell phone records could still be used to track your position."

"All the cell phone records say is where my cell phone was. I could have ditched my cell phone in the alley, gone to the cemetery, bashed Brian's head in, come back, and retrieved my cell phone."

"All that in half an hour?"

"It's a ten-minute cab ride."

"It sounds far-fetched…" Jeanne's voice trailed off. Far-fetched, yes. But not impossible.

"Anyway," he said brusquely. "She didn't do it. My wife and I have a great relationship. She would never betray me."

"She's cheating on you with Jorge!"

He flicked his wrist dismissively, then hurriedly tugged his sleeve over the Rolex. "He gives her what I can't. After all" –he peered at her intently—"would you want to be married to a gay man?"

"No," she said weakly. She wanted to add that she would in all likelihood die an old maid, now that Fergus was out of the picture, but she held her tongue.

"Have you ever been married?"

"No."

"Ah," he said as if this explained everything. "Then you have much to learn. In my first marriage, I made the mistake of pretending to be straight. Trying to be faithful. But I just made my wife unhappy in the end, and we divorced. The second time, I resolved to be truthful. Meaghan jumped in with both feet, eyes wide open. Marriage works a lot better when you understand what it really is—a partnership. It's beautiful, really—a partnership that transcends everything. I pity straight couples, really. Sex just muddies the waters, turns people's heads so that they don't focus on what's really important."

"The partnership," Jeanne repeated, incredulous.

"Exactly," he said. "The partnership. Meaghan and I are like two peas in a pod. We're single-minded in the pursuit of what we want, we love power, we appreciate beauty and the finer things in life. We can be ruthless but also fiercely loyal. She's my equal in every way, and we have a relationship built on honesty and trust."

She winced. The strength of his conviction rattled her. A gay man in a sham marriage was lecturing her on the true meaning of marriage—and it had the ring of truth. She had hoarded her secrets, meting out a few small truths to Fergus when absolutely necessary. But she hadn't really let him in. Not all the way.

Luckily, Congressman Robert's musings on marriage were unlikely to solve the case, so she had the perfect excuse to change the subject. "So" –Jeanne cleared her throat, as if to signal that they needed to get back to business—"the murder weapon was owned by you and has your prints on it. Your whereabouts are not strictly accounted for between twelve-fifteen and twelve-forty-five so your alibi has a hole in it, unless we can pinpoint the time of death more exactly. Your wife and Jorge have no alibi—although the police don't know that Meaghan doesn't have an alibi. Yet, anyway."

He nodded and shuffled his feet uncomfortably.

"For the moment, at least," Jeanne continued, "I won't tell them about the hole in Meaghan's alibi. Unless, of course, they ask."

"I appreciate that."

"Does Ana María have any reason to be resentful? Unpaid wages, that kind of thing?"

He shook his head.

"And besides her, you, and Meaghan, does anyone else have access to the coach house? Workmen perhaps?" She peered at him intently. "Lovers? Ex-lovers?"

For an instant, his Adam's apple tensed. "Not to where the bat was stored."

"But to the apartment?"

"Yes," he said tersely.

"I'm going to need names."

"Can't do that," he said. "How do I know you're not going to sell my list of lovers to *The Post*?"

"You don't. But you know I've been the soul of discretion so far. And besides, you need this case solved. And the best way to get you off the hook is to find out who really killed Brian Schwartz."

"No lover of mine has a motive to kill Brian," he muttered.

"No? Not even as a little love token? After all, what's more romantic than getting your blackmailer out of the way? It sure beats a box of chocolates or"—she looked pointedly at his wrist—"a Rolex for the man who has everything."

"I didn't tell anyone," he said, and it had the ring of true conviction. "Not a soul, I swear. And besides, there was a separate locked entrance to the lower level—and no lover of mine had access."

Jeanne sighed. "Then you're looking pretty good for this murder. It's only a matter of time before the investigators figure out Brian Schwartz was blackmailing Meaghan."

By now, night had fallen. The crowd had thinned considerably; red brake lights twinkled around the edges of the traffic circle.

Yawning, Jeanne turned to him and suddenly said, "Besides, why should I believe anything you say?"

"Because everything I've said to you has been true."

She considered this. "Maybe. But hardly revealing. All very safe."

"Okay," he countered. "Well here's an inconvenient truth for you. Do you want to know who put the cameras inside the 'wall of eyes' as you so picturesquely put it?"

Now he had her attention.

He tapped a finger to his chest. "Me."

Chapter Twenty-One

For a moment, Jeanne was speechless. She had assumed that Brian had made an alliance with some shadowy workman who'd done work at the Richardsons' house. She had meant to probe that angle—get a list of workmen and try to find a connection to Brian—but Brian had been murdered before she got that far.

"Whatever for?" she gasped.

"Evidence. In case she ever tried to leave me. I'm fine with being a gay man in a passionless but loving marriage. And Meaghan says she's fine with it." He squinted and rubbed his hands together. Now that the sun was down, it was getting cold. "But with women, you never know. Maybe someday someone would turn her head."

"Like Jorge?"

"Oh, no. He's harmless. A perfect boyfriend for her really. I approve."

"Did you—did you arrange this with Brian?" she stammered.

"Hell, no. I didn't know he existed until you looked into this. He must have just figured out how to hack the security company's server."

Jeanne grunted. "A relationship built on honesty and trust, huh?"

He shrugged. "As with all that is precious in life, one always needs insurance." He stood up. "So will you help me?"

"Yes." The word tumbled out of her mouth, an almost unconscious admission that—in spite of herself, in spite of all evidence to the contrary—she, strangely enough, believed him.

"You don't think much of me, do you?"

"Should I?" she asked. "You're a closeted gay man cheating on his wife with a rotating cast of young men—and yet you voted for the Defense of Marriage Act. You rant about keeping the government out of citizens' lives and yet you label Snowden a traitor for pointing out that the government is spying on us. Of course, you're strangely consistent there. You do believe in spying on everyone and everything—including your own wife." She whistled. "It's a slippery slope, though. You can't invade others' privacy without giving up your own right to privacy. And if you hadn't bugged your wife, Brian might not be dead." She sucked in a breath of cold night air. "And you wouldn't be suspected of murder."

He turned his collar up against the wind and leaned towards her. "I admire you, Jeanne. You're very sure of your principles. Quite the straight arrow, really. The universe arcs towards justice and all of that. Such youthful idealism. I was like that once."

"You don't know me," she growled.

"Oh, no? As you said, there is no such thing as privacy any more. I can google you as well as anyone else. You're Jeanne Pelletier, daughter of the woman who killed five teens and a little girl in a drunk driving accident. Even in your family, human beings are weak."

"I wouldn't call it weak," Jeanne said. "I'd call it guilty."

"So I take it you're not going to the parole hearing."

Through clenched teeth, she said, "That's none of your business."

"No," he agreed affably. "It's not."

"For what it's worth, I like you more than I like your wife."

"Ah, she'd probably say that you're just jealous."

"But I'm not."

"No, I can see that," the congressman said. "Nor should you be." Shaking her hand firmly, he clapped her on the back. "I appreciate your help. I fear the next time we talk, I may be in jail."

She watched him stumble across the circle, back in character as just one more drug-addled homeless man in a city of thousands, and she was struck by the fact that in other circumstances, this would be a great publicity stunt—a powerful congressman goes undercover to investigate the plight of the homeless first-hand.

Dodging traffic, he lurched across the street and tottered over to the Metro escalator. Where would he go? Surely not home. Into the arms of a sympathetic lover? She wondered.

When his black-clad figure slipped out of sight, she got up and walked to the opposite side of the circle, crossed the street, and made her way to Kramerbooks.

After ordering shrimp and grits, a cup of coffee, and a slice of Goober Pie, Jeanne texted Lily, who was out having a drink with a humorlessly earnest political appointee and was ecstatic to have a reason to call it a night.

"Oh, thank goodness," Lily huffed fifteen minutes later as she slid into a seat across from Jeanne and ordered a slice of Goober Pie for herself. "He was a 'crashing bore' as Fergus would say. He was the assistant to the assistant to the deputy of the secretary, or something like that, but he acted like he ran the place." Lily bit her lip. "Oh, sorry," she said. "I didn't mean to mention Fer—"

"Don't worry about it." Jeanne was eager to change the subject. She swallowed a delicious mouthful of peanut butter mousse and stabbed the air with her fork. "You're not going to believe this," she said, "but Congressman Richardson just admitted to bugging his own house to get evidence of Meaghan's adultery in case she ever files for divorce."

Jeanne enjoyed watching Lily's jaw drop. Her fork fell on her plate with a clatter.

"And" –Jeanne licked her lips—"he just hired me to get him off the hook. Brian Schwartz was killed with a baseball bat owned by Congressman Richardson, and the congressman's fingerprints are all over it."

Now she really had her friend's attention. For the next hour, Lily shoveled Goober Pie in her mouth while Jeanne filled her in on the details. "So what do you make of all this?"

"Two things stand out to me," Jeanne said as she scraped up every last crumb of chocolate cookie crust. "If

I'm right that Curtis is not the murderer, but instead is just a stooge who was lured to the scene by the murderer in order to provide police with a plausible suspect, then it seems the real killer changed his or her mind after the murder was committed and decided to pin the murder on the congressman instead."

"Meaning that the congressman pissed off the murderer after the murder but before the bat was discovered."

"Right: so the question is: what did the congressman do in that timeframe and who got mad as a result?"

"He announced his re-election bid."

Jeanne nodded. "Which unfortunately opens the door to any number of rivals who have a motive."

"But," Lily said slowly, "how would they know that Brian was going to be in the cemetery at that time, and that the police would discover a plausible motive for Richardson to kill him?"

"That's the million-dollar question, isn't it?"

Lily smiled. "Well, loaded as they are, I don't think the Richardsons will pay you a million." She licked the chocolate off her fork. "And what's the second thing that occurs to you?"

"That the time of death is critical. It won't necessarily tell us who committed the murder, but if it's before twelve-fifteen, or between twelve-forty-five and one-thirty, we can eliminate the congressman."

"Well then I think it's time for a visit with Mary Sue. She told you she likes mysteries, right?"

"Right."

"Then let's get her to help us solve one."

MAUREEN KLOVERS

****

That night, Jeanne could not sleep. Her odd conversation with the congressman played over and over again in her mind. The rational part of her—the lawyer in her, who knew that any inconsistency in the witness's testimony rendered it unreliable, and therefore she shouldn't give any credence to the matrimonial theories of a man who secretly videotaped his wife as some sort of warped "insurance policy"—told her to disregard what he had said. But still, it rankled her. He had been talking about his relationship with Meaghan, but he may as well have been lecturing her about her relationship with Fergus.

Had she been open and honest with Fergus? Not really. Sure, he knew the broad outlines of her story—she had told him, at last, that her mother had killed her little sister Annie and several classmates in a drunk driving accident—but it was in the same antiseptic way that a doctor tells a patient, in a strictly professional way, all stiff and formal, that he or she is dying. She had given him the once-over-lightly, just-the-facts version, but she didn't want him to see her past—to see her—up close. As long as it was something that happened far away, a long time ago, it was sanitized somehow. But inviting him to the parole hearing and the reunion would bring that whole messy episode right into the present. It was the difference between talking about death and staring it in its face, inhaling its putrid stench, watching the life force of a loved one draining inexorably away.

Up there, she would turn into a creature that Fergus wouldn't even recognize. She would feel small and insignificant, swallowed up by the towering pines that blocked out the sky. How beautiful, Fergus would say, admiring the pristine, slow-moving river with its mirror-like sheen and the deep, dark woods—like something out of a Robert Frost poem—and she would nod and pretend. Pretend not to feel suffocated by the trees that blocked the sun, pretend not to feel choked off by the nameless bend in the river that snaked past her family's miserable trailer. Pretend not to feel small and insignificant, trapped in that beautiful but brutal land, the latest in her family's long line of embittered and disillusioned romantics. He would insist on driving past her trailer, and she would comply, white-knuckled and tight-lipped. It would all look the same to him, one vast expanse of woods bisected by a weed-choked gravel road, but around each bend she would see the entrance to the mining shaft where she and Annie would hide out during their mother's drunken rages, or the stump where her father would leave her food when her mother had banished her. Every stump, every rock, and every wild blueberry bush, the pine-scented air, the *chut-chut-chut* of the white-winged crossbills—it was all part of her, a strange mix of exquisite pain, nostalgia, and wonder. The landscape, this topography of her memory, had represented the known world of her childhood, with all of its beauty and brutality. She had both respected its limits and tested them—slowly venturing further and further—until the forest could contain her no more.

Her little girl voice—high-pitched and tentative—would come back, antiquated Acadian French would creep into her speech, and her "r"'s would fade into the vastness of the landscape.

Even now—even after moving to the big city and earning a law degree, even if her mother were shackled and wearing an orange jumpsuit—she would shrink beneath her mother's withering gaze. Her mother was like that—she could reduce Jeanne to the meekest, mousiest version of herself without saying a word.

Jeanne shuddered. She didn't want Fergus to see this side of her, ever.

And yet.

Was the truth—the whole bitter ugly, unflinching truth, up close and staring Fergus in the face—the price to pay for a remote chance at happiness?

She trusted only one person to give her the answer.

Jerry broke the silence after they had spent half an hour staring at each other, brooding over two steaming mugs of inky black coffee.

"Well the answer is yes, obviously."

"What's the question?" Jeanne asked, startled. She hadn't asked him anything—she hadn't had the nerve yet—other than to come in (at four in the morning no less, but what was a little sleeplessness between two insomniac friends?) and have a cup of Turkish coffee.

"To all the questions in your head. Should you reach out to Fergus? Yes. Should you apologize? Yes. Should you try to be happy? Yes."

Jeanne set her mug down on the coffee table and stared at him. "You really can read my mind."

He laughed. "There are only four things on your mind. Fergus, your crazy family, crime, and belly dancing. And if you were thinking about belly dancing, you certainly wouldn't talk to me. I wouldn't know the difference between a shimmy and a shake. And if you were ruminating about the case, you'd come right out with it. It's only in matters of the heart that you clam up. Plus, I didn't believe your excuse at the closing for a moment. You didn't go through with it because it didn't seem right to pour your life savings into something that you blame for tearing you and Fergus apart."

Tears welled up in her eyes. "If only Fergus understood me like—"

"Like me?"

She nodded and a tear rolled down her cheek and splashed onto the table.

"He will if you give him a chance. I understand you because you've never hidden anything from me. You see me as equally damaged goods. Someone who won't judge you." He grunted. "Trust me, Twinkletoes, he won't judge you. Let him in."

He leaned over and shook her slightly. His big brown eyes bored into her. "Let him in."

Chapter Twenty-Two

At first light, she bounded out of her apartment with Scarlett in tow. Slightly queasy, she felt the bile welling up in her throat. Was it the three cups of Turkish coffee, the two glasses of orange juice she'd just downed, or nerves? Probably all three.

She had spent an hour agonizing over her outfit—longer than she had spent to glam up for one of Vivienne's Charity League events—and ended up with a green fleece, slightly frayed at the neck, and some loose-fitting jeans. She had arranged her hair into a ponytail, then a bun, then a messy braid, all to give the impression of casualness.

As Scarlett nudged her out the door, she took a quick peek in the hall mirror. Perfect, she thought. I look as though I just rolled out of bed to take Scarlett for a quick walk, not as though I spent an hour getting ready.

They walked up to the cathedral, whose stone façade matched the slate-gray sky, and then cut into the neighborhood. She circled the dog park in a desultory fashion, and Scarlett obliged by sniffing every bush and tree, as if trying to solve some great mystery herself.

"Magnus?" Jeanne asked Scarlett. "Do you smell Magnus?"

Scarlett just looked at her. Did she understand? Her tail wagged slightly, as if to say that she anticipated that something good could happen, but it had not happened yet.

Jeanne felt her pulse racing. So Magnus hadn't been there. Yet.

She threw Scarlett a few sticks, but Scarlett was not much of a retriever. Scarlett lay down and yawned. How much longer do we need to wait, she seemed to say.

Jeanne knew that they could not stay much longer without attracting the attention of some nosy neighborhood watchman—or, more likely, watchwoman. It would look suspicious if they hovered too long.

So she reluctantly tugged at Scarlett's leash and they started across the street. She figured she'd walk around the block and then casually circle back.

She was halfway across the street when a familiar brogue stopped her in her tracks.

"Jeanne."

He said her name warmly, and the leash went slack in her hands. She turned to see him staring intently at her, Magnus straining at his leash.

"Fergus."

She stood there stupidly, slack-jawed. Where was her courage? She and Jerry had practiced last night, over and over, but now the words stuck in her throat.

"Magnus really misses Scarlett," Fergus stammered. "The poor bloke's been just mooning about the house."

"Oh, well, I'm sure he's met someone else. Other dogs, that is."

"Oh, some very fine bitches, I'll grant you that." Was it her imagination, or was he fighting a smile? "He misses Scarlett, though. And," he added pointedly, "you."

"He has Pamela to take my place. Who's very pretty, by the way. And charming, very agreeable, quite amiable, really—"

"Jeanne," he chided her gently, "you sound like you're trying out for one of those Jane Austen films you forced me to watch."

"Well, she is amiable. Quite. I can see why your family liked her."

"They liked her because I liked her. They would like anyone that I liked. Or loved."

Jeanne held her breath as Fergus and Magnus stepped off the curb. Scampering up to Scarlett, Magnus nuzzled her gently and rubbed his big wet nose against hers. Then they circled each other slowly, first cautiously sniffing each other's posterior, then proceeding to yips of delight and finally frantic tail-wagging.

Somehow, though, she and Fergus could not do the same. It was as though there were an invisible steel wall between them.

"Well, I'm sure Pamela is taking him on lots of walks," Jeanne babbled, anxious to fill the silence. "All over the city. Or I guess he's taking her. I mean, since she doesn't know her way around." As if it were an afterthought, she casually asked, "How long is she staying?"

"That depends."

Jeanne did not want to ask what it depended on. No, in this case, ignorance was bliss, so she prattled on, "Yes, I'm sure Magnus is very fond of her. She seems very uncomplicated. She's a three-walks-a-day, one-trip-to-the-dog-park kind of woman."

"She's not you, if that's what you mean." He kept one eye fixed on Jeanne as he reached down and patted Scarlett on the head. "How does Scarlett like her new home?"

"She doesn't. I mean she didn't—we didn't—move in. I got cold feet. I just couldn't do it."

He stared at her. "Why not?"

She felt her heartbeat racing, her palms starting to sweat. "Well, it seemed such a waste to spend all of that money on an empty apartment."

His hand rested on Scarlett's fur, just behind the ears, as if it were glued in place. "Go on."

She felt panic welling up in her chest. This was her moment to tell him why she hadn't gone through with the closing. But the words just wouldn't come, so instead she babbled about the case, stalling for time. "I figured out who was blackmailing Meaghan—I mean, I think I did at least—and then I told Meaghan and he ended up dead."

Fergus looked confused by the change of subject. He blinked. "Dead?"

Jeanne sighed. "Yes, unfortunately. I found his body on the tomb of Major Willard when Everett and I were hunting for dinosaur eggs—"

"As one does, naturally." His eyes crinkled in amusement. "Everyone knows that dinosaurs hide their eggs in cemeteries."

"Er, yes—"

"Pamela wouldn't do that," he interrupted. "Hunt for dinosaur eggs. Or find dead bodies for that matter."

"No," Jeanne said ruefully. "Nor would she buy a place on her own. Nor would she be the daughter of a backwoods lush who single-handedly tripled the county's murder rate. Nor" -her lips trembled and tears sprang to her eyes—"would she push you away. She—"

Her words were suddenly drowned out by the screech of brakes. Jeanne looked up to see Pamela leaning out of Aunt Margaret's ancient Buick.

"Oh, hullo there, Jeanne," Pamela cooed in her perfect plummy accent. So British, so proper. As if she hadn't practically run Jeanne over. Was there a wicked gleam in Pamela's eyes, or was Jeanne imagining things?

The fact that Pamela had arrived—and nearly run over Jeanne and Scarlett—did not seem to register with Fergus. He just stood there, rooted to the spot, staring at Jeanne as if he were seeing her—really, really seeing her— for the first time. Only Jeanne couldn't tell if he liked what he saw.

"Come along now, Fergus. We'd better hurry so we're not late for Aunt Margaret's doctor appointment." Pamela gave an impatient little shake of her head, and her shiny brown bob swung forward and then settled back perfectly into place.

"Are you all right, Jeanne?" Fergus asked.

"Yes," she said, but inside she whispered "no." She would never be all right again without him.

"Fergus," Pamela wheedled.

When he didn't answer, she balled her hands into two little fists and banged on the steering wheel petulantly. "Fergus!"

"Aye, all right." He opened the back door for Magnus, who landed with a plop on the pea green seats. "Maybe we can continue this interesting conversation about dinosaur eggs some other time. Take care, Jeanne. Cheerio."

They sped off, and Jeanne and Scarlett just stood there, in the middle of the street.

Jeanne sighed. "Well that didn't go as planned. But there's nothing like a little crime to take one's mind off things, right?" she lied to Scarlett as her heart sank in her chest and the bile rose in her throat. She felt pathetic. Who tries to keep a stiff upper lip for their dog? Scarlett gave her a reproachful look as if to say, you don't fool me.

"Oh, fine. I'm forlorn and depressed," Jeanne admitted. "Now let's go find Mary Sue and forget this ever happened."

She cried intermittently on the way to the cemetery, but by the time they arrived, Jeanne was in some semblance of order. Ignoring the "no dogs allowed" sign, she and Scarlett slipped through the front gate and went around to the back door of the little brick house that served as the administration building. Jeanne was just rapping on the door a third time when Mary Sue's heavy frame appeared in the doorway. Clapping her hands, she exclaimed, "Mercy! Don't tell me there's another dead body!"

"Oh, no," Jeanne reassured her, and Mary Sue let out a sigh of relief. "I'm here about the last one."

With a wave of her hands, Mary Sue ushered them inside and produced a plate of chocolate chip cookies for Jeanne and a water bowl for Scarlett. "What do you want to know?" she asked as she brushed a few crumbs off her ample, fuchsia-swathed bosom.

"I'm not sure exactly. But did you notice anything out of the ordinary that morning? Before, that is, I came and told you there'd been a murder."

Mary Sue scrunched her nose and sighed. "Well there was that trail of jelly beans."

"You mean there were more jelly beans than just the ones near the body?"

"Oh, yes. They started at the front gate and continued right down the road until—well, I don't really know how far. But at least as far as I could see from here. There were quite a few burials that day so I didn't have time to investigate. And then the next thing I knew, you were here telling me there was a murder."

"All yellow?"

"Yes, now that you mention it. All yellow."

Jeanne could picture it now—the jelly beans carefully arranged to lead Curtis, dim-witted and trusting, right into a trap. Only the real murderer hadn't counted on a witness to Curtis's visit. Or had he?

"Kind of like a treasure map." Jeanne laughed ruefully. "With a dead body at the end."

"You don't think...?" Mary Sue's voice trailed off as she pushed her glasses further up her nose. "Yes, I see it now."

Jeanne showed Mary Sue the photo she'd snapped of Curtis. "Did you see this guy?"

Mary Sue brought Jeanne's phone very close to her face. "I think so." She laughed. "Obviously, I'm quite near-sighted. So it's hard to say. But I saw someone with his build, wearing a coat like this, picking up the jelly beans. I thought he was just doing me a favor."

"And I think he was sent here by the murderer," Jeanne said. "What better way to lead the cops astray than sending someone who's already in the system to contaminate the crime scene? Hairs, fingerprints. He must have left something behind."

"But that only proves he was at the scene of the crime. But it doesn't prove what time he was there. In fact, if anything," Mary Sue said, "your chance encounter helps him. It shows he was there hours after the murder occurred."

"Ah, but the prosecution will say that he was just returning to the scene of the crime. Admiring his handiwork. That kind of thing." Jeanne took a last bite of cookie and stood up. Scarlett got to her feet too. "So, the real question is, who else was here that night? And where would they have gotten in? And who would have seen them?"

Strolling along the inner perimeter of the cemetery, with Scarlett trudging along beside her, Jeanne kept her eyes glued to the chain-link fence. Six feet high and rusty, topped with barbed wire, it would have been very difficult to scale. Directly on the other side was a thicket of tall, scraggly bushes and, beyond that, the grassy lawns of Montrose Park. So someone would have had to vault over the brick wall of Montrose Park, creep through the exposed grassy area, somehow crawl through the bushes, and then climb up and over the fence without getting snagged in the barbed wire. After a few hundred yards, the ground sloped sharply downwards, towards Rock Creek, and a precarious flight of slate steps led downwards past an avenue of monumental tombs. "Tombs" did not even seem the right word—they were more like imposing stone cottages, lined with marble slabs containing the remains of some of Washington's most illustrious families.

Two-thirds of the way down the hill, Scarlett sniffed at a hole in the fence. It was about two feet tall, with a makeshift length of barbed wire dragging along the ground to deter trespassers. Jeanne squinted. Could someone have entered the cemetery here? Only if they were very small, she concluded, and if they were fit enough to climb down the steep forested slope on the other side—or ford Rock Creek and come staggering up the precipitous hill.

The hole was directly opposite the Carroll tomb, a gray granite edifice in which Willie Lincoln's body had been temporarily laid to rest. The plaque inside rather morbidly recounted President Lincoln's visits to the tomb, during which he apparently would order his son's coffin to be pried open so that he could hold him once more. Jeanne imagined the doomed president embracing the putrefying remains of his favorite son, and shuddered.

Just below, the cemetery fence took a sharp right, paralleling the stream. Jeanne and Scarlett followed alongside, winding their way along the dirt path that skirted yet more grandiose tombs, before dropping down a little stone walkway inscribed with the names of the deceased. Jeanne assumed that each stone rested on top of an urn. At the bottom of the walkway, there was a small clearing around a maintenance shed and, below that, a steep drop-off and then the rushing waters of Rock Creek. Someone could, she supposed, have been dropped off along the Rock Creek Parkway, waded across the creek, and then—perhaps with rock-climbing equipment—scrambled up the cliff.

Jeanne and Scarlett retraced their steps to the top of the stone path, and then followed the fence as it curled around to the right. At last they came to a right angle, where the fence turned back towards the entrance. Just outside the fence was a footbridge connecting the Rock Creek Parkway bike path to a little footpath that curved up the hill, paralleling the fence and leading to R Street.

Jeanne's heart began to race. This was clearly the most likely entry point. Someone could have been dropped off on the parkway, quickly run across the bridge, and then either scaled the fence or climbed a tree and then dropped over the other side. There were no hedges on the other side—there were no obstacles at all really except a six-foot fence and a thin line of barbed wire.

Suddenly, Scarlett bounded ahead, in hot pursuit of a squirrel, who zigged and zagged along the fence line before scampering up a maple tree. It branches were mostly bare, but a few hardy crimson leaves wavered bravely in the wind.

"You're not going to get him, Scar," Jeanne said impatiently, tugging at her leash. "Come on, let's go."

But Scarlett just strained at the leash, teeth bared, claws digging into the tree's bark. The squirrel was not intimidated. With an insouciant, almost impertinent, shake of his bushy black tail, he leapt from the trunk to a branch and then, with a final swish, disappeared into an enormous squirrel nest.

Jeanne smiled, admiring the ingenuity of its construction. Twigs were the main material, of course, but there were also condoms, gum wrappers, scraps of paper, and even a piece of red cloth fluttering faintly in the wind. Frowning, Jeanne began climbing the tree to get a better look. She hadn't climbed a tree in years—not since she'd left Maine, in fact—but it came back to her at once, the exhilaration of being above it all, the quiet satisfaction of having broken the rules. Resting her right foot on the large branch below the one supporting the nest, she lunged forward and grabbed the upper branch, then steadied both feet on the lower branch. She wobbled for a second, and Scarlett whimpered below her, although whether from concern or jealousy Jeanne could not tell. She was close enough to hear the chirping of the little baby squirrels, the scratching of their little paws against the twigs.

And close enough to spot a gold cufflink in the shape of the letter "S" and a strip of red silk embossed with mustard-yellow vines and matching yellow flowers. The center of each flower was a vivid green dot.

She may not have seen that exact swatch of fabric before, but she'd seen a similar pattern once before.

At Brian's funeral.

Chapter Twenty-Three

It was an excruciatingly boring day at the law firm of Higgins, Higgins, and Applebaum—and a supremely frustrating one.

"How'd the closing go?" Jim, her boss, boomed as he came storming into her cubicle.

"Fine," she lied and quickly closed her browser.

"Welcome to home ownership." He slapped her on the back, hard enough that she nearly choked, and cackled. "The golden handcuffs, as they say. Now you can't quit. Gotta pay that mortgage. Isn't that right?"

"You make it sound like high-paid slavery," she muttered.

"The best kind." He fixed her with a sudden look of alarm. "You're not thinking of asking for any time off, are you? To paint the walls or decorate or something ridiculous like that?"

She shook her head.

"Good for you. White walls are best. Very clean and restful. And we really need all hands on deck until this merger is completed. Every day that goes by—"

"—is a million in lost revenues for the client. I know."

"Well keep up the good work, Jeanne. I know I can count on you to stay focused and not get all, er, squishy. You know, caught up in one's personal life."

He shot a contemptuous look at Kara, her cubicle mate, who had had the audacity to ask for two weeks off for her upcoming wedding, and thundered out. Jeanne wouldn't get caught up in decorating her new condo or dealing with her personal life, because she didn't have either. But she couldn't help but think that it would behoove Jim to pay more attention to what he called "those squishy things." Last year, his long-suffering wife had insisted that they go on a marriage counseling retreat in Utah. The idea was to drop the bickering couple in the desert and have them work together to get back to civilization. Jeanne was a bit surprised to see him turn up the following week—she half-expected his wife to off him in some dried-up streambed fifty miles from the closest highway and then claim he died of thirst.

Jeanne held her breath as Jim barreled back down the corridor, poking his head into every second or third cubicle and terrorizing its inhabitants. His booming voice eventually receded into the distance, and slowly the office buzzed back to life.

Kara yawned one of her big, slow, ostentatious yawns, the kind one might expect to see in a melodramatic silent film from the twenties. "I guess I need coffee," Kara muttered apologetically, covering her mouth with her left hand, her enormous diamond glittering beneath the fluorescent lights.

Jeanne knew that Kara was not in the least bit tired, having already consumed two giant mugs of coffee, but it was in Jeanne's best interest to play along. She knew for a fact that Kara would cross the street to Starbuck's, stand in line for twenty minutes, and then spend another twenty making frantic phone calls to find someone to make fifty organic peach pies—made out of heritage varietals no longer commercially available, no less—for her over-the-top Southern wedding on a plantation in Georgia.

Jeanne grunted in acknowledgement, which was what Kara wanted. The minute her cubicle mate was gone, Jeanne re-opened her browser and dialed the first seamstress on the list.

"Marti Shaw." The woman sounded old, but not frail.

"Uh, hello, Marti. This is Amanda Weston, and I'm a re-enactor and—"

"Which group?"

Jeanne had not counted on this, so she blurted out the name of the only group she knew. "The Pennsylvania 16th Reserve Volunteers." She added hastily, "I just joined."

"Oh, you're one of them, are you? Well, here's my advice, dearie. Get out while you still can."

"What do you mean?"

"What do I mean?" Marti sputtered and started coughing. She had the raspy, dull hack of a lifelong smoker. "That outfit's cursed. Two years ago, their reenactment of the Battle of Dranesville managed to coincide with the coldest day of the year. It had rained the day before, then the temperature plummeted, resulting in a crust of ice on the snow-covered battlefield. So the battle turned into more of a slip and slide. One set of cracked ribs, one broken fibula, and two twisted ankles later, they finally outflanked the Confederates and won. 'Course, that was supposed to happen—the Union forces winning, that is, not the broken bones."

"How terrible," Jeanne murmured, hoping Marti would go on.

Marti grunted. "And that's not all."

Jeanne could hear her light a cigarette; she could picture the older woman settling deeper into her couch, wreathed in smoke, deriving a certain grim pleasure from her tale.

"It wasn't just those four that ended up in the emergency room," Marti continued. "It was everyone." She lowered her voice another octave. "The Brunswick stew was poisoned. With rat poison, the doctor said. Not enough to kill. But they were all sick—sick as dogs."

"Who made the stew?"

"The ladies. That's what they do, you know. Make the stew, keep the fires going. While the men do battle."

The ladies, Jeanne thought. Which included Chloe. Why she would want to poison them all was a mystery. But perhaps the poison was meant only for Edith.

"Well, enough with the gossip," Marti said, suddenly all business. "What can I do for you?"

"I'm looking for someone to make me a dress, but not just any dress. I really have my heart set on a pattern I saw once—a red background with mustard-yellow vines and flowers. The center of each flower was a bright green dot. Do you know anyone who could supply you with that kind of fabric?"

Marti snorted. "Sure. Suzanne Latimer. But trust me, you don't want that fabric."

"Why not?"

"It's the fabric I used to make Chloe Simpson a dress. And you don't want to be caught dead" -she emphasized the last word—"wearing the same dress as Chloe. Especially if you look better in it. She might try to poison you—or worse."

Jeanne's pulse was racing. Her hunch was correct. The fabric in the squirrel's nest wasn't from just any dress—it was from Chloe's dress. "You think she's behind the poisoned Brunswick stew?"

"That, and the tampering with Edith's corset so that the stays—or that is, what she replaced them with—nearly punctured her spleen when she tightened them. No one can prove it, but if you ask me, that Chloe's one homicidal maniac."

Yes, Jeanne thought, but did Chloe want Brian dead, or only Edith?

She thanked Marti and promised to get back in touch once she had selected an alternate print. By the time Kara slid back in her chair, Jeanne had her nose buried in a sheaf of documents and looked every bit the model employee.

She worked steadily until her mid-afternoon dark chocolate break, when she had a sudden epiphany and called Vivienne on her speed dial.

"Hey, sis. Who was volunteering at the Charity League toy drive?"

"Well, there was Sarah O'Brien, Tabitha Edwards, I think Samantha was there for a bit..."

So, basically, Jeanne thought as she jotted each name down, all of the mean girls were there.

At exactly six p.m., she slipped out the door and met Lily in the parking garage for a road trip to Baltimore. As they inched along New York Avenue, Jeanne recounted her conversation with Marti. Lily suddenly interrupted her with a tap on the arm and turned the radio way up.

"Breaking news just in," the NPR correspondent was saying. "Congressman Richardson has been arrested for the murder of Brian Schwartz, an NSA employee found dead in Oak Hill Cemetery on November first. So far, police have not released any information about a motive. However, a preliminary hearing is expected in the next day or two, and we expect more details may be available then."

Lily whistled. "Well, then I guess it's about time we interview an alternate suspect. So how do we play this? Who are we today?"

"I think we play it straight for a change."

"And you think that will work?"

"I think Chloe's dying to talk to someone about what she saw."

In a peach polyester dress and a white pinafore speckled with tomato sauce, with her hair piled into an unraveling beehive, she bore only a passing resemblance to the Civil War belle Jeanne had seen at the funeral.

"You sure that's her?" Lily muttered as they perused the laminated menu, a strange mishmash of Greek home cooking, Italian pasta dishes, and diner classics.

"Same pinched nose, too-close eyes. Quiet, here she comes."

Chloe approached, notepad in hand. Her lips curled into the mandatory smile, but her eyes weren't smiling. "What can I get you, hon?"

Jeanne bet that the management told staff to call everyone "hon." Very Baltimore.

"The Maryland crab soup and chicken and waffles," Lily said.

"Moussaka." Jeanne slid the menu across the table toward Chloe, placing a photo of the squirrel nest on top. "Why don't you take a little break and come sit with us?"

Chloe's hand froze above her notepad.

"We know you didn't" –Jeanne lowered her voice– "er, harm Brian, but we also know you were there."

Chloe plopped into the booth and stared at them. "How did you—?"

"It's a piece of your dress, isn't it? And now it's in a squirrel nest in a tree in Oak Hill Cemetery. Plus," Jeanne lied, "we've got witnesses that place you in Georgetown, right outside the cemetery on Halloween. Hard to miss that hoop skirt."

If Chloe were smarter, she might have tried to argue that the squirrel found it outside the cemetery and dragged it inside for its nest. But, as Jeanne surmised, she wasn't.

"Who are you?"

"Private investigators," Lily said, stretching the truth. "We know you didn't do it, but we think you can help us find out who did."

Chloe wrung her hands and stared at her lap. "I really don't know," she said.

"What time did you arrive at the cemetery?"

"Eleven forty-five. Well, that is to say, we parked at eleven forty-five. I wanted to be there at midnight on the dot. That's when Brian always lays the flowers on the grave. He's very punctual."

Jeanne leaned forward. "We?"

"Brian's brother offered to drive me."

Jeanne and Lily exchanged a glance. Could this be the same brother who threatened to kill Brian over Edith?

"Sam?"

"Yes, that's the one."

"Why did he offer to drive you?"

Chloe seemed to have never considered this. "Well, he was just being nice, I suppose. He said that now that Edith was dead, there was no longer an obstacle to Brian and me being together. He said he wanted Brian to be happy."

"He wanted the brother whom he threatened to kill—the one who stole his girlfriend—to be happy?"

Chloe tittered uncomfortably. "When you put it like that, it does sound a little odd."

Lily couldn't help herself. "A little?" she sputtered, and Jeanne gave her friend a swift kick under the table.

"So," Jeanne said as casually as possible, trying her best to sound like a sympathetic friend, "he just calls you up and offers to drive you to Georgetown on Halloween in order to accost Brian in the cemetery while he conducts his little annual ritual of putting flowers on the Willards' graves."

"That's right."

"So what was your plan?"

"Well—I know it sounds silly now—but I thought that Sam could boost me over the wall—and then I could meet him at the Willards' grave. And I'd be dressed as Antonia, you see, and then he'd realize—he'd realize—"

"That you were meant to be together?" Jeanne finished helpfully.

"Right."

"But that's not what happened, is it?"

"No." Chloe's eyes filled with tears and she started scribbling furiously on her notepad. "I got stuck on the fence, first of all, and it took a while to free me. I didn't realize it at the time, but my dress must have been torn then. Then I got a little lost. I'd been there during the day, but it looked so different at night."

"So what time did you get to the gravesite?"

She shuddered. "I don't know. Civil War re-enactors don't exactly wear wristwatches. But maybe twelve-fifteen, twelve-thirty."

"But it was too late."

"Yes." She groped about frantically, grabbed Lily's water glass, and took a big gulp. "It was too—too late."

"Did you notice anything else at the grave?"

"Just this trail of yellow jelly beans glistening in the moonlight. Isn't that odd? At first, I thought they had fallen out of Brian's pocket, but that didn't make sense. He was an M&M guy." She smiled immodestly. "I know everything about him."

217

"So I've heard," Jeanne said. "What happened next?"

"I ran, I just ran. I didn't know what to do. I—"

"Where did you run?"

"Back to the spot where I came over the fence. I climbed back over it and then ran up the path and down R Street."

"You climbed back over yourself?" Jeanne asked skeptically. "In a hoop skirt?"

"Oh, no. Sam boosted me."

"So Sam went into the cemetery with you?"

"He boosted me over the fence, then jumped down himself. He waited for me, then boosted me back over the fence."

Jeanne replayed the scene in her mind. Sam, who had said he wanted to kill Brian, was in the cemetery that night. And Chloe was delayed in getting to the gravesite because she got lost.

Jeanne squeezed Chloe's hand and shot her a sympathetic look. "Do you think it's possible Sam could have killed him?"

Chloe shook her head vehemently. "He was waiting for me when I came back. Right at the same spot."

"Yes," Jeanne said gently, "but you admitted that you got lost. What if he got to the grave while you were still wandering in the dark, killed Brian, then hurried back to your meeting place?"

"No!" Chloe nearly shouted the word, then clapped her hand over her mouth. "No," she said in a softer tone. "I don't think so. But..."

"It's possible," Lily said flatly.

Chloe's voice dropped to a hoarse whisper. "It's possible."

"Did you see anyone," Jeanne asked, "when you got back on the street?"

Chloe gave a little snort. "It was Halloween in Georgetown."

"Meaning?"

"Meaning I saw dozens of people. Daffy Duck, Michelle Obama, Tiger Woods, a few witches, a princess, a ghost—you name it, I saw it."

"Anyone with a baseball bat?"

"Well not just then, but then I realized I dropped my lipstick—"

Lily looked at her, incredulous. "Civil War re-enactors wear lipstick?"

Chloe bristled. "Well, I wanted to look nice. And, yes, many women did wear lipstick in that era. Of course, you usually had to make it yourself with wax, alkanet root, which is what makes it red, spermaceti—that's this waxy stuff found in the head of a sperm whale—"

"Okay, enough with the nineteenth century cosmetic recipes." Jeanne shuddered and pushed her moussaka away. "So you realized you dropped your lipstick and you doubled back?"

"Yes, but I'd only gone maybe fifty yards before I collided with a man dressed in a baseball uniform and carrying a bat."

"Collided, you say?"

"I was distracted and the hoop skirt is enormous."

"Enormous," Lily said. "Big enough to hide a baseball bat in."

"Which I didn't," Chloe said primly.

"What did this baseball player look like?" Jeanne prompted her.

"Hard to say. He was wearing a mask—probably of some famous baseball player, but I don't really know. I don't follow baseball."

"Tall? Short? Thin? Fat? Hair color? Something?"

"Maybe between five-eight and five-ten. Slender definitely."

"Could it have been a woman?"

Chewing her lip, Chloe said slowly, "I suppose it could have been. I really didn't pay too much attention. Really, I was just in a hurry to get away. The only thing that I can tell you is that he—or she—was wearing a platinum blond wig. And the number on his shirt was 66. I remember thinking that it was oddly sinister. Here, I'd just found Brian murdered. You know?" She looked up at Jeanne. "And the number of the devil is 666?"

"Uh-huh." Jeanne had never put much stock in Revelations, but now wasn't the time to argue. "Did you find your lipstick?"

Chloe nodded. "About half a block further down."

"Outside the cemetery?"

"Yes."

"And what time," Jeanne asked, "did the car clock say that it was when Sam started the engine?"

"Twelve fifty-two."

Jeanne wrote that down. "Do you know Congressman Richardson or his wife Meaghan?"

Chloe looked genuinely bewildered. "No. What business would I have with a congressman?"

The manager snapped his fingers in Chloe's direction and she stood up wearily. "That's all I can tell you."

"You've been very helpful," Jeanne said. "One last question: did Brian ever brag about getting even with someone? Maybe even blackmailing them?"

Chloe just shook her head and went to retrieve an eggplant parmesan from under a heat lamp.

Chapter Twenty-Four

Jeanne called Mitch at eight the next morning.

"I didn't know my sister-in-law was even capable of getting up so early," he joked.

"Ex sister-in-law."

"Not yet," he chirped. "Not ever, hopefully."

Ignoring him, Jeanne said, "Ask him about jelly beans."

"Come again?"

"Jelly beans. Ask Curtis who called and told him to follow the jelly beans. There was a trail of yellow jelly beans to the body, and I have reason to think that Curtis was following that trail. Like someone told him to."

She hung up and tried to concentrate on her memo, some claptrap about how these two companies would not corner the market for a particular medical device if they merged, even though obviously they would. After a half hour of staring at the screen, she allowed herself a break to research Sam Schwartz's schedule for the day. According to the overeager junior analyst that Jeanne spoke to—who quickly puffed up with importance when Jeanne explained that she wanted to get in touch with

Sam about an urgent procurement need at Higgins, Higgins, and Applebaum—Sam was going to give the lunchtime address at a conference for federal government IT managers, which was being held at the Mayflower Hotel.

Jeanne thanked her profusely and went back to her memo. At twelve-forty, she slipped out of the office and ran the five blocks to the Mayflower. Slowing to a walk as she approached the registration table, she discretely glanced at the few nametags left. "Alex Levinson," she announced, reading the only name that could possibly be a woman, and was relieved when the young woman failed to ask for an ID.

She followed the signs to the ballroom and slid into an empty seat at the table in the back, between two middle-aged men in nearly identical navy blue suits and red ties. Sam was striding across the stage, touting the success of his firm's work with a certain DOD agency. He's good, Jeanne thought. Smooth but not smarmy, he oozed competence. And he clearly knew his audience. He reeled off all of the right acronyms and sympathetically ticked off all of the challenges facing the managers in the room. The shape of his face had a certain resemblance to Brian's, but he was clean-shaven, slimmer, and much more polished. Jeanne could only imagine how much it must have rankled him to see Edith gravitate towards his brother instead.

When he finished his presentation to thunderous applause, Jeanne sprang up and rushed to accost him before he could rejoin his table.

"Mr. Schwartz," she called out, thrusting a gold cuff link in the shape of a letter "S" towards him, "I just wanted to give this back to you."

He recoiled as if she were handing him a rattlesnake. But his recovery was swift. In one deft move, he clasped her shoulder and began steering her towards the exit. "Let's get some air, shall we?"

His grin was wide and his tone affable, but there were little worry lines around his eyes. Once in the hallway, he poured himself a cup of coffee and then offered one to Jeanne. "I really do appreciate Good Samaritans who return lost items, but I'm afraid that's not mine."

"Really?" Jeanne turned the cuff link in her palm so that it glinted in the light. "I'm quite sure I saw you drop this."

He hastily spit out a sip of coffee. "Oh that's—that's hot. Where did you see me—that is, someone who looked like me—drop it?"

"Inside Oak Hill Cemetery. You see, I was walking my dog, Miss Moneypenny, late on Halloween night. It must have been a little after midnight. We were walking down R Street, and I had my binoculars." She preened a little for effect. "I'm an amateur ornithologist, and you'd be amazed at the kinds of birds you see at night in Georgetown. They are so elusive during the day. And I heard some rustling along that little path that starts at R and then goes down the hill to the bridge over Rock Creek. I thought it might be a Great Horned Owl, but then I saw you in the moonlight, and you were assisting a young lady in a hoop skirt over the fence, and then I saw you drop the cuff link."

Sam had turned white. "Most extraordinary," he mumbled.

"So when I saw your bio for this conference, with your head shot, I realized that I could return the cuff link to its owner!" She beamed up at him.

"Oh, so that's how you recognized me." The color began to return to his cheeks.

Not from TV, was what he didn't say. Not from the news conference about Brian's death.

He dumped three lumps of sugar into his cup. "I'm sorry to disappoint you, but there must be a look-alike out there. I was home handing out Halloween candy."

"At midnight?"

"Well, earlier. And then I went to bed. I had to fly to Atlanta the next day. We've got a big project with the CDC." He shook her hand, and she noticed his strong grip. "Good luck finding your mystery man," he said as he re-entered the ballroom.

But Jeanne did not need to look any further; she knew that she had found him. Smiling, she felt her empty palm, still warm from his touch. The man who had insisted it was not his had taken the precaution of palming it during their handshake.

But if he thought he had destroyed all evidence of his presence there, he was wrong. They had made a thousand of those cuff links, and she had purchased one on the way to work this morning. His cuff link was still safely in the squirrel nest, just waiting for the police to find if and when she alerted them.

****

Mitch returned her call later that afternoon. "His buddy, Caspar, was the one who told him to follow the jelly beans. Apparently, Caspar used to visit him when he was at Red Onion."

"Last name?"

"No last name. And I'm not even sure that's a first name. Might be a nickname, even a gang name. Who knows?"

"What does Caspar look like?"

Mitch laughed. "A white dude. He says we white people all look the same. Except for our hair color."

"And what color is Caspar's hair?"

"Yellow, almost white. That's Curtis's description."

Jeanne thought for a moment. "And when did this Caspar pay him a visit?"

"The day Mrs. Washington's poodle got loose. Which according to Mrs. Washington was Thursday the 30th."

"And this Caspar told him to go to Oak Hill?"

"He told him that he had a secret treasure hunt planned for him with a big surprise at the end."

"Well I'd say a corpse is a surprise. But probably not what Curtis had in mind." Jeanne unwrapped a piece of dark chocolate and popped it in her mouth. "How did he get to Oak Hill?"

"Taxi. Caspar gave him a voucher and everything. Told Curtis to arrive at one a.m. on Saturday."

"So within an hour of the murder."

"But Curtis got tired and fell asleep and didn't end up going until eleven the next morning." He laughed. "Which is great news for me. I can easily get the cab driver to corroborate when Curtis arrived and it's well after the time of death. The prosecutor might try to say Curtis was also there earlier, but I think I can make the case that with no car and no friends, it would have been hard for him to get there."

"Metro?"

"I don't think someone with his IQ could figure out how to make that trip."

"But would a judge agree during a preliminary hearing? I don't know," Jeanne said. "Did any of the neighbors see this Caspar?"

"Yeah. Mrs. Washington. She was out looking for her poodle. Says he was a white guy, average height, slim build, blond hair."

"Sounds like our murderer."

Congressman Richardson's prediction had come true. Fox Five News, Nine News Now, Seven on Your Side—the "vultures" as he called them—were all camped outside his home. The correspondents tried to look serious, but did little to conceal their glee between takes. This story had all the hallmarks of a good D.C. scandal—wealth, power, espionage—minus the sex. But they were sure they would find that angle eventually.

Jeanne caught snatches of their reports, the same words coming to the fore over and over again. "Sources caution that, like the Gary Condit case, the congressman may eventually be cleared of all charges....Sources confirm that the murder weapon was owned by Congressman Richardson...The victim, Brian Schwartz, was an employee of NSA, and Congressman Richardson is the Chair of the powerful Judiciary Committee and has been an outspoken advocate of extraordinary rendition for Edward Snowden...The Richardsons' home is just a five-minute walk from the Oak Hill Cemetery, where Brian Schwartz was found, and incidentally is just blocks away from the home of socialite Viola Drath, who was brutally murdered by her husband."

Smoothing the creases in the ridiculous French maid's costume she had borrowed from Lily, Jeanne reflected that D.C. was a very underrated city—for murder. Yes, the city's once spectacular murder rate—over four hundred homicides a year under its crackhead mayor, Marion Barry—had come tumbling down, but it was hard to beat the city's murderers' flair for the dramatic. Some, of course, stumbled into a juicy scandal—like Ingmar Guandique, the Salvadoran immigrant who killed Chandra Levy, an attractive twenty-four-year-old intern, during her morning jog—and in the process torpedoed the career of Congressman Gary Condit, who was both married and having an affair with the unfortunate Chandra. But others really seemed to seek the limelight, like forty-nine-year-old Albrecht Muth, a homosexual German gold-digger who variously styled himself as Count Albi and an Iraqi general and hinted to police that an Iraqi assassin had murdered his wife, ninety-one-year-old Georgetown socialite Viola Drath. Or Daron Wint, who in the course of just twenty-four hours, took his former employer and his wife and housekeeper hostage, extorted money from them, murdered them, and set fire to their mansion—and was only caught because he got the munchies during the ordeal and left his DNA on a pizza crust.

Pushing her way through the gaggle of reporters, she offered a shy smile and an apologetic "*no hablo inglés*" to the barrage of questions shouted in her direction.

"Is Mr. Richardson at home?" a tall elegant blonde shouted.

"How was he acquainted with Mr. Schwartz? Did you ever see Mr. Schwartz at the Richardsons' residence?"

"Is your employer gay? Is this a lover's spat gone awry?"

Ah, so Maggie—or someone else—had been talking to the press. Jeanne tried not to react in the slightest to this last question, or any of the others.

In the background, she could hear a poofy-haired brunette summoning her cameraman José to translate. Jeanne quickened her step, lunged at the front gate, quickly turned the key in the lock, and bounded up the path. She rang the bell twice and then pushed her way in as soon as the door opened a crack.

A small dark woman in a much more sensible maid's uniform than Jeanne's grabbed her by the arm and pulled her quickly out of sight. "*Venga,*" she said in a hoarse whisper.

As Jeanne followed her into the living room, she was struck by how oppressive the air felt. With every blind shut and every curtain drawn, the atmosphere was as close as Jeanne would ever get to experiencing a medieval siege. And, in a sense, they were under siege.

As if to underscore the point, Ana María motioned for her to sit on the leather divan, poured her a cup of tea from a silver teapot on a silver tray—after all, a media frenzy was no excuse to let appearances slip—and then turned the volume all the way up, until Jeanne's eardrums began to hurt.

Ana María smoothed her skirt and sat so close to Jeanne that their legs were touching. "*Para que nadie nos oiga*," she said right into Jeanne's ear. "Mrs. Richardson's orders."

Mrs. Richardson gave lots of orders, Jeanne suspected, and most of them were probably sheer whims. But this one came from a deep wellspring of well-founded paranoia. After all, thanks to Jeanne, Mrs. Richardson knew she had been bugged once before.

What she didn't know, however, was that it was by her own husband.

Jeanne nodded and squirmed slightly. Ana María smelled of chili peppers and bleach, and Jeanne felt surprisingly self-conscious in her French maid's outfit, which was too tight and too short, the gaping slit in the back artfully covered by a black cardigan; that was the problem with borrowing an outfit from a size two Asian woman. What must Ana María think of her?

Taking a notebook and a pen from her bag, Jeanne turned and shouted in her ear in Spanish. "Were you here the night of the thirty-first?"

"Yes, watching Grayson. Mrs. Richardson paid me extra. She was busy that night."

"And what time did she leave?"

"Ten-thirty. And she returned after two-thirty."

"Was there a baseball bat in the box when you put it in the car?"

"No." Ana María's voice was firm.

"Did you make any stops on the way to the toy drive?"

"Just to get gas."

"Did you pay at the pump?"

"Yes."

"And when you arrived at the toy drive, did you notice a baseball bat?"

"No." Ana María shook her head firmly. "There was no baseball bat when I picked up the box, and there was no baseball bat when I left it at the toy drive."

Jeanne took a moment to process this. If Ana María was telling the truth, the baseball bat must have been added to the box at the toy drive. While that would in theory exponentially increase the number of suspects—by Vivienne's account, more than one hundred people stopped by with donations—it seemed unlikely that just anyone would know to put the murder weapon in the Richardsons' box.

It must have been someone who knew the Richardsons had a motive for murdering Brian Schwartz, and who could recognize—from the contents of the box alone—which box was theirs.

Jeanne was so caught up in her reverie that she was startled when Ana María nudged her. Looking up, she saw Meaghan standing in the doorway. In a white silk jumpsuit silhouetted against the encroaching gloom, she was a mesmerizing, almost spectral, appearance. Meaghan crooked her finger, and Jeanne followed the gently sashaying white figure up the stairs with a mounting sense of dread.

There was no denying that her client had a motive to kill Brian, she had access to the area where the baseball bat was stored, and the alibi she had given police—that she was at the Charity League fundraiser all night—was false.

And she also had a motive to frame her husband. With him in prison, she could act shocked—*shocked*—that she had married a man so violent, so ruthless. Then she could divorce him with her head held high, without losing any prestige; probably argue successfully that their pre-nuptial agreement was null and void; and maybe even run for his Congressional seat.

Or would that look petty if he had killed Brian to protect his wife from a malicious blackmailer?

Jeanne wasn't sure but she rummaged through her purse nonetheless, pulling out her cell phone and clutching it in her hand.

Just in case.

Extending her hand over the edge of the bannister, she left a trail of sweaty little fingerprints along the outer edge, the side that no one would ever leave fingerprints on when going up and down the stairs.

The side Meaghan would never think to wipe clean if she killed Jeanne. Which, Jeanne consoled herself, was very unlikely with Ana María in the house and a throng of reporters outside.

Meaghan led her into the master bedroom, crossed to the stereo, and turned up the classical music until it was just as loud as Ana María's *bachata* CD. To Jeanne's surprise, they were not alone.

Sprawled out on the king-sized bed like an overindulged house cat getting in a last stretch before devouring a bowl of cream, was Jorge. He had neither the decency to be embarrassed nor the foresight to be concerned. He just lay there, serene and self-satisfied, and gave her the slightest nod of acknowledgement. When Mrs. Richardson motioned Jeanne over to the bed, he begrudgingly made room for them.

"I figured there's no point in keeping up the pretense," Mrs. Richardson said, cupping her hand over Jeanne's ear. "My husband told me that you found out about our little domestic arrangement." Her dark blue eyes flashed, as if daring Jeanne to disapprove. When Jeanne said nothing and maintained a perfect mask of indifference, Mrs. Richardson added, "And I also hear that you know I wasn't actually at the benefit."

She pulled away from Jeanne for a moment to collect her thoughts, and the scent of strong rum and pineapple juice filled Jeanne's nostrils. Her client had clearly been drinking. Drowning her sorrows, or celebrating? That was the question.

Jeanne flinched. She hadn't expected the congressman to tell his wife, whom he mistrusted enough to spy on, everything. Especially since Meaghan was the most plausible alternative suspect.

And she had counted on getting out of their home alive by not revealing that she knew Mrs. Richardson's alibi was false. Because that would give Meaghan a motive for murdering Jeanne.

Mrs. Richardson's mouth twisted into a caustic little smile. Pulling Jeanne roughly towards her, she said into her ear, "Ah, you couldn't hide your surprise this time, could you? Mason and I tell each other everything. We're very, very close. I love him dearly, and I will do anything to save him."

Jeanne took a deep breath and tried to relax. She gently pried Mrs. Richardson's fingers off her arm and leaned in. "Even admitting that you have no alibi? That would make you the number one suspect."

Mrs. Richardson's eyes flashed once again. "If it would help, I most certainly would. But I don't think it would help. Because I do have an alibi—just not the one they think I have. Jorge and I were celebrating our anniversary—with Mason's blessing of course."

She reached out and caressed Jorge's bicep.

"And where were you two between twelve and twelve-thirty?" Jeanne shouted in her ear.

"At Bourbon. Celebrating."

"Can anyone vouch for that?"

"Liam, the bartender."

"Then I guess that won't help," Jeanne said, making a mental note to check this new alibi later. "What time did you leave the house on the night of the thirty-first?"

"Ten forty-five."

"And what time did you return?"

Meaghan frowned. "I was pretty drunk." She leaned over and spoke in Jorge's ear. He turned and shouted something back.

"Around two-forty-five," she relayed back to Jeanne.

Jeanne made a mental note that Meaghan's timeline roughly tallied with Ana María's. But was this because it was the truth, or because Ana María had been coached?

"Did you notice anything odd earlier in the evening, when you were home?"

"As a matter of fact, yes. The security alarm went off repeatedly. By the third time, I decided it must just have been a deer that wandered over from Rock Creek Park and tripped the alarm, and so I turned the security system off." She added, rather smugly as she cast an appraising glance over Jorge's muscular frame, "It was interrupting things, you see."

"I can imagine," Jeanne said uncomfortably. "Did you see any deer?"

"No."

"So how do you know there were deer? How do you know that there wasn't a burglar?"

"I sent Jorge to check it out. He didn't see anything."

Jeanne considered this for a moment. By Meaghan's own admission, Jorge was roaming the property repeatedly that night, allegedly looking for prowlers. That would have given him plenty of opportunities to enter the storage area and retrieve the baseball bat. But, if he really was with Meaghan the whole night, he couldn't have committed the murder.

But an accomplice could have.

And if the congressman did go to prison, Jorge could console Meaghan until she married him and showered him with the Richardsons' fortune.

"And other than these brief forays to look for a potential prowler, was Jorge with you all night?"

"Of course," Mrs. Richardson shot back indignantly.

"Did Jorge know about the blackmail?"

"Yes."

"And did you mention that Brian had this habit of going to Oak Hill Cemetery every Halloween to Jorge? Or at least in front of Jorge?"

Meaghan shook her head.

"Maybe while you were a bit tipsy?" Jeanne asked as delicately as possible.

Mrs. Richardson froze for a moment. She shook her head no, eventually, but she wasn't very convincing. Jeanne could almost smell her client's fear and vulnerability and in a flash she realized why she had always loathed Mrs. Richardson. With all of her first-hand experience, she should have been able to spot an alcoholic a mile away. But Mrs. Richardson, unlike her mother, had the resources to hide it well. Yet underneath the fancy clothes and the gym bunny physique, she was the same: an insecure woman who lamented her lost youth and beauty, despised Jeanne for seeing through her—and lived with the nagging suspicion that she had said some very inadvisable things while drunk.

"So besides you, Jorge, Ana María, and the congressman, who had access to the lower level of the coach house?"

"No one."

"What about the apartment above?"

"Well my parents stay there when they visit. And Cassandra, the congressman's daughter. And the rest of the time, when we don't have family staying, it's a love nest."

"For you and Jorge?"

"Oh, no, for Mason and whoever is the flavor of the moment."

"So who's been there?"

Meaghan sighed. "I can't remember all of them. But in the last six months or so, since we had the locks changed, there have been three, as far as I know: Dan

236

someone-or-other, a bouncer at JR's; Simon, some Brit who was only here on a two-week boondoggle of a work trip; and Mark Miller, who is" –she hesitated for a moment—"an intern in his office. I trust you to use this information discretely." Then she added in a rather defensive tone, "He's a graduate student intern. He's twenty-four."

Jeanne fished a notepad and a pen out of her purse and jotted down the names. "Why'd you have the locks changed?"

"Oh, Mason dated a real drama queen last year. Some young lobbyist named Tim—or was it Tom?—Malbork. He didn't take it well when Mason broke it off."

Jeanne dutifully added the name to her list. "But could any of them have gotten in the storage area? Is there any way to access the lower level from the coach house apartment?"

Mrs. Richardson thought for a moment, and then motioned for Jeanne to stay put. Meaghan slipped out of the room, and Jeanne found herself in the uncomfortable position of being alone with Jorge.

Whom she had not ruled out as a suspect.

A few minutes later, she was relieved to see Mrs. Richardson walk back through the door, clutching Lucinda's leather-bound diary. Taking a seat next to Jeanne, Meaghan thumbed furiously through the stiff, rippled pages. At last, she found the page she was looking for, read it over once or twice with a deeply furrowed brow, then shoved it under Jeanne's nose.

Jeanne had to read it several times before she understood its import. At first, it seemed like a veiled reference to an assignation in the coach house, interesting only for its titillating aspects. Imagine, a woman in that era carrying on an affair right under her father's nose, in his own coach house! Surely, the servants must have been in on it.

But then the words jumped out at her, just as they must have jumped out at Mrs. Richardson.

He came through the stables, then stole up to the coachman's quarters. Dear old Henry! He does help us so.

The stables must have been where the garage was now. If he could enter through the stables and sneak up to the apartment above, that meant that there must have been a staircase connecting the two.

And if it existed then, might it exist now?

Chapter Twenty-Five

Jeanne and Mrs. Richardson just stared at each other. Then Meaghan nodded and they padded off downstairs to borrow Ana María's maid uniform.

When Meaghan emerged from the downstairs bathroom, she looked ridiculous. The uniform was absurdly short, revealing her shapely legs in a way no real maid ever would, and yet the dress hung on her spare frame like a potato sack. Short, rotund Ana María just stood there in her slip with a bemused smile on her face.

Jeanne and Meaghan crept out the back door, tiptoed across the grass, and leapt over the narrow gravel driveway. As quietly as possible, they scrambled up the stairs and crept into the apartment.

Tastefully decorated, with contemporary artwork on the walls and crisp white curtains, it had the ambience of a honeymoon suite in an exclusive B&B. The four-poster mahogany bed was draped with an heirloom quilt, a dozen red roses were carefully arranged in a vase on an end table, and the dark wood built-in bookshelves were filled to the brim with old classics.

"Mason's book collection," Meaghan explained, following Jeanne's gaze. "He's got several first editions."

Jeanne's glanced back at the roses. "Those look relatively fresh. When was the last time someone stayed here?"

"Oh, I think Mason had a guest three or four days ago."

"Name?"

"I think it was the intern."

"Ah."

Jeanne looked around the contours of the room for a moment, then went back down the stairs to contemplate the outside dimensions. She walked back in and cast an appraising eye about. No doubt about it, she thought—the left side of the room opposite the door was not as big as it should be. She walked along that wall, tapping, leaning against the bookshelves, stomping her foot.

At first, nothing.

Then, as she reached behind a tattered old book with a teal spine, she finally felt something. It was a slight change in the wood, nothing more, but when she pressed firmly, the bookcase swung open.

Only a foot and a half wide, the space had stairs which led down below. The stairs creaked beneath them as Jeanne and Mrs. Richardson descended into the abyss.

"What was this for?" Mrs. Richardson wondered aloud. "Hiding liquor during Prohibition? An Underground Railroad stop?"

"Well, more importantly, who knows it is here?"

Meaghan sighed. "I wish I knew. Maybe one of his guests discovered it by accident."

"Or someone else read Lucinda's journal."

"I doubt it. I've been meaning to transcribe it for publication, but I haven't gotten around to it yet."

"And the antiquarian who sold it to you?"

"He might have read it, but what motive would he have? None."

They reached the bottom of the stairs. Jeanne felt around in the dim light and finally found a small latch.

She pulled it and suddenly they were bathed in sunlight.

And they were in the storage area.

Jeanne's first stop after leaving the Richardsons was Bourbon. The bartender, a muscle-bound twenty-something with frosted blond hair and an Australian accent, was quick to confirm Mrs. Richardson's alibi. He didn't seem to bat an eye when Jeanne claimed to be a private investigator and flashed a fake ID manufactured by one of Jerry's shady friends.

"Oh, yeah, they're regulars," he said. "Good tippers. And they were here that night."

"What time?"

"I'd say they got here around eleven-thirty and left at twelve-thirty."

"What makes you so sure of the time?"

"The woman said 'it's twelve-thirty, we'd better call so-and-so and let her know we're going to be late.'"

Well that's pretty convenient, Jeanne thought. Meaghan had established the time for the bartender.

"But you didn't actually check the time yourself?" she pressed.

"What's the point?" he said. "Unless it's closing time, it's all the same to me."

A group of Georgetown students crowded in just then, and he cut their conversation short with a "cheers" and an apologetic wave.

She walked to the corner of Wisconsin and Q, caught the #D2 bus, and rode past the mansions of Q Street to Dupont Circle. She had a strange sense of déjà vu as she crossed the circle, half-expecting to be accosted by Congressman Richardson in the guise of a homeless man. But then she reminded herself that he was in custody.

On the other side of the circle, she continued down P Street, which along this stretch was lined with stately hundred-year-old apartment buildings, and turned left onto 17th Street. The rainbow-colored flag made it easy to spot JR's Bar and Grill, and today she was in luck—Dan was working.

"Can I help you?" he asked gruffly.

"I'm working for Congressman Richardson's defense team. And I heard you could help us."

Dan slid behind the bar, poured two glasses of ice water, and barked "back in five" to the bartender. He led her to a dark table along the far exposed brick wall, beneath a big screen TV. "Okay, you've got four minutes now," he said.

"Do you know who might want to harm the congressman?"

"He's a politician, right?"

"Is that an answer?"

"It means, I dunno. Probably a lot of people."

"How was your relationship with him?"

"Great. Simple. No strings attached."

"You weren't ever jealous?"

He guffawed, which made the little gold key affixed to the dog collar around his neck shake. "More like the other way around, don't you think? I'm a bouncer. At a gay bar. He's a closeted old man. Who do you think gets more action?"

Jeanne considered this for a moment. He had a point. "That's a cool key you've got there," she said, craning her neck to see better. She saw some initials scratched onto the surface. "MR. Mason Richardson, huh?"

He smiled sardonically. "Well, you've got me there. I like keeping it around my neck. My connection to the rich and powerful, you know?"

"What's it to?"

"Our meeting place." He dropped the gruff expression for a moment. "Look, he's a good guy. Really, he is. But I don't think I know anything that can be of use. We didn't talk about personal problems—we got together to escape our everyday lives. So I don't know anything about who would want to harm him."

But as she walked out into the sunshine, she actually thought that he had given her a useful bit of information.

****

It was toasty inside Eastern Market as Jeanne and Mark Miller strolled the aisle, pretending to admire the hand-rolled pasta, expensive charcuterie, and other delicacies in a desultory fashion. Looking younger than his twenty-four years, with a broad, slightly freckled face and big green eyes, Mark worked nervously at loosening the knot in his tie.

"You seem upset," she observed. "Because your lover—and employer—may go to prison? Or because of something else?"

"All of the above," he said through gritted teeth, pulling her away from the pastry case. "I care about him as a person. I don't want him to go to prison for a crime he didn't commit. And it's a good job and I'd like to keep it."

"And if he loses his seat, you're out of a job. And?"

"And I'm not out yet. Not to my family. Not to anyone. I don't want to get mixed up in this. I'll be the gay Monica Lewinsky."

Jeanne sighed. He seemed to be telling the truth on all accounts, but she suspected that this last reason was the most important.

"How do you meet him? Secretly, I mean."

"At his" –Mark gulped–"at the coach house on his property."

Jeanne tried to look surprised. "And how do you get in?"

"With a key. He gave it to me."

"Is it gold and incised with the initials MR?"

He gasped. "How did you know?"

She decided not to ruin it for him. He didn't need to know that for his lover, he was just one of many. The only person Congressman Richardson was loyal to, strangely enough, was his wife. "He told me," she assured him. "I'm just making sure everything's consistent. Where do you keep your key?"

"On my key chain."

"And where do you keep the key chain?"

"Oh, on me."

"All the time?"

"Well sometimes," he conceded, "I might leave it on my desk at work."

So anyone, Jeanne thought, who works in—or visited—the office could have snatched the key.

But it would only have been useful to the killer if he knew that it led to the congressman's coach house.

Jeanne thanked Mark for his time, bought an almond croissant, and headed to the Metro station. While waiting for the train, she sent a quick text to Meaghan: "Need to talk. Number of suspects could be much larger. Meet me by waterfront fountains in one hour."

Meaghan's reply was nearly instantaneous and quite surprising. "Dupont Circle. He will meet you."

Chapter Twenty-Six

As Jeanne trudged up the escalator next to the Krispy Kreme, she couldn't help but feel a frisson of excitement. Who was "he"? The congressman? Would he really risk a media frenzy to meet with her in public?

On a whim, she bought a doughnut and then crossed to the circle.

"Spare a doughnut, lady?" a familiar voice asked her.

Jeanne thrust it into his hands—still too clean, she noted—and sat down next to him on the fountain's marble lip.

"Surprised?" he asked.

"A little."

"Meaghan posted bail an hour ago. Two million dollars." He whistled. "She figured I could tell you more about my enemies than she could. That, or she wanted me out of the house already."

"Mark admits that he kept the key to the coach house on a key chain that he occasionally left on his desk at work. So I'm thinking that someone who knew the significance of that key could have copied it when Mark was out, used it to gain access to the coach house, then accessed the secret staircase to retrieve the baseball bat. Probably the night of the murder, since Meaghan and Jorge admit they disabled the alarm after it repeatedly malfunctioned—or so it seemed. I think someone kept deliberately tripping the alarm so that they'd turn it off."

She waited for a cop on a Segway to pass before continuing. "And then this person—or an accomplice— put it in the box that you donated, all but ensuring the murder weapon would be tied to you. So the question is, who in your office both knows the significance of the little gold key and needed both you and Brian out of the way?"

He sighed. "The only person currently in the office who used to have a key is Scott."

She looked up at him sharply. "Your chief of staff?"

Congressman Richardson nodded. "He was one of my first, um, relationships with staff," he said delicately.

"Did he have a reason to kill Brian?"

"None that I know of. I don't think he had ever heard of him."

"So you never mentioned to him that Meaghan was being blackmailed?"

"Of course not."

"And does he have a grudge against you?"

"No." He hesitated for a second. "Well not a grudge, really. But I suppose he does have a reason to want me out of the way. He thought I wasn't running for re-election you see—and I wasn't intending to with the shadow of blackmail hanging over me. But then you did such a good job of identifying the blackmailer and then— what a stroke of good luck, as horrible as it is of me to say…"

"The blackmailer was murdered," Jeanne said flatly. "And you decided to run for re-election after all."

"Yes," he said ruefully. "Which probably didn't make Scott too happy. You see, he was planning to run for my seat when I retired."

"But that's crazy! He's never held elective office."

"No, but he's a real master of politics. He's made a lot of friends as my chief of staff. And he's very good at constituent relations. Little old ladies love him. He's always helping them track down some missing Social Security check. Plus,"—he looked away from her—"he was counting on my endorsement."

"And were you going to endorse him?"

"Yes," he said weakly. "Partly out of loyalty. He was, after all, an excellent chief of staff. And then partly out of fear. He never threatened me—nothing like that at all. But it is always in the back of my mind that he could expose our little affair."

Jeanne's head was swimming. Scott could have made a copy of the key, let himself into the coach house, gotten the baseball bat, and killed Brian. But he was nowhere near the toy drive and, if Ana María could be believed, the baseball bat was not in the box when she dropped it off.

Plus, Scott had no reason to go to the cemetery and kill Brian. If he had wanted to frame Mrs. Richardson, it would have been far more straightforward to kill Mark, then claim it was a lover's spat gone awry.

And, as far as she could tell, he had no way of even knowing that Brian was in the cemetery, or that Congressman Richardson had a motive to kill him.

Jeanne's phone rang. At first, no one spoke. All she could hear was some ragged breathing, crickets chirping, and then a few popping sounds. Was it a car backfiring? A gunshot?

She was about to hang up when she heard a hoarse whisper. "Jeanne," Carlos rasped, "Tonio—or one of his *sicarios*—found me."

"Where are you?"

"In the woods near Route 50."

"Can you be more specific?"

"I'm about a hundred meters from a white sign."

"A sign? Like a historical marker?"

"I think so. It said something about the Battle of Middleburg."

"Don't move," she said. "I should be there in about an hour and a half."

There was another pop, and then the line went dead.

With trembling hands, she placed the phone back in her purse. *Sicario* somehow sounded even more menacing than its English equivalent, hit man.

Tonio's *sicario* was after Carlos.

"Gotta go," she mumbled with a curt nod to Congressman Richardson and then broke into a run.

True to her word, Jeanne was idling by the site of the Battle of Middleburg an hour and ten minutes later. A moment later, Carlos ran up to the passenger side door and yanked it open. "Just drive," he pleaded, sliding all the way down in the seat, and Jeanne obeyed.

He didn't relax until they were on Interstate 66, heading west. Jeanne wasn't quite sure where they were going, but she figured it was best to head away from the city.

When he at last dared to sit up, he asked, "How'd you find me?"

"Your tax dollars at work. There's a database of every historical marker in the state."

He raised an eyebrow. "*Eres muy lista, sabes?*"

Which meant that she was smart, clever, always prepared for any eventuality. All true, she thought ruefully. Except in matters of the heart. But all she said was, "Well, I try." Turning down the heat several notches, she asked, "How was your stay at the safe house?"

"Great, although a little lonely. Until they found me."

"How do you think they found you?"

He shrugged. "Who knows?"

At Front Royal, Jeanne took the first exit and then turned into the parking lot of a strip mall. She nodded in the direction of a garishly lit storefront with a bright red neon "takeout" sign and an aquarium teeming with squirming crabs. "Chinese?"

He looked nervously over his shoulder and then quickly scanned the deserted parking lot. "Sounds good."

They were greeted by an elderly Chinese woman with jet-black hair and a shuffling gait. "You sit in front," she insisted, flashing a gap-toothed smile. "Everyone see beautiful couple, think they want to eat here, too."

Carlos shook his head and pointed at the table further from the window, in the corner. "That one."

She relented and led them to the back, where Jeanne ordered the kung pao chicken. Carlos ordered a whole fish sautéed with black bean sauce, a bowl of egg drop soup, a side of eggplant, and extra rice. They sat in companionable silence until the food came.

Looking glum, Carlos slurped his soup. "I'll never be safe again. If they found me at your safe house, they'll find me anywhere."

"What are you going to do?"

He shrugged. "Keep running, I guess."

He asked about the case, and she filled him in, struck by how seemingly normal their dinner was. It felt very domestic, like an old married couple discussing their respective work days over takeout.

Only his day had involved a near-miss with death.

And hers had involved interviewing a trio of suspects in a grisly murder.

Maybe they were meant for each other.

Carlos was particularly interested in Curtis's welfare. "So he's in the clear?" he asked.

"For now, anyway." Jeanne pushed a few grains of fried rice around her plate. "But I still don't understand how someone could have lured Curtis to the cemetery with some jelly beans."

"It must have been someone he trusted."

"Like who?"

Carlos shrugged. "A guard, a lawyer, a volunteer."

Jeanne mulled this over as she cracked open a fortune cookie and extracted the tiny slip of paper warily. "Count on an old friend," it said. "Your lucky numbers are 22, 17, and 99."

She grunted. "What's yours?"

"You will go on a journey soon."

Normally, Jeanne didn't believe in omens. Putting blind faith in tea leaves, horoscopes, tarot cards—that was Lily's specialty. But in this case, it wasn't blind faith. It was a confluence of events pushing her towards one logical step—which happened to dovetail with Carlos's fortune. Biting into the fortune cookie, she asked, "Are you up for a trip to southwestern Virginia?"

"Anywhere that gets me farther away from Tonio and his *sicarios* is fine with me."

"Good."

Jeanne made a quick call to Jerry and jotted down the name and address that he gave her in teeny-tiny letters on the back of her fortune. Then she punched the address into her phone. According to GPS, they would arrive at three fifty-two in the morning.

By one, Carlos was fast asleep and Jeanne, who was fighting to keep her eyes open, decided to call it a night. She took the next exit and pulled into an old motor hotel with a flashing "vacancy" sign and three cars in the parking lot. Despite the empty parking lot, the shifty-eyed clerk insisted that there was only one room left—at least if they wanted a working toilet and heat. "Aren't you lucky?" he said, peering over his spectacles at her and carefully counting out Jeanne's thirty-seven dollars as if expecting some sleight of hand. Then he slapped an old-fashioned metal key on the counter. "One-oh-seven," he barked. "Next to the ice machine."

She went back to the car, nudged Carlos awake, and led him to their room, her hand shaking slightly as she slid the key into the lock. Sharing a room with Carlos had not been part of the plan.

She flicked on a light and stared at the lone double bed in the middle of the room. Her eyes flew to the threadbare carpet, which was studded with cigarette burns. Should she offer to sleep on the floor? Would he?

But Carlos did not appear the least bit discomfited. He crossed the room, kicked off his shoes, pulled back the cheap maroon bedspread, and dove under the covers, fully clothed. Then he patted the bed, as if expecting Jeanne to do the same.

Jeanne had the sinking realization that there was no bedtime ritual to hide behind. She had no pajamas, no toothbrush. She had nothing to busy herself with, to delay this decision.

Reluctantly, she tiptoed forward, pulled back a corner of the coverlet, slid gingerly between the coarse sheets, and scooted to the edge of the mattress. The box springs creaked beneath her. She reached out, turned off the lamp, and held her breath in the darkness.

Their bodies did not touch, but even so, she was acutely aware of his presence—the heat of his body, the gentle rising and falling of his chest, his cologne wafting across the bed. The moonlight stole through the thin curtains, illuminating the delicate sweep of his cheekbones. Was he asleep, or only pretending?

His dark eyes suddenly flew open and, in a single fluid motion, he closed the gap between them. As if it were the most natural thing in the world, he nestled his chin in the crook of her neck.

"*Dime un cuento*," he said drowsily, his hot breath shooting into her ear.

She began to tell him a story rather like one she might tell Everett—about a little girl who lived in the woods and had a pet deer. But as Carlos drifted off to sleep, the story stopped being about just any little girl. The story was about her, and she spared no details.

When she was done, it was nearly three in the morning. She felt strangely at peace. It did not matter that the only person she had ever told her whole life story to was fast asleep and on the run from a killer. She had told the story to someone, and he had not judged her. In fact, it hadn't even been interesting enough to keep him awake.

When she awoke, Carlos was nowhere to be seen.

"Carlos? Carlos?" she called with mounting alarm as she rushed into the dingy pink and yellow bathroom. She shoved the plastic shower curtain aside in a single sweeping motion, half expecting to find him slumped over with a bullet in his head.

It didn't take long to search their cramped hotel room, and when she was done, she was almost inclined to think it had all been a dream. There was not a scrap of evidence that Carlos had ever been there.

Except by the sink. There, in surprisingly neat cursive, was a note written on the back of a badly crinkled receipt.

"Because I love you," she read aloud, the words catching in her throat, "I am going to leave you alone. You are the strongest, kindest, smartest person that I know and it has been a great honor to call you a friend. Take care of yourself and I am sure that the story will have a happy ending."

The note fell out of her hands and fluttered onto the countertop.

He had been listening the whole time.

Chapter Twenty-Seven

Mrs. Brown had not exaggerated Red Onion's remoteness. An angry brown scar in an otherwise stunning landscape, the prison had been gouged into one of the area's highest peaks. A winding road circled its flanks, culminating in an enormous parking lot and, beyond that, concentric security perimeters enclosing a warren of low-slung, interconnected buildings that gleamed in the sunlight. It reminded Jeanne of a very ugly version of a medieval fortress.

The tiny town of Pound was ten minutes down the sinuous country road, nestled in a U-shaped bend in the Pound River and backing onto an expanse of seemingly endless hazy blue ridges. Jeanne drove to the edge of town and turned onto a dirt road that meandered through a dense thicket of trees, pitched down into a dark hollow, and then followed the curve of a rocky stream until dead-ending in front of a white clapboard house.

As she peered through the windshield, Jeanne's heart sank. The only sign of life was in the form of a scrawny hen pecking her way through knee-high weeds.

The house reminded her of her *grand-père* in his final years, a listless shell of his former self, his left side drooping, his right angry and defiant. The house listed to the left, towards fallow fields of rocky black earth, and its weather-beaten shutters tilted inward, flanking the upstairs windows—which seemed to glare at her in the morning sun—like eyebrows knitted into angry v's. With each gust of wind, the screen door creaked open and then banged shut.

Jeanne took a deep breath, got out of the car, and slammed the door loudly to announce her presence. Dragging her feet through the gravel, she walked slowly up the path and then, with an anxious glance at the crater in the floorboards, stepped gingerly onto the porch. She rapped twice on the door, which still retained a few traces of red paint, and held her breath.

At first, it seemed that her only response was the wind. But then she leaned in and heard a slightly high-pitched, nasal voice with a distinct twang. "Door's open."

She turned the knob and stepped into a musty corridor lined with peeling wallpaper. "In here," the voice said, and she followed the sound through an old kitchen, with metal cabinets and a black and white tiled floor, and out into a surprisingly pleasant little sunroom. While the rest of the house appeared mired in a Depression-era time warp, this room had a seventies vibe, with its cheap faux wood paneling and fuzzy, mismatched furniture. Against the wall was a rust-colored couch and there, surrounded by hanging houseplants and a fat tabby cat, was a tall, lanky, middle-aged man with thinning brown hair and a wispy moustache. With his beady eyes blinking out at her from behind owlish glasses, he reminded Jeanne of an accountant—the kind that crunched numbers into the wee hours of the night and was never allowed to interact with clients. She could not imagine him as a guard.

"Hello." He looked in her direction, but not really at her, and he leaned forward, hunching his shoulders. "I'm Mike. Jerry tells me you've got some questions for me."

"Jeanne," she stammered, taking a seat next to him. She turned towards him in a vain attempt to make eye contact. "Thank you seeing me."

"I'd do anything for Jerry," he said, his voice swelling with conviction. "He saved me from an IED. Did he tell you that?"

"No."

"He's very modest."

Jeanne nodded. "He's a great guy. One of my best friends, actually."

"You want to know about Red Onion." Mike shuddered and looked past her, out the window. "What's to tell? It's a horrible place. When I realized that I liked the prisoners more than my fellow guards, it was time to go."

"Do you remember an inmate named Curtis Brown?"

Nodding slowly, he scratched the tabby behind the ears. "One of my favorites. He was very agreeable. Never caused any problems for me, unlike a lot of the rest of them." He gave a half-hearted little chuckle. "Which was kind of surprising, given that he was a cop killer."

258

"He wasn't really a cop killer. He just was the look-out in a drug deal in which a cop happened to get killed."

Mike formed his long bony fingers into a steeple and looked directly at her for the first time. "That makes more sense. But we were told he was a cop killer. And the other guards treated him accordingly. Those prisoners are at the bottom of the pecking order—cop killers and pedophiles." He winced. "They did some terrible things to him. I have nightmares about it sometimes. I've tried everything to cope—medication, talk therapy, art therapy. Nothing really works, but at least I enjoy painting. I paint a lot of fruit. Peaches, mostly."

"Uh-huh," Jeanne murmured politely, trying to think of something to say about still lifes. "I painted an apple in sixth grade."

"Red or green?"

"Red, I think, but with a little spot of green. It wasn't very good. I think my mom threw it right in the trash." She drummed her fingers on the coffee table. "Did Curtis ever mention jelly beans to you?"

"Oh, yes." Mike pushed his glasses further up his nose. "He really liked jelly beans. Especially the yellow ones."

"Did anyone in particular bring him jelly beans?"

"I only remember one person. A UVA law student who took his case as some sort of student project."

"Do you remember his name?"

He sighed. "Unfortunately not. Curtis called him Caspar, but I don't think that was his real name."

Caspar. Jeanne's heart began to race. "Could you draw him?"

Mike bit his lip. "I think so. It's a little harder than fruit, but I could try."

He went into the kitchen. Jeanne could hear drawers being opened and slammed shut. When he re-emerged a minute later, he was clutching a pad of construction paper and a blue pen. He sat down next to her, selected a bubble gum pink sheet, placed it over an old magazine on his lap, and began to draw. "I'm not so good at the eyes," he murmured apologetically as he sketched in two delicate wispy eyebrows, large round pupils, and a thick fringe of eyelashes.

Jeanne watched with rapt attention. With each stroke, his confidence seemed to grow, and what began to emerge was the portrait of an elegant young man. More beautiful than handsome, he bore a striking resemblance to a Greek statute, with high cheekbones, a chiseled jawline, and nearly perfectly symmetrical features. But when Mike began to draw in the nose and mouth, the man's personality began to leap off the page. The base of the nose was wide, the nostrils flared. Beneath this, his thin fish lips curled almost imperceptibly downwards. Unusually, the upper lip was slightly longer than the lower lip.

When Mike finished, he placed it in the middle of the coffee table and they hunched forward to study it. The overall effect was arresting. No matter how Jeanne shifted her position, she felt herself shrinking beneath the young man's gaze. He seemed somehow dangerous, with his all-knowing stare and arrogant tilt of the head, the flared nostrils and slight snarl hinting at the rage bottled up within.

And he seemed disconcertingly familiar.

Squinting, she covered up his hair with one hand and tried to imagine him with other hairstyles, ten years older. She mentally added a couple of lines around the eyes and across the forehead and tried out the standard D.C. men's haircut—short and singularly uninteresting.

Suddenly she gasped. "Scott Ferrer."

Mike frowned. "Who?"

"Someone who may have framed Curtis and then Congressman Richardson for murder."

Mike shot her a bewildered look. Snatching up her purse, Jeanne hurriedly shook his hand. "You've been a great help, Mike. You really should do more portraits. You've got talent."

She rushed back through the kitchen and down the hallway, the front door banging behind her. The porch creaked beneath her, and the hen gave her a half-hearted cluck good-bye. Yanking the car door open, Jeanne snatched the phone out of her purse and flung the purse onto the passenger seat. Pulling the door shut, she gunned the motor, scrolled to her client's number, and headed back down the dirt road.

The house was just a speck in her rearview mirror when the congressman's voicemail invited her to leave a message with a loud beep. The words tumbled out of her mouth, rushed and breathless. "Don't go near Scott Ferrer," she said. "He's Caspar—the guy who lured Curtis to the cemetery, which means he either committed the murder or conspired with the person who did. I'm still trying to figure out why he killed Brian—or how he knew you'd have a motive to kill Brian. But in the meantime, don't go near him."

The voicemail cut off with an angry beep, and she swerved suddenly to avoid a pothole. "That's what they mean by distracted driving," she muttered. With one eye on the road, she scrolled to the congressman's office number and gave it a ring.

His perky, twenty-two-year-old receptionist answered. "He's on the floor," she said apologetically. "They're in the middle of a vote on the energy bill."

"I didn't think they ever voted on anything anymore."

"Can I take a message, ma'am?"

"Oh, just put me through to his voicemail," Jeanne grumbled.

She left the same message and then had a sudden inspiration. At the bottom of the hollow, she pulled into a little clearing and fumbled with her phone until she located the number of Maggie Cooper, the Hill staffer.

"This is Maggie."

"Maggie, it's Jeanne."

There was a long pause, so Jeanne cleared her throat and added, "Jeanne Pelletier. We met—"

"I remember," Maggie broke in curtly. "I just don't think we have anything more to discuss."

"I'm sorry if we didn't get off on the right foot. I'm just trying to help Congressman Richardson beat the rap for a murder he didn't commit. And for what it's worth, I don't think he was behind that quid pro quo you overheard. I think that was all Scott."

She heard what sounded like a sigh of relief on the other end of the line.

"I'm glad to hear that," Maggie said softly. "He always seemed like a good man to me."

"Look, I don't have a lot of time to talk right now, but could you tell me anything about Scott?"

"Like what?"

Jeanne racked her brain. "I don't know. Maybe how Scott met the congressman."

Maggie snorted. "It's Capitol Hill, Jeanne. It's all about the connections. Scott is the brother—or maybe half-brother or stepbrother, I forget—of some friend of Mrs. Richardson's. Someone" -a note of bewilderment crept into her voice—"with the name of a fish. Or maybe a nickname. Piranha, no, it's, um—"

"Barracuda?" Jeanne crossed her fingers over the steering wheel. "Sarah the Barracuda?"

"That's it."

Chapter Twenty-Eight

Driving ten miles over the speed limit and limiting herself to one pit stop, Jeanne made it back to Georgetown in just seven hours. The sun was just setting as she maneuvered into a tight spot within sight of the cemetery. As she walked the three blocks to the Richardsons' mansion, she left Jerry a quick message. "Mike was very helpful. I'm going to the Richardsons now. Thanks for looking after Scarlett. I'll be home soon."

As she walked up the path to the front door, she noticed that the news vans had departed. Apparently, the energy bill vote—or something else—was a better story now. Both of the Richardsons' cars—her Mercedes, his Aston-Martin—were parked in the driveway, but no one responded to Jeanne's frantic knocks. The shades were drawn.

Could they have gone for a walk like a normal couple?

She doubted it.

Harder and harder she knocked, until her knuckles began to hurt. "Congressman!" she shouted. "Congressman—"

At last the door opened and she was surprised to find herself face to face with the congressman, who somehow managed to look pale beneath his tan. "Uh, hullo," he drawled, fixing her with an intense stare. "Oh, I see you're from the Environmental Defense Fund," he said, and Jeanne looked at him with alarm. Had a night in jail sparked delusions? "I couldn't give a fig about global warming," he rambled on. "Human activity has nothing to do with it. It's all the methane from those tasty cows. So move along, young lady. The Wallaces next door will probably eat up that liberal claptrap."

"But I—"

"Sorry," he said firmly, pushing the door shut.

Only a crack remained when a gloved hand and an arm clad in an expensive navy blue sports coat thrust it open again.

And the man that the arm belonged to was Scott Ferrer.

"Jeanne," he trilled. "So nice to see you again. You played a little disappearing act last time."

His lips twisted into a little smile, but his eyes remained icy.

"Sorry about that," she said weakly.

He waved his left hand dismissively. His right hand was firmly grasping Congressman Richardson's arm, and Jeanne spotted the glint of the barrel of a handgun in Scott's waistband.

"Don't be," Scott said. "I can see why you'd want to impersonate someone so much younger, thinner, and prettier. Pity. You look nothing like the real Olivia Van Sant."

Jeanne couldn't see a whole lot of resemblance between Sarah and Scott, but he certainly had his sister's snark.

"Do come in and join us," he cooed. He phrased it as an invitation, but the strong grip on her arm told her it was actually a command. Leaving the door just slightly ajar, he yanked her roughly across the foyer and into the living room, to the edge of the leather divan, where she took a seat next to Meaghan, whose wrists were bound with what appeared to be a giant lavender ribbon. On closer inspection, Jeanne saw that it was one of Meaghan's beauty pageant sashes.

"Well, isn't this cozy?" Scott enthused, slipping a scarlet sash over Jeanne's wrists and expertly tying a knot. "I really couldn't have planned this any better myself. After the tragic murder-suicide, I was going to have to track Jeanne down. But how much more convenient for her to come to me! You've saved me a step, dear. And it was really so nice of you to call the congressman's office and leave that message. It really helps to know when someone's on to you."

"How did you—?"

"Really, Jeanne. Didn't you realize that a congressman's chief of staff has access to his voicemail?" He furrowed his brow. "Now how are we going to work Jeanne into the suicide note?"

He bounds Jeanne's calves with a yellow sash, then roughly pulled Congressman Richardson across the room and flung him into an antique wooden chair so that he was seated in front of the desk where Meaghan had stored Lucinda's diary. Craning her neck, Jeanne could see a sheet of heavy white card stock. It appeared to be some sort of half-completed hand-written letter, and with a sinking heart Jeanne realized this was the suicide note.

"Could Jeanne be yet another blackmailer?" Scott mused as he tied Congressman Richardson's left hand to the chair, then bound his feet together. "That would very neatly explain the payments to Jeanne's account."

"Yes, that will do nicely." He pulled a box cutter out of his pocket, flipped open the blade, and caressed it gently. Bringing it alongside Congressman Richardson's neck, he growled, "Now, write 'I can no longer live with the tyranny of blackmail—first, the perfidious Brian Schwartz, who tormented my dear wife, then the vile Jeanne Pelletier, who is bleeding me dry over a minor indiscretion committed years ago. My wife and I can no longer live with this shame.'" He shivered with pleasure. "Man, I'm good. I guess there are dividends to being your speechwriter. It really does sound like you."

"You may as well finish with a 'live free or die'," Jeanne grunted.

"That's New Hampshire's motto, you dimwit," Scott snapped. "But yes, we should add something that's very states' rights, individual liberty, that sort of thing. That's exactly what our hypocritical public servant would do— try to make a cowardly suicide sound like heroic self-sacrifice. Just finish with 'sic semper tyrannis.' Yes, that will do nicely."

Scott leaned over to inspect Congressman Richardson's handiwork. "Very good," he murmured and patted him on the head patronizingly. The congressman flinched ever so slightly, forcing his flesh against the point of the blade. A trickle of blood seeped down his neck.

"Pity," Scott said, fingering the congressman's starched collar. "This looks like a designer shirt. Now"— he pulled him to his feet roughly—"hop towards the couch. There you go. Hop, hop, hop. Like a bunny."

The congressman did as he was told.

"Now stop," Scott said when the congressman was about ten feet away. "Meaghan, recline. Like you're, you know, exhausted from your day swanning about as a society lady pretending to be a serious historian."

"I am a serious historian," Meaghan huffed.

"Oh, touchy, touchy. Now be a good girl and lie down. Jeanne, dear, get up so Meaghan can lie down. Come stand by the window."

Struggling to her feet, Jeanne hopped to the window as instructed. Meaghan lay down and stared impassively at Scott.

"You're not going to get away with this, you know," Meaghan said as she smoothed her black hair so it fanned out across the couch.

Scott chuckled. "What a very unoriginal thing to say. But I think I will. Everything's gone according to plan so far—well, except for Jeanne showing up." He took the gun out of his waistband. "Here, hold this," he said, thrusting it towards the congressman, who kept his fists tightly clenched. "Ah, so now the man with the ninety-nine percent approval rating from the N.R.A. is afraid to handle his own weapon."

Out of the corner of her eye, Jeanne saw something that nearly made her faint. On the other side of the far

268

back left window, creeping through the hedges, was Fergus.

She had to remind herself to breathe. And then to look somewhere, anywhere else.

Scott grabbed the congressman's right hand and forcibly curled his fingers around the handle. The chief of staff stood behind his boss, so close that Jeanne was sure Congressman Richardson could feel Scott's heartbeat. Then Scott raised his arm and put his finger on the trigger. Just as Scott squeezed the trigger, the congressman suddenly lurched backwards, sending Scott's arm skywards. As Scott fell to the gleaming wooden floor with a thud, the bullet grazed the chandelier and lodged in the crown molding, sending a crack spreading across the ceiling. The gun clattered across the floor, landing just a few feet from Jeanne. She flung her body towards it, and the cold metal barrel dug into her shoulder blade. Rolling to her side, she wiggled away from it until the barrel was within reach. She reached out her bound hands, grasped the barrel, curled her knees, and then rocked over to a kneeling position. She was about to stand up when she heard Fergus shout from behind her, "Watch out!"

Then she felt a sharp pain shoot through her neck, and the gun slid out of her hand.

"I'm a black belt," Scott said smugly as he grabbed the gun and jumped back up. He waved the gun in their direction. "Who's your friend?"

Fergus stood in the doorway, wide-eyed and frozen to the spot. To Jeanne's relief, he seemed incapable of speaking.

"Captain Smith," Jeanne said. "A D.C. off-duty police officer."

Scott seemed unimpressed. "Badge?" When Fergus failed to produce one, he sighed. "I thought so. You, too—on the couch. In fact, let's get Jeanne over here too."

He brandished the gun in his left hand and, all out of sashes, sliced a strip of upholstery off the armchair. Scott hurled it in Fergus's direction and ordered him to tie his hands and feet.

"What are you doing here?" Jeanne hissed.

"Jerry told me you were here." He twisted to look right at her and rested his bound hands on hers. "And I didn't want to wait to continue our conversation."

"About dinosaur eggs?"

"No, about us."

"What about Pamela?"

"I told her it was no use pretending that I would ever feel for her what I feel for you. And I dropped her off at Dulles this morning. She should be home, in front of the telly, drinking a cup of tea by now."

"Ah, isn't this sweet?" Scott interjected. "Deathbed confessions."

Fergus ignored him. "I love you, Jeanne. Yes, you can be mysterious and complicated and distant— sometimes maddeningly so—but you're so much more interesting than anyone else. And even if you have a funny way of showing it, I think you love me—"

"I do," she said quickly. "I do love you."

He sighed happily. "Okay, I *know* you love me, and I'm willing to wait as long as it takes to get you to trust me as well."

Scott lugged a can of gasoline from behind the couch and began pouring it around the room. "That's sweet," he said, "although I wouldn't count on living long enough for that to happen."

"I want you to come with me to Maine," Jeanne said quickly, "to the reunion, to the parole hearing. From now on, I'm all in."

"No more secrets," Fergus whispered.

"No more secrets," Jeanne promised.

She leaned it and nuzzled Fergus's cheek. A jolt of electricity shot through her as she felt his stubble against her cheek. This—not some miserable trailer in the Maine woods—was home. Suddenly her eyes widened. "Jerry's here," she breathed into his ear.

Fergus's blue-gray eyes flitted to the window and registered just the briefest acknowledgement. Jeanne reached up and ran her hands through Fergus's hair, then locked eyes with Jerry. "Front door," she finger-spelled.

"Can we at least play Twenty Questions with our last couple of minutes?" Jeanne called out to Scott.

Her ruse worked, as he momentarily looked up—and narrowly missed seeing Jerry slipping past the windowsill.

"Don't see why not." Scott shot her one of his malicious little upside-down smiles. "But let's make it interesting. You tell me what you know, and I'll tell you if you are right."

"Okay." Jeanne tried not to follow Jerry with her eyes as he briefly came into view again. "You're Sarah O'Brien's stepbrother," she guessed.

"Half-brother," he corrected her.

"Okay, half-brother. And she was being blackmailed by Brian Schwartz, and out of family loyalty you decided to do her a favor and kill him."

"Well, that, and she'd bankroll my campaign in return."

Now that, Jeanne thought, made more sense. Family honor didn't seem like a strong enough motivation for a mercenary like Scott.

"So," Jeanne continued, "you figured Curtis would be the perfect fall guy. Criminal record, mentally handicapped, easily lured to the scene of the crime."

"And it would have worked perfectly if you hadn't been traipsing through the cemetery the next day."

"Because that fixed the time of Curtis's visit several hours after you bludgeoned Brian to death with the baseball bat you stole from the Richardsons' garage." She bit her lip. "But how did you get into the garage?"

Scott chuckled. "I found the staircase years ago. Sheer dumb luck. I was stumbling from the bed to the shower after the congressman left for some floor vote when I bumped into the bookcase at just the right angle."

"So," Jeanne said, picking up the thread, "you recognized the gold key on Mark's key chain, made a copy, repeatedly set off the security alarm on Halloween night—maybe by rolling a ball over the trip wire—until Jorge and Meaghan turned it off, then crept into the apartment, went down the secret staircase, and retrieved the bat."

Scott whistled. "Very good, Jeanne. Two gold stars for you."

"You crept into the cemetery, sprinkled a trail of yellow jelly beans to the gravesite, lay in wait for Brian, then bashed his head in with Congressman Richardson's baseball bat. Wearing gloves, of course."

"Of course."

"Prior to that, you visited Curtis and told him to take a cab to the cemetery at one a.m. and follow a trail of jelly beans to some sort of prize. Only it led him to the scene of the crime, where you were hoping he'd leave some hairs, fingerprints, something."

"Bravo, Jeanne."

"But later you decided to pin it on Congressman Richardson."

"Tsk, tsk," Scott said, wagging a finger in his boss's direction. "Odd things happen when people break their promises. Like not running for re-election."

"You were angry when he went back on his word and announced his bid for re-election. So you seized the opportunity for Sarah to slip the bloodied baseball bat in the Richardsons' box of donated toys, knowing it would soon be discovered as the murder weapon."

"Very good." Scott's voice was soft as velvet, and he looked very pleased with himself. "Too bad a jury will never hear that." Setting the gasoline can down, he came up behind the congressman, slit the sash with the box cutter, and in a single swift motion, grasped the congressman's trembling hand, curled it around the gun handle, and raised it to the congressman's head.

A single shot rang out. But to Jeanne's surprise, the congressman did not fall to the ground. Instead, Scott's body slumped onto the sumptuous Oriental carpet, and then, except for a strangled cry and a gurgle, there was silence. Scott's blood seeped into the carpet, into an ever-growing crimson puddle.

Whipping around, Jeanne got a glimpse of Jerry's outstretched arm; his hand trembled as he slowly lowered his firearm. Jeanne just sat there, rocking back and forth. Her cheeks were wet with tears, and she could feel Fergus's jaw tensed against her own.

They were both alive.

They had Jerry to thank.

And they were back together.

Epilogue

True to her word, Jeanne took Fergus to her mom's parole hearing, her high school reunion, and even her family's ancestral land by the bend in the river.

"Very quaint," Fergus murmured as they picked their way through the blackberry brambles, dodging immense puddles left by the thunderstorm from the night before, and the trailer came into view.

It was smaller than Jeanne had remembered. Long vines crept up the sides and curled onto the roof. Before long, it would be swallowed up into the forest and exist only in Jeanne's memory. Jeanne's mother would be released soon—thanks in part to Jeanne's decision not to oppose her parole—but she had made it clear that she had no intention to return. No, she had said, it was time to start a new chapter, preferably in a place far away from her drinking buddies. Jeanne's father had left long ago and died shortly after moving to an apartment in Portland. There was nobody left—nobody, that is, except Annie.

Jeanne heard the cemetery plot before she saw it— the dull clanking of the rusting metal gate in the late

November bluster. Winter is coming, the wind seemed to howl, you'd better hurry. And, indeed, the animals seemed to heed the call. Deer went slip-sliding through the muddy forest floor, tense and skittish; squirrels bounded through the puddles, gathering a few last acorns before the Arctic winds swept down and buried the landscape in snow.

But Jeanne resisted the urge to hurry. She showed Fergus the log where she and Annie had carved their initials, the cave where they had pretended their fairy godmother lived, and the abandoned mine shaft where they had hidden out during their mother's drunken rages.

As they slogged through the mud, the sound of rushing water grew louder. Between the bare branches, the cemetery gate came into view and then, as Jeanne and Fergus rounded a small knoll, the tops of the rough-hewn, pockmarked tombstones, which jutted out from the waterlogged earth at all sorts of alarming angles.

Normally, the final resting place of the Pelletier clan was a green mossy plot that sloped gently down towards the languid waters of the St. John River. Jeanne and Annie had spent hours puzzling over the inscriptions, carefully scraping away the lichen that oozed across the slabs like cancerous growths to reveal some aristocratic-sounding French name, the s's distended to look like f's.

But today, the St. John enveloped it with the full fury of Mother Nature. Swollen from the storm last night, the normally placid waters had been whipped into a raging, seething torrent the color of chocolate. The flood waters surged higher and higher, lapping at the tombstones, crashing against the twisted beech tree, which groaned under the assault. Jeanne stood there, transfixed, as the obelisk atop her great-grandmother's gravestone, which had been rent by a terrific crack for as long as she could remember, toppled over.

"Jeanne," Fergus yelled about the din, tugging at her hand, "We have to get to higher ground."

The noise was almost deafening now. She recognized the remnants of the Michauds' old barn as it floated past, then the Martins' chicken coop with its iconic fluorescent pink paint job. It was as if her whole childhood were floating past.

Reluctantly, she let Fergus pull her back from the edge, back over the grassy knoll, through the thicket of blackberry bushes, back down the gravel road, and back to Lily's waiting Crown Vic, which she had generously lent them for the occasion. But Jeanne turned back at the top of a small ridge just in time to see a coffin emerge from the mire, beneath the watchful gaze of the little stone angel that had been lovingly carved by her father.

She held her breath. That was Annie's coffin.

The coffin bobbed once or twice on the roiling waters, almost as if to test its seaworthiness, then began to float gracefully down the river. Towards the sea, Jeanne thought with a smile. Annie had always loved the shore.

Fergus pretended not to see this for her sake. She knew that he would expect her to be horrified, revolted by the desecration of her sister's remains.

But Jeanne had never felt more at peace. Annie seemed to be bidding her good-bye, liberating Jeanne even as she freed herself from the damp, piney earth. In just a few moments, the coffin was a mere speck on the horizon, and then it was gone.

And then Jeanne was able to see the land the way Fergus did—no longer a place of misery but simply of sheer savage beauty.

Jeanne, Fergus, Vivienne, Everett, and Lily crowded into a dark wooden booth at The Tombs, a cozy student hangout in the bowels of a Georgetown townhouse.

"Well we certainly have a lot to celebrate," Lily marveled as she took a swig of beer. "The dropping of all charges against the Richardsons plus—thanks to Jerry—you guys are alive." She clinked her glass with Jeanne's. "And you and Fergus are back together."

Fergus kissed her on the forehead and she leaned closer to him. "For good," she said, curling her fingers around his.

"Where is Jerry, by the way?" Vivienne asked. "He really should be here with us."

"Agreed." Jeanne dialed Jerry's number and clutched the phone close to her ear.

"Hello," he shouted. Jeanne could barely hear him over the chatter in the background.

"Jerry, where are you? We're celebrating the fact that, thanks to you, we're still alive and not charged with killing Scott."

She said a silent prayer of thanks that Jerry had had the foresight to record her game of Twenty Questions with Scott; without that recording, the police might have found their story just a tad too convenient. Of course, it had helped that the police were able to match one of the hairs from the crime scene—which had hitherto been classified as from some unknown John Doe—with the hair from Scott's lifeless body.

"Come celebrate with us," she shouted. "We're at The Tombs."

"Sure thing, Twinkletoes. I'll just catch a cab and be there in ten minutes."

She hung up and a minute later was engrossed in a game of dominoes with Everett. Suddenly, out of the corner of her eyes, she glimpsed Jerry's stocky frame slipping past.

To her surprise, he was coming from the back of The Tombs towards the entrance.

And he didn't seem to want to be seen.

"Jerry?"

He froze for a moment, then turned around and greeted her with a smile. "Oh, Jeanne, there you are. I thought maybe you were in the back and so I went back there and you weren't there and then I—then I—"

Gesticulating wildly, he had an idiotic grin plastered on his face.

"Jerry," Jeanne said impatiently, "stop pretending. I'm a sleuth, remember? Clearly, you were already here when I called."

"Well, I...I..." His voice trailed off and he seemed incapable of finishing the sentence.

A small smile played at the corners of Jeanne's lips and began to spread into a grin. "Are you here alone?"

"Oh, yeah, of course. I mean, who do I know besides you? I'm practically a hermit."

What he said was true. And yet she suspected that he was lying.

"Okay, Jerry," she said smugly. "I'm going to just walk back there and find the table with the half-eaten rare burger with fries and we'll just see if there's anyone else there."

A bead of sweat formed on his upper lip. Before he could stop her, she bolted from the table and raced to the back. In the far corner, there was an empty seat with a half-eaten burger, blood red in the center. And across from the empty seat, eating a taco salad, was Roxy.

Jeanne's mouth fell open. "Jerry? Roxy? You're an item?"

Jerry shrugged sheepishly. "Are you mad?"

She shook her head, partly to indicate that no, she wasn't mad, partly in sheer disbelief. She wasn't angry in the slightest. Shocked, definitely. Bemused, a little. But most of all she was delighted—and slightly irritated with herself for not having recognized a perfect match when she saw one. Jerry and Roxy had a lot in common: an earthy sense of humor, refreshing candor, and rather checkered pasts. Jerry wouldn't judge Roxy for having spent—and enjoyed—her heyday at The Frisky Puss. Roxy would take Jerry under her slightly crass maternal wing and shower him with affection.

"Congratulations," Jeanne murmured, kissing each of them on the cheek. "I'm so happy."

And she was happy. Happy about everything, really. Her classmates had been strangely, inexplicably, happy to see her—and the subject of the car accident had not even come up. She and her mother had reached an uneasy détente. Annie was at peace, floating around somewhere in the Atlantic Ocean. She and Fergus were back together. And now one of her dearest friends in the world had finally found the perfect mate.

Jerry breathed a sigh of relief.

"We're glad that you're glad," Roxy said. "And we're glad that you and Fergus are back together. I was a little worried about you when you ran out of the closing."

"Sorry about that."

Roxy waved a liver-spotted hand. "Don't be, hon. It worked out terrifically for us. I snapped the condo up and, if all goes well"—she blushed and shot a furtive glance at Jerry, who beamed—"Jerry will move in one of these days."

Jeanne could hardly believe her ears. They had met at her closing only a week before, and they were already talking about moving in together. But rash as that seemed, she had more immediate concerns. "Oh, no," she moaned, "I'm going to miss Jerry so much."

Jerry slipped his arm in hers. "Well now that, Twinkletoes, could be remedied. You see, there's another unit upstairs that just came on the market. And it's perfect for you, Braveheart, and Scarlett."

"I think I've learned my lesson," she said. "This time I'll consult Fergus."

"Very wise." Jerry winked. "But I think he'll approve, and nothing could make me happier. You and I, kid, are meant to be neighbors."

"And friends."

"And friends," he agreed. "The very best of friends."

ABOUT THE AUTHOR

Maureen Klovers is the author of the first in the Jeanne Pelletier mystery series, *Hagar's Last Dance*, as well as the memoir *In the Shadow of the Volcano: One Ex-Intelligence Official's Journey through Slums, Prisons, and Leper Colonies to the Heart of Latin America*. A former student of belly dance, she lives outside of Washington, D.C., with her husband, Kevin; her daughter, Kathleen; and their black Labrador Retriever, Nigel.

For more information on Maureen and her writing, or to schedule her for a book signing or book club event, please visit www.maureenklovers.com.

AND IF YOU ENJOYED THIS BOOK...

Please post a review on amazon.com, goodreads.com, or your own blog! Thank you!